His brother would always be with them,

like a darkness hovering over them. What could possibly thrive in such shadow? Certainly not love.

Love? No, what Chase felt as he held Miranda's slim, warm body to his, had far more to do with lust. *Maybe it runs in my family,* he thought. *This propensity for reckless, hopeless affairs.*

Pulling away, they stared at each other. The confusion he felt was mirrored in her eyes.

"I shouldn't have let you do that," she said. "You'll say I led you on. You think that's how I got hold of your brother, don't you? Temptation. Seduction."

"But is it true?"

"You've just proved it. Get me alone in a room—and another Tremain male bites the dust." Her voice took on a cold edge. "But what I want to know is, who's really seducing whom?"

ABOUT THE AUTHOR

Tess Gerritsen lives in Camden, Maine, with her husband and two sons. Formerly a physician, Tess now writes full-time. She has just added a new occupation to her résumé: professional musician. The Scottish dance band, in which she plays fiddle, recently performed at its first paid gig—for which she received a grand total of twenty dollars!

Books by Tess Gerritsen

Presumed Guilty

Tess Gerritsen

Harlequin Books

TORONTO • NEW YORK • LONDON
AMSTERDAM • PARIS • SYDNEY • HAMBURG
STOCKHOLM • ATHENS • TOKYO • MILAN
MADRID • WARSAW • BUDAPEST • AUCKLAND

To Terrina and Mike, with aloha

Harlequin Intrigue edition published August 1993

ISBN 0-373-22238-6

PRESUMED GUILTY

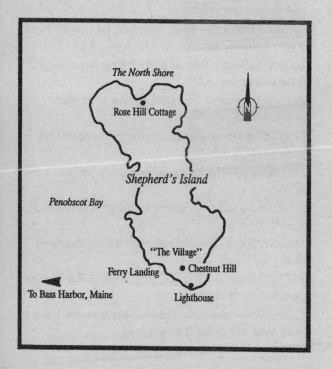

The North Shore

• Rose Hill Cottage

Shepherd's Island

Penobscot Bay

"The Village"

Ferry Landing   • Chestnut Hill

• Lighthouse

To Bass Harbor, Maine

CAST OF CHARACTERS

Miranda Wood—She claimed innocence—but the body was found in *her* bed.

Chase Tremain—He wanted his brother's murderess behind bars.

Richard Tremain—Even in death, he couldn't keep away from Miranda.

Tony Graffam—Desperately trying to salvage a land deal gone sour.

Evelyn Tremain—''...no fury like a woman scorned''?

Noah Debolt—He'd do *anything* to protect his daughter.

Jill Vickery—The editor who tried to see both sides of the story.

Annie Berenger—A savvy reporter—with inside knowledge.

Miss St. John—Would curiosity be the death of her?

Phillip Tremain—The heir apparent to the Tremain publishing dynasty.

Cassandra Tremain—How eager had she been to take over her dead father's job?

Chapter One

He called at ten o'clock, the same time he always did.

Even before Miranda answered it, she knew it was him. She also knew that if she ignored it the phone would keep on ringing and ringing, until the sound would drive her crazy. Miranda paced the bedroom, thinking, *I don't have to answer it. I don't have to talk to him. I don't owe him a thing, not a damn thing.*

The ringing stopped. In the sudden silence she held her breath, hoping that this time he would relent, this time he would understand she'd meant what she told him.

The renewed jangling made her start. Every ring was like sandpaper scraping across her raw nerves.

Miranda couldn't stand it any longer. Even as she picked up the receiver she knew it was a mistake. "Hello?"

"I miss you," he said. It was the same whisper, resonant with the undertones of old intimacies shared, enjoyed.

"I don't want you to call me anymore," she said.

"I couldn't help it. All day I've wanted to call you. Miranda, it's been hell without you."

Tears stung her eyes. She took a breath, forcing them back.

"Can't we try again?" he pleaded.

"No, Richard."

"Please. This time it'll be different."

"It'll never be different."

"Yes! It will—"

"It was a mistake. From the very beginning."

"You still love me. I know you do. God, Miranda, all these weeks, seeing you every day. Not being able to touch you. Or even be alone with you—"

"You won't have to deal with that any longer, Richard. You have my letter of resignation. I meant it."

There was a long silence, as though the impact of her words had pummeled him like some physical blow. She felt euphoric and guilty all at once. Guilty for having broken free, for being, at last, her own woman.

Softly he said, "I told her."

Miranda didn't respond.

"Did you hear me?" he asked. "I told her. Everything about us. And I've been to see my lawyer. I've changed the terms of my—"

"Richard," she said slowly. "It doesn't make a difference. Whether you're married or divorced, I don't want to see you."

"Just one more time."

"No."

"I'm coming over. Right now—"

"*No.*"

"You have to see me, Miranda!"

"I don't have to do anything!" she cried.

"I'll be there in fifteen minutes."

Miranda stared in disbelief at the receiver. He'd hung up. Damn him, he'd hung up, and fifteen minutes from now he'd be knocking on her door. She'd managed to carry on so bravely these past three weeks, working side by side with him, keeping her smile polite, her voice neutral. But now he was coming and he'd rip away her mask of control and there they'd be again, spiraling into the same old trap she'd just managed to crawl out of.

She ran to the closet and yanked out a sweatshirt. She had to get away. Somewhere he wouldn't find her, somewhere she could be alone.

She fled out the front door and down the porch steps and began to walk, swiftly, fiercely, down Willow Street. At ten-thirty, the neighborhood was already tucked in for the night. Through the windows she passed she saw the glow of lamplight, the silhouettes of families in various domestic poses, the occasional flicker of a fire in a hearth. She felt that old envy stir inside her again, the longing to be part of the same loving whole, to be stirring the embers of her own hearth. Foolish dreams.

Shivering, she hugged her arms to her chest. There was a chill in the air, not unseasonable for August in Maine. She was angry now, angry about being cold, about being driven from her own home. Angry at *him*. But she didn't stop; she kept walking.

At Bayview Street she turned right, toward the sea.

The mist was rolling in. It blotted out the stars, crept along the road in a sullen vapor. She headed through it, the fog swirling in her wake. From the road she turned onto a footpath, followed it to a series of granite steps, now slick with mist. At the bottom was a wood bench—she thought of it as her bench—set on the beach of stones. There she sat, drew her legs up against her chest and stared out toward the sea. Somewhere, drifting on the bay, a buoy was clanging. She could dimly make out the green channel light, bobbing in the fog.

By now he would be at her house. She wondered how long he'd knock at the door. Whether he'd keep knocking until her neighbor Mr. Lanzo complained. Whether he'd give up and just go home, to his wife, to his son and daughter.

She lowered her face against her knees, trying to blot out the image of the happy little Tremain family. *Happy* was not the picture Richard had painted. *At the breaking point* was the way he'd described his marriage. It was love for

Phillip and Cassie, his children, that had kept him from divorcing Evelyn years ago. Now the twins were nineteen, old enough to accept the truth about their parents' marriage. What stopped him from divorce now was his concern for Evelyn, his wife. She needed time to adjust, and if Miranda would just be patient, would just love him enough, the way he loved her, it would all work out....

Oh, yes. Hasn't it worked out just fine?

Miranda gave a little laugh. She raised her head, looked out to sea and laughed again, not a hysterical laugh but one of relief. She felt as if she'd just awakened from a long fever, to find that her mind was sharp again, clear again. The mist felt good against her face, its chill touch sweeping her soul clean. How she needed such a cleansing! The months of guilt had piled up like layers of dirt, until she thought she could scarcely see herself, her real self, beneath the filth.

Now it was over. This time it was really, truly over.

She smiled at the sea. *My soul is mine again,* she thought. A calmness, a serenity she had not felt in months, settled over her. She rose to her feet and started for home.

Two blocks from her house she spotted the blue Peugeot, parked near the intersection of Willow and Spring Streets. So he was still waiting for her. She paused by the car, gazing in at the black leather upholstery, the sheepskin seat covers, all of it too familiar. *The scene of the crime,* she thought. *The first kiss. I've paid for it, in pain. Now it's his turn.*

She left the car and headed purposefully to her house. She climbed the porch steps; the front door was unlocked, as she'd left it. Inside, the lights were still on. He wasn't in the living room.

"Richard?" she said.

No answer.

The smell of coffee brewing drew her to the kitchen. She saw a fresh pot on the burner, a half-filled mug on the countertop. One of the kitchen drawers had been left wide open. She slammed it shut. *Well. You came right in and made yourself at home, didn't you?* She grabbed the mug and tossed the contents into the sink. The coffee splashed her hand; it was barely lukewarm.

She moved along the hall, past the bathroom. The light was on, and water trickled from the faucet. She shut it off. "You have no right to come in here!" she yelled. "It's my house. I could call the police and have you arrested for trespassing."

She turned toward the bedroom. Even before she reached the doorway she knew what to expect, knew what she'd have to contend with. He'd be sprawled on her bed, naked, a grin on his face. That was the way he'd greeted her the last time. This time she'd toss him out, clothes or no clothes. This time he'd be in for a surprise.

The bedroom was dark. She switched on the lights.

He was sprawled on the bed, as she'd predicted. His arms were flung out, his legs tangled in the sheets. And he was naked. But it wasn't a grin she saw on his face. It was a frozen look of terror, the mouth thrown open in a silent scream, the eyes staring at some fearful image of eternity. A corner of the bed sheet, saturated with blood, sagged over the side. Except for the quiet tap, tap of the crimson liquid slowly dripping onto the floor, the room was silent.

Miranda managed to take two steps into the room before nausea assailed her. She dropped to her knees, gasping, retching. Only when she managed to raise her head again did she see the chef's knife lying nearby on the floor. She didn't have to look twice at it. She recognized the handle, the twelve-inch steel blade, and she knew exactly where it had come from: the kitchen drawer.

It was her knife; it would have her fingerprints on it.

And now it was steeped in blood.

CHASE TREMAIN DROVE straight through the night and into the dawn. The rhythm of the road under his wheels, the glow of the dashboard lights, the radio softly scratching out some Muzak melody all receded to little more than the

fuzzy background of a dream—a very bad dream. The only
reality was what he kept telling himself as he drove, what
he repeated over and over in his head as he pushed onward
down that dark highway.

Richard is dead. Richard is dead.

He was startled to hear himself say the words aloud.
Briefly it shook him from his trancelike state, the sound of
those words uttered in the darkness of his car. He glanced
at the clock. It was four in the morning. He had been driving for four hours now. The New Hampshire-Maine bor-
der lay ahead. How many hours to go? How many miles?
He wondered if it was cold outside, if the air smelled of the
sea. The car had become a sensory deprivation box, a self-
contained purgatory of glowing green lights and elevator
music. He switched off the radio.

Richard is dead.

He heard those words again, mentally replayed them
from the hazy memory of that phone call. Evelyn hadn't
bothered to soften the blow. He had scarcely registered the
fact it was his sister-in-law's voice calling when she hit him
with the news. No preambles, no are-you-sitting-down
warnings. Just the bare facts, delivered in the familiar Evelyn half whisper. *Richard is dead,* she'd told him. *Murdered. By a woman....*

And then, in the next breath, *I need you, Chase.*

He hadn't expected that part. Chase was the outsider, the
Tremain no one ever bothered to call, the one who'd picked
up and left the state, left the family, for good. The brother
with the embarrassing past. Chase, the outcast. Chase, the
black sheep.

Chase, the weary, he thought, shaking off the cobwebs
of sleep that threatened to ensnare him. He opened the
window, inhaled the rush of cold air, the scent of pines and
sea. The smell of Maine. It brought back, like nothing else
could, all those boyhood memories. Scrabbling across the
beach rocks, ankle deep in seaweed. The freshly gathered
mussels clattering together in his bucket. The foghorn,

moaning through the mist. All of it came back to him in that one whiff of air, that perfume of childhood, of good times, the early days when he had thought Richard was the boldest, the cleverest, the very best brother anyone could have. The days before he had understood Richard's true nature.

Murdered. By a woman.

That part Chase found entirely unsurprising.

He wondered who she was, what could have ignited an anger so white-hot it had driven her to plunge a knife into his brother's chest. Oh, he could make an educated guess. An affair turned sour. Jealousy over some new mistress. The inevitable abandonment. And then rage, at being used, at being lied to, a rage that would have overwhelmed all sense of logic or self-preservation. Chase could sketch in the whole scenario. He could even picture the woman, a woman like all the others who'd drifted through Richard's life. She'd be attractive, of course. Richard would insist on that much. But there'd be something a little desperate about her. Perhaps her laugh would be too loud or her smile too automatic, or the lines around her eyes would reveal a woman on the downhill slide. Yes, he could see the woman clearly, and the image stirred both pity and repulsion.

And rage. Whatever resentment he still bore Richard, nothing could change the fact they were brothers. They'd shared the same pool of memories, the same lazy afternoons drifting on the lake, the strolls on the breakwater, the quiet snickerings in the darkness. Their last falling-out had been a serious one, but in the back of his mind Chase had always assumed they'd smooth it over. There was always time to make things right again, to be friends again.

That's what he had thought until that phone call from Evelyn.

His anger swelled, washed through him like a full-moon tide. Opportunities lost. No more chances to say, *I care about you.* No more chances to say, *Remember when?* The road blurred before him. He blinked and gripped the steering wheel tighter.

He drove on, into the morning.

By ten o'clock he had reached Bass Harbor. By eleven he was aboard the *Jenny B,* his face to the wind, his hands clutching the ferry rail. In the distance, Shepherd's Island rose in a low green hump in the mist. *Jenny B*'s bow heaved across the swells and Chase felt that familiar nausea roil his stomach, sour his throat. *Always the seasick one,* he thought. In a family of sailors, Chase was the landlubber, the son who preferred solid ground beneath his feet. The racing trophies had all gone to Richard. Catboats, sloops, you name the class, Richard had the trophy. And these were the waters where he'd honed his skills, tacking, jibbing, shouting out orders. Spinnaker up, spinnaker down. To Chase it had all seemed a bunch of frantic nonsense. And then, there'd been that miserable nausea....

Chase inhaled a deep breath of salt air, felt his stomach settle as the *Jenny B* pulled up to the dock. He returned to the car and waited his turn to drive up the ramp. There were eight cars before him, out-of-state license plates on every one. Half of Massachusetts seemed to come north every summer. You could almost hear the state of Maine groan under the the weight of all those damn cars.

The ferryman waved him forward. Chase put the car in gear and drove up the ramp, onto Shepherd's Island.

It amazed him how little the place seemed to change over the years. The same old buildings faced Sea Street: the Island Bakery, the bank, FitzGerald's Café, the five-and-dime, Lappin's General Store. A few new names had sprung up in old places. The Vogue Beauty Shop was now Gorham's Books, and Village Hardware had been replaced by Country Antiques and a realty office. Lord, what changes the tourists wrought.

He drove around the corner, up Limerock Street. On his left, housed in the same brick building, was the *Island Herald.* He wondered if any of it had changed inside. He remembered it well, the decorative tin ceiling, the battered desks, the wall hung with portraits of the publishers, every one a Tremain. He could picture it all, right down to the Remington typewriter on his father's old desk. Of course, the Remingtons would be long gone. There'd be computers now, sleek and impersonal. That's how Richard would run the newspaper, anyway. Out with the old, in with the new.

Bring on the next Tremain.

Chase drove on and turned onto Chestnut Hill. Half a mile up, near the highest point on the island, sat the Tremain mansion. A monstrous yellow wedding cake was what it used to remind him of, with its Victorian turrets and gingerbread trim. The house had since been repainted a distinguished gray and white. It seemed tamer now, subdued, a faded beauty. Chase almost preferred the old wedding-cake yellow.

He parked the car, grabbed his suitcase from the trunk and headed up the walkway. Even before he'd reached the porch steps the door opened and Evelyn was standing there, waiting for him.

"Chase!" she cried. "Oh, Chase, you're here. Thank God you're here."

At once she fell into his arms. Automatically he held her against him, felt the shuddering of her body, the warmth of her breath against his neck. He let her cling to him as long as she needed to.

At last she pulled away and gazed up at him. Those brilliant green eyes were as startling as ever. Her hair, shoulder length and honey blond, had been swept back into a French braid. Her face was puffy, her nose red and pinched. She'd tried to cover it with makeup. Some sort of pink powder caked her nostril and a streak of mascara had left a dirty shadow on her cheek. He could scarcely believe this was his beautiful sister-in-law. Could it be she truly was in mourning?

"I knew you'd come," she whispered.

"I left right after you called."

"Thank you, Chase. I didn't know who else to turn to...." She stood back, looked at him. "Poor thing, you must be exhausted. Come in, I'll get you some coffee."

They stepped into the foyer. It was like stepping back into childhood, so little had changed. The same oak floors, the same light, the same smells. He almost thought that if he turned around and looked through the doorway into the parlor, he'd see his mother sitting there at her desk, madly scribbling away. The old girl never did take to the typewriter; she'd believed, and rightly so, that if a gossip column was juicy enough, an editor would accept it in Swahili. As it turned out, not only had the editor acquired her column, he'd acquired *her* as well. All in all, a practical marriage.

His mother never did learn to type.

"Hello, Uncle Chase."

Chase looked up to see a young man and woman standing at the top of the stairs. Those couldn't be the twins! He watched in astonishment as the pair came down the steps, Phillip in the lead. The last time he'd seen his niece and nephew they'd been gawky adolescents, not quite grown into their big feet. Both of them were tall and blond and lean, but there the resemblance ended. Phillip moved with the graceful assurance of a dancer, an elegant Fred Astaire partnered with—well, certainly not Ginger Rogers. The young woman who ambled down after him bore a closer resemblance to a horse.

"I can't believe this is Cassie and Phillip," said Chase.

"You've stayed away too long," Evelyn replied.

Phillip came forward and shook Chase's hand. It was the greeting of a stranger, not a nephew. His hand was slender, refined, the hand of a gentleman. He had his mother's stamp of aristocracy—straight nose, chiseled cheeks, green eyes. "Uncle Chase," he said somberly. "It's a terrible reason to come home, but I'm glad you're here."

Chase shifted his gaze to Cassie. When he'd last seen his niece she was a lively little monkey with a never-ending supply of questions. He could scarcely believe she'd grown into this sullen young woman. Could grief have wrought such changes? Her limp hair was pulled back so tightly it seemed to turn her face into a collection of jutting angles: large nose, rabbity overbite, a square forehead unsoftened by even a trace of bangs. Only her eyes held any trace of that distant ten-year-old. They were direct, sharply intelligent.

"Hello, Uncle Chase," she said. A strikingly business-like tone for a girl who'd just lost her father.

"Cassie," said Evelyn. "Can't you give your uncle a kiss? He's come all this way to be with us."

Cassie moved forward and planted a wooden peck on Chase's cheek. Just as quickly she stepped back, as though embarrassed by this false ceremony of affection.

"You've certainly grown up," said Chase, the most charitable assessment he could offer.

"Yes. It happens."

"How old are you now?"

"Almost twenty."

"So you both must be in college."

Cassie nodded, the first trace of a smile touching her lips. "I'm at the University of Southern Maine. Studying journalism. I figured, one of these days the *Herald*'s going to need a—"

"Phillip's at Harvard," Evelyn cut in. "Just like his father."

Cassie's smile died before it was fully born. She shot a look of irritation at her mother, then turned and headed up the stairs.

"Cassie, where are you going?"

"I have to do my laundry."

"But your uncle just got here. Come back and sit with us."

"Why, Mother?" she shot back over her shoulder. "You can entertain him perfectly well on your own."

"Cassie!"

The girl turned and glared down at Evelyn. "What?"

"You are embarrassing me."

"Well, that's nothing new."

Evelyn, close to tears, turned to Chase. "You see how things are? I can't even count on my own children. Chase, I can't deal with this all alone. I just can't." Stifling a sob, she turned and walked into the parlor.

The twins looked at each other.

"You've done it again," said Phillip. "It's a lousy time to fight, Cassie. Can't you feel sorry for her? Can't you try and get along? Just for the next few days."

"It's not as if I *don't* try. But she drives me up a wall."

"Okay, then at least be civil." He paused, then added, "You know it's what Dad would want."

Cassie sighed. Then, resignedly, she came down the steps and headed into the parlor, after her mother. "I guess I owe him that much...."

Shaking his head, Phillip looked at Chase. "Just another episode of the delightful Tremain family."

"Has it been like this for a while?"

"Years, at least. You're just seeing them at their worst. You'd think, after last night, after losing Dad, we could pull together. Instead it seems to be driving us all apart."

They went into the parlor and found mother and daughter sitting at opposite ends of the room. Both had regained their composure. Phillip took a seat between them, reinforcing his role as perpetual human buffer. Chase settled into a corner armchair—his idea of neutral territory.

Sunshine washed in through the bay windows, onto the gleaming wood floor. The silence was filled by the ticking of the clock on the mantelpiece. It all looked the same, thought Chase. The same Hepplewhite tables, the same Queen Anne chairs. It was exactly the way he remembered it from childhood. Evelyn had not altered a single detail. For that he felt grateful.

Chase launched a foray into that dangerous silence. "I drove by the newspaper building, coming through town," he said. "Hasn't changed a bit."

"Neither has the town," said Phillip.

"Just as thrilling as ever," his sister deadpanned.

"What's the plan for the *Herald?*" asked Chase.

"Phillip will be taking over," said Evelyn. "It's about time, anyway. I need him home, now that Richard..." She swallowed, looked down. "He's ready for the job."

"I'm not sure I am, Mom," said Phillip. "I'm only in my second year at college. And there are other things I'd like to—"

"Your father was twenty when Grandpa Tremain made him an editor. Isn't that right, Chase?"

Chase nodded.

"So there's no reason you couldn't slip right onto the masthead."

Phillip shrugged. "Jill Vickery's managing things just fine."

"She's just a hired hand, Phillip. The *Herald* needs a real captain."

Cassie leaned forward, her eyes suddenly sharp. "There are others who could do it," she said. "Why does it have to be Phil?"

"Your father wanted Phillip. And Richard always knew what was best for the *Herald.*"

There was a silence, punctuated by the steady ticking of the clock on the mantelpiece.

Evelyn let out a shaky breath and dropped her head in her hands. "Oh, God, it all seems so cold-blooded. I can't believe we're talking about this. About who's going to take his place...."

"Sooner or later," said Cassie, "we have to talk about it. About a lot of things."

Evelyn nodded and looked away.

In another room, the phone was ringing.

"I'll get it," said Phillip, and left to answer it.

"I just can't *think,*" said Evelyn, pressing her hands to her head. "If I could just get my mind working again...."

"It was only last night," said Chase gently. "It takes time to get over the shock."

"And there's the funeral to think of. They won't even tell me when they'll release the—" She winced. "I don't see why it takes so long. Why the state examiner has to go over and over it. I mean, can't they *see* what happened? Isn't it obvious?"

"The obvious isn't always the truth," said Cassie.

Evelyn looked at her daughter. "What's that supposed to mean?"

Phillip came back into the room. "Mom? That was Lorne Tibbetts on the phone."

"Oh, Lord." Evelyn rose unsteadily to her feet. "I'm coming."

"He wants to see you in person."

She frowned. "Right this minute? Can't it wait?"

"You might as well get it over with, Mom. He'll have to talk to you sooner or later."

Evelyn turned and looked at Chase. "I can't do this alone. Come with me, won't you?"

Chase didn't have the faintest idea where they were going or who Lorne Tibbetts was. At that moment what he really wanted was a hot shower and a bed to collapse onto. But that would have to wait.

"Of course, Evelyn," he said. Reluctantly he stood, shaking the stiffness from his legs, which felt permanently flexed by the long drive from Greenwich.

Evelyn was already reaching for her purse. She pulled out the car keys and handed them to Chase. "I—I'm too upset to drive. Could you?"

He took the keys. "Where are we going?"

With shaking hands Evelyn slipped on her sunglasses. The swollen eyes vanished behind twin dark lenses. "The police," she said.

Chapter Two

The Shepherd's Island police station was housed in a converted general store that had, over the years, been chopped up into a series of hobbit-size rooms and offices. In Chase's memory, it had been a much more imposing structure, but it had been years since he'd been inside. He'd been only a boy then, and a rambunctious one at that, the sort of rascal to whom a police station represented a distinct threat. The day he'd been dragged in here for trampling Mrs. Gordimer's rose bed—entirely unintentional on his part— these ceilings had seemed taller, the rooms vaster, every door a gateway to some unknown terror.

Now he saw it for what it was—a tired old building in need of paint.

Lorne Tibbetts, the new chief of police, was built just right to inhabit this claustrophobic warren. If there was a height minimum for police work, Tibbetts had somehow slipped right under the requirement. He was just a chunk of a man, neatly decked out in official summer khaki, complete with height-enhancing cap to hide what Chase suspected was a bald spot. He reminded Chase of a little Napoleon in full dress uniform.

Though short on height, Chief Tibbetts was long on the social graces. He maneuvered through the clutter of desks and filing cabinets and greeted Evelyn with the overweening solicitousness due a woman of her local status.

"Evelyn! I'm so sorry to have to ask you down here like this." He reached for her arm and gave it a squeeze, an intended gesture of comfort that made Evelyn shrink away. "And it's been a terrible night for you, hasn't it? Just a terrible night."

Evelyn shrugged, partly in answer to his question, partly to free herself from his grasp.

"I know it's hard, dealing with this. And I didn't want to bother you, not today. But you know how it is. All those reports to be filed." He looked at Chase, a deceptively casual glance. The little Napoleon, Chase noted, had sharp eyes that saw everything.

"This is Chase," said Evelyn, brushing the sleeve of her blouse, as though to wipe away Chief Tibbetts's paw print. "Richard's brother. He drove in this morning from Connecticut."

"Oh, yeah," said Tibbetts, his eyes registering instant recognition of the name. "I've seen a picture of you hanging in the high school gym." He offered his hand. His grasp was crushing, the handshake of a man trying to compensate for his size. "You know, the one of you in the basketball uniform."

Chase blinked in surprise. "They still have that thing hanging up?"

"It's the local hall of fame. Let's see, you were class of '71. Star center, varsity basketball. Right?"

"I'm surprised you know all that."

"I was a basketball player myself. Madison High School, Wisconsin. Record holder in free throws. And points scored."

Yes, Chase saw it clearly. Lorne Tibbetts, rampaging midget of the basketball court. It would fit right in with that bone-crushing handshake.

The station door suddenly swung open. A woman called out, "Hey, Lorne?"

Tibbetts turned and wearily confronted the visitor, who looked as if she'd just blown in from the street. "You back again, Annie?"

"Like the proverbial bad penny." The woman shifted her battered shoulder bag to her other side. "So when am I gonna get a statement, huh?"

"When I have one to make. Now scram."

The woman, undaunted, turned to Evelyn. The pair of them could have posed for a magazine feature on fashion make-overs. Annie, blowsy haired and dressed in a lumpy sweatshirt and jeans, would have earned the label Before. "Mrs. Tremain?" she said politely. "I know this is a bad time, but I'm under deadline and I just need a short quote—"

"Oh, for Chrissakes, Annie!" snapped Tibbetts. He turned to the cop manning the front desk. "Ellis, get her out of here!"

Ellis popped up from his chair like a spindly jack-in-the-box. "C'mon, Annie. Get a move on, 'less you wanna write your story from the inside lookin' out."

"I'm going. I'm going." Annie yanked open the door. As she walked out they heard her mutter, "Geez, they won't let a gal do her job around here...."

Evelyn looked at Chase. "That's Annie Berenger. One of Richard's star reporters. Now a star pest."

"Can't exactly blame her," said Tibbetts. "That's what you pay her for, isn't it?" He took Evelyn's arm. "Come on, we'll get started. I'll take you into my office. It's the only private place in this whole fishbowl."

Lorne's office was at the far end of the hallway, past a series of closet-size rooms. Almost every square inch was crammed with furniture: a desk, two chairs, a bookcase, filing cabinets. A fern wilted, unnoticed, in a corner. Despite the cramped space, everything was tidy, the shelves dusted, all the papers stacked in the Out box. On the wall, prominently displayed, hung a plaque: *The smaller the dog, the bigger the fight.*

Tibbetts and Evelyn sat in the two chairs. A third chair was brought in for the secretary to take accessory notes. Chase stood off to the side. It felt good to stand, good to straighten those cramped legs.

At least, it felt good for about ten minutes. Then he found himself sagging, scarcely able to pay attention to what was being said. He felt like that wretched fern in the corner, wilting away.

Tibbetts asked the questions and Evelyn answered in her usual whispery voice, a voice that could induce hibernation. She gave a detailed summary of the night's events. A typical evening, she said. Supper at six o'clock, the whole family. Leg of lamb and asparagus, lemon soufflé for dessert. Richard had had a glass of wine; he always did. The conversation was routine, the latest gossip from the paper. Circulation down, cost of newsprint up. Worries about a possible libel suit. Tony Graffam upset about that last article. And then talk about Phillip's exams, Cassie's grades. The lilacs were lovely this year, the driveway needed resurfacing. Typical dialogue from a family dinner.

At nine o'clock Richard had left the house to do some work at the office—or so he'd said. And Evelyn?

"I went upstairs to bed," she said.

"What about Cassie and Phillip?"

"They went out. To a movie, I think."

"So everyone went their separate ways."

"Yes." Evelyn looked down at her lap. "And that's it. Until twelve-thirty, when I got the call...."

"Let's go back to that dinner conversation."

The account went into replay. A few extra details here and there, but essentially the same story. Chase, his last reserves of alertness wearing thin, began to drift into a state of semiconsciousness. Already his legs were going numb, sinking into a sleep that his brain longed to join. The floor began to look pretty good. At least it was horizontal. He felt himself sliding....

Suddenly he jerked awake and saw that everyone was looking at him.

"Are you all right, Chase?" asked Evelyn.

"Sorry," he muttered. "I guess I'm just more tired than I thought." He gave his head a shake. "Could I, uh, get a cup of coffee somewhere?"

"Down the hall," said Tibbetts. "There's a full pot on, plus a couch if you need it. Why don't you wait there?"

"Go ahead," said Evelyn. "I'll be done soon."

With a sense of relief Chase fled the office and went in search of the blessed coffeepot. Moving back down the hall, he poked his head into the first doorway and discovered a washroom. The next door was locked. He moved on and glanced into the third room. It was unlit. Through the shadows he saw a couch, a few chairs, a jumble of furniture off in a corner. In the sidewall there was a window. It was that window that drew his attention because, unlike a normal window, it didn't face the outside; it faced an adjoining room. Through the pane of glass he spied a woman, sitting alone at a small table.

She was oblivious to him. Her gaze was focused downward, on the table before her. Something drew him closer, something about her utter silence, her stillness. He felt like a hunter who has quite unexpectedly come upon a doe poised in the forest.

Quietly Chase slipped into the darkness and let the door close behind him. He moved to the window. A one-way mirror—that's what it was, of course. He was on the observing side, she on the blind side. She had no idea he was standing here, separated from her by only a half inch of glass. It made him feel somehow contemptible to be standing there, spying on her, but he couldn't help himself. He was drawn in by that old fantasy of invisibility, of being the fly on the wall, the unseen observer.

And it was the woman.

She was not particularly beautiful, and neither her clothes nor her hairstyle enhanced the assets she did have.

She was wearing faded blue jeans and a Boston Red Sox T-shirt a few sizes too big. Her hair, a chestnut brown, was gathered into a careless braid. A few strands had escaped and drooped rebelliously about her temples. She wore little or no makeup, but she had the sort of face that needed none, the sort of face you saw on those Patagonia catalog models, the ones raking leaves or hugging lambs. Wholesome, with just a hint of sunburn. Her eyes, a light color, gray or blue, didn't quite fit the rest of the picture. He could see by the puffiness around the lids that she'd been crying. Even now, she reached up and swiped a tear from her cheek. She glanced around the table in search of something. Then, with a look of frustration, she tugged at the edge of her T-shirt and wiped her face with it. It seemed a helpless gesture, the sort of thing a child would do. It made her look all the more vulnerable. He wondered why she was in that room, sitting all alone, looking for all the world like an abandoned soul. A witness? A victim?

She looked straight ahead, right at him. He instinctively drew away from the window, but he knew she couldn't see him. All she saw was a reflection of herself staring back. She seemed to take in her own image with passive weariness. Indifference. As though she was thinking, *There I am, looking like hell. And I couldn't care less.*

A key grated in the lock. Suddenly the woman sat up straight, her whole body snapping to alertness. She wiped her face once more, raised her chin to a pugnacious angle. Her eyes might be swollen, her T-shirt damp with tears, but she had determinedly thrown off that cloak of vulnerability. She reminded Chase of a soldier girded for battle, but scared out of her wits.

The door opened. A man walked in—gray suit, no tie, all business. He took a chair. Chase was startled by the loud sound of the chair legs scraping the floor. He realized there must be a microphone in the next room, and that the sound was coming through a small speaker by the window.

"Ms. Wood?" asked the man. "Sorry to keep you waiting. I'm Lieutenant Merrifield, state police." He held out his hand and smiled. It said a lot, that smile. It said *I'm your buddy. Your best friend. I'm here to make everything right.*

The woman hesitated, then shook the offered hand.

Lieutenant Merrifield settled into the chair and gave the woman a long, sympathetic look. "You must be exhausted," he said, maintaining that best-friend voice. "Are you comfortable? Feel ready to proceed?"

She nodded.

"They've read you your rights?"

Again, a nod.

"I understand you've waived the right to have an attorney present."

"I don't have an attorney," she said.

Her voice was not what Chase expected. It was soft, husky. A bedroom voice with a heartbreaking quaver of grief.

"We can arrange for one, if you want," said Merrifield. "It may take some time, which means you'll have to be patient."

"Please. I just want to tell you what happened. . . ."

A smile touched Lieutenant Merrifield's lips. It had the curve of triumph. "All right, then," he said. "Let's begin." He placed a cassette recorder on the table and pressed the button. "Tell me your name, your address, your occupation."

The woman sighed deeply, a breath for courage. "My name is Miranda Wood. I live at 18 Willow Street. I work as a copy editor for the *Island Herald.*"

"That's Mr. Tremain's newspaper?"

"Yes."

"Let's go straight to last night. Tell me what happened. All the events leading up to the death of Mr. Richard Tremain."

Chase felt his whole body suddenly go numb. *The death of Mr. Richard Tremain.* He found himself pressing forward, against that cold glass, his gaze fixed on the face of Miranda Wood. Innocence. Softness. That's what he saw when he looked at her. What a lovely mask she wore, what a pure and perfect disguise.

My brother's mistress, he thought with sudden comprehension.

My brother's murderer.

In terrible fascination he listened to her confession.

"LET'S GO BACK a few months, Ms. Wood. To when you first met Mr. Tremain. Tell me about your relationship."

Miranda stared down at her hands, knotted together on the table. The table itself was a typically ugly piece of institutional furniture. She noticed that someone had carved the initials JMK onto the surface. She wondered who JMK was, if he or she had sat there under similar circumstances, if he or she had been similarly innocent. She felt a sudden bond with this unknown predecessor, the one who had sat in the same hot seat, fighting for dear life.

"Ms. Wood? Please answer my question."

She looked up at Lieutenant Merrifield. The smiling destroyer. "I'm sorry," she said. "I wasn't listening."

"About Mr. Tremain. How did you meet him?"

"At the *Herald.* I was hired about a year ago. We got to know each other in the course of business."

"And?"

"And..." She took a deep breath. "We got involved."

"Who initiated it?"

"He did. He started asking me out to lunch. Purely business, he said. To talk about the *Herald.* About changes in the format."

"Isn't it unusual for a publisher to deal so closely with the copy editor?"

"Maybe on a big city paper it is. But the *Herald*'s a small-town paper. Everyone on the staff does a little of everything."

"So, in the course of business, you got to know Mr. Tremain."

"Yes."

"When did you start sleeping with him?"

The question was like a slap in the face. She sat up straight. "It wasn't like that!"

"You didn't sleep with him?"

"I didn't—I mean, yes, I did, but it happened over the course of months. It wasn't as if we—we went out to lunch and then fell into bed together!"

"I see. So it was a more, uh, *romantic* thing. Is that what you're trying to say?"

She swallowed. In silence she nodded. It all sounded so stupid, the way he'd phrased it. A more romantic thing. Now, hearing those words said aloud in that cold, bare room, it struck her how foolish it all had been. The whole disastrous affair.

"I thought I loved him," Miranda whispered.

"What was that, Ms. Wood?"

She said, louder, "I thought I loved him. I wouldn't have slept with him if I didn't. I don't *do* one-night stands. I don't even do affairs."

"You did this one."

"Richard was different."

"Different than what?"

"Than other men! He wasn't just—just cars and football. He cared about the same things I cared about. This island, for instance. Look at the articles he wrote—you could see how much he loved this place. We used to talk for hours about it! And it just seemed the most natural thing in the world to..." She gave a little shudder of grief and looked down. Softly she said, "I thought he was different. At least, he seemed to be...."

"He was also married. But you knew that."

She felt her shoulders droop. "Yes."

"And did you know he had two children?"

She nodded.

"Yet you had an affair with him. Did it mean so little to you, Ms. Wood, that three innocent people—"

"Don't you think I thought about that, every waking moment?" Her chin shot up in rage. "Don't you think I hated myself? I never *stopped* thinking about his family! About Evelyn and the twins. I felt evil, dirty. I felt—I don't know." She gave a sigh of helplessness. "Trapped."

"By what?"

"By my love for him. Or what I thought was love." She hesitated. "But maybe—maybe I never really *did* love him. At least, not the real Richard."

"And what led to this amazing revelation?"

"Things I learned about him."

"What things?"

"The way he used people. His employees, for instance. The way he treated them."

"So you saw the real Richard Tremain and you fell out of love."

"Yes. And I broke it off." She let out a deep breath, as though relieved that the most painful part of her confession was finished. "That was a month ago."

"Were you angry at him?"

"I felt more . . . betrayed. By all those false images."

"So you must have been angry."

"I guess I was."

"So for a month you walked around mad at Mr. Tremain."

"Sometimes. Mostly I felt stupid. And then he wouldn't leave me alone. He kept calling, wanting to get back together."

"And that made you angry, as well."

"Yes, of course."

"Angry enough to kill him?"

She looked up sharply. "No."

"Angry enough to grab a knife from your kitchen drawer?"

"No!"

"Angry enough to go into the bedroom—your bedroom, where he was lying naked—and stab him in the chest?"

"No! No, no, no." She was sobbing now, screaming out her denials. The sound of her own voice echoed like some alien cry in that stark box of a room. She dropped her head into her hands and leaned forward on the table. "No," she whispered. She had to get away from this terrible man with his terrible questions. She started to rise from the chair.

"Sit down, Ms. Wood. We're not finished."

Obediently she sank back into the chair. "I didn't kill him," she cried. "I told you, I found him on my bed. I came home and he was lying there. . . ."

"Ms. Wood—"

"I was on the beach when it happened. Sitting on the beach. That's what I keep telling all of you! But no one listens. No one believes me. . . ."

"Ms. Wood, I have more questions."

She was crying, not answering, not able to answer. The sound of her sobs was all that could be heard.

At last Merrifield flicked off the recorder. "All right, then. We'll take a break. One hour, then we'll resume."

Miranda didn't move. She heard the man's chair scrape back, heard Merrifield leave the room, then the door shut. A few moments later the door opened again.

"Ms. Wood? I'll take you back to your cell."

Slowly Miranda rose to her feet and turned to the door. A young cop stood waiting, nice face, friendly smile. His name tag said Officer Snipe. Vaguely she remembered him from some other time, from her life before jail. Oh, yes. Once, on a Christmas Eve, he'd torn up her parking ticket. It had been a kind gesture, gallantry offered to a lady. She wondered what he thought of the lady now, whether he saw *murderer* stamped on her face.

She let him lead her into the hall. At one end she saw Lieutenant Merrifield, huddled in conference with Chief Tibbetts. The polite Officer Snipe guided her in the opposite direction, away from the pair. Miranda had gone only a short distance when her footsteps faltered, stopped.

A man was standing at the far end of the hall, watching her. She had never seen him before. If she had, she certainly would have remembered him. He stood like some unbreachable barrier, his hands jammed in his pockets, his shoulders looming before her in the cramped corridor. He didn't look like a cop. Cops had standards of appearance, and this man was on the far edge of rumpled—unshaven, dark hair uncombed, his shirt a map of wrinkles. What disturbed her the most was the way he looked at her. That wasn't the passive curiosity of a bystander. No, it was something far more hostile. Those dark eyes were like judge and jury, weighing the facts, pronouncing her guilty.

"Keep moving, Ms. Wood," said Officer Snipe. "It's right around the corner."

Miranda forced herself to move forward, toward that forbidding human barrier. The man moved aside to let her pass. As she did, she felt his gaze burning into her and heard his sharp intake of breath, as though he was trying not to breathe the same air she did, as if her very presence had somehow turned the atmosphere to poison.

For the past twelve hours she'd been treated like a criminal, handcuffed, fingerprinted, intimately searched. She'd had questions fired at her, humiliations heaped upon her. But never, until this man had looked at her, had she felt like a creature worthy of such disgust, such loathing. Rage suddenly flared inside her, a rage so fierce it threatened to consume her in its flames.

She halted and stared up at him. Their gazes locked. *There, damn you!* she thought. *Whoever you are, take a look at me! Take a good, long look at the murderess. Satisfied?*

The eyes staring down at her were dark as night, stony with condemnation. But as they took each other in, Miranda saw something else flicker in those depths, a hint of uncertainty, almost confusion. As if the picture he saw was all wrong, as if image and caption were terribly mismatched.

Just down the hall, a door swung open. Footsteps clicked out and stopped dead.

"Dear God," whispered a voice.

Miranda turned.

Evelyn Tremain stood frozen in the washroom doorway. "Chase," she whispered. "It's her...."

At once the man went to Evelyn and offered her his steadying arm. Evelyn gripped it with both hands, as if holding on to her only lifeline. "Oh, please," she murmured helplessly. "I can't stand to look at her."

Miranda didn't move. She felt paralyzed by guilt, by what she'd done to this woman, to the whole family. Though her crime might not be murder, still she had committed a sin against Evelyn Tremain and for that she would always be tormented.

"Mrs. Tremain," she said quietly. "I'm sorry...."

Evelyn buried her face against the man's shoulder. "Chase, please. Get her out of here."

"He loved you," said Miranda. "I want you to know that. I want you to know that he never stopped loving—"

"Get her out of here!" cried Evelyn.

"Officer," said Chase quietly. "Please. Take her away."

Officer Snipe reached for Miranda's arm. "Let's go."

As she was led away Miranda called over her shoulder, "I didn't kill him, Mrs. Tremain! You have to believe that—"

"You tramp!" shouted Evelyn. "You filthy whore! You ruined my life."

Miranda glanced back and saw the other woman had pulled away from Chase and was now facing her like some avenging angel. Strands of blond hair had fallen free and her face, always pale, was now a stark white.

"You ruined my life!" Evelyn screamed.

That accusing shriek echoed in Miranda's ears all the way down that long walk to the jail.

Drained of resistance, she quietly entered the cell. She stood there, frozen, as the door clanged shut. Officer Snipe's footsteps faded away. She was alone, trapped in this cage.

Suddenly she felt as if she were suffocating, as if she would smother without fresh air. She scrambled over to the one small window and tried to pull herself up by the bars, but it was too high. She ran to the cot, dragged it across the cell and climbed on top. Even then she was barely tall enough to peek over the sill, to gulp in a tantalizing taste of freedom. Outside the sun was shining. She could see maple trees beyond the fenced yard, a few rooftops, a sea gull soaring in the sky. If she breathed in deeply, she could almost smell the sea. Oh, Lord, how sweet it all seemed! How unattainable! She gripped the window bars so tightly they dug into her palms. Pressing her face against the sill, she closed her eyes and willed herself to stay in control, to keep panic at bay.

I am innocent. They have to believe me, she thought.

And then, *What if they don't?*

No, damn it. Don't think about that.

She forced herself to concentrate on something else, anything else. She thought of the man in the hallway, the man with Evelyn Tremain. What had Evelyn called him? Chase. The name stirred a memory; Miranda had heard it before. She snatched desperately at that irrelevant strand of thought, concentrated hard on dredging up the memory, anything to crowd the fears from her mind. Chase. Chase. Someone had said it. She tried to bring back the voice, to match it to the utterance of that name.

The memory hit her like a blow. It was Richard who'd said it. *I haven't seen my brother in years. We had a fall-*

ing-out when my father died. But then, Chase was always the problem kid in the family....

Miranda's eyes flew open with the revelation. Was it possible? There'd been no resemblance, no hint of familial ties in that face. Richard had had blue eyes, light brown hair, a weathered face always on the verge of sunburn. This man called Chase was all darkness, all shadow. It was hard to believe they were brothers. But that would explain the man's coldness, his look of condemnation. He thought she'd murdered Richard, and repulsion was exactly what he would feel, coming face-to-face with his brother's killer.

Slowly she sank onto the cot. Lying there beneath the window she could catch glimpses of blue sky and cloud. August. It would be a hot day. Already her T-shirt was damp with sweat.

She closed her eyes and tried to imagine soaring like a sea gull in that bright blue sky, tried to picture the island far below her.

But all she could see were the accusing eyes of Chase Tremain.

Chapter Three

He truly was the ugliest dog on earth.

Miss Lila St. John regarded her pet with a mixture of affection and pity. Sir Oscar Henry San Angelo III, otherwise known as Ozzie, was a rare breed known as a Portuguese Water Dog. Miss St. John was not quite clear as to the attributes of this particular breed. She suspected it was some sort of geneticist's joke. Her niece had presented the dog to her—"to keep you company, Auntie"—and Miss St. John had been trying to remember ever since what that niece could hold against her. Not that Ozzie was entirely without redeeming value. He didn't bite, didn't bother the cat. He was a passable watchdog. But he ate like a horse, twitched like a mouse and was absolutely unforgiving if you neglected to take him on his twice-daily walk. He would stand by the door and whine.

The way he was doing now.

Oh, Miss St. John knew that look. Even if she couldn't actually see the beast's eyes under all that fur, she knew what the look meant. Sighing, she opened the door. The black bundle of fur practically shot down the porch steps and took off for the woods. Miss St. John had no choice but to follow him, and so off into the woods she went.

It was a warm evening, one of those still, sweet twilights that seem kissed with midsummer magic. She would not be surprised to see something extraordinary tonight. A doe and fawn, perhaps, or a fox cub, or even an owl.

She moved steadily through the trees in pursuit of the dog. She noticed they were headed in a direct line toward Rose Hill Cottage, the Tremains' summer camp. Such a tragedy, Richard Tremain's death. She hadn't particularly liked the man, but theirs were the last two cottages on this lonely road, and on her walks here she had occasionally seen him through his window, his head bent in concentration at his desk. He'd always been polite to her, and deferential, but she'd suspected much of it was automatic and not, in any sense, true respect. He'd had no use for elderly women; he simply tolerated them.

But as for young women, well, she'd heard that was a different story.

It troubled her, these recent revelations about his death. Not so much the fact of his murder, but the identity of the one accused. Miss St. John had met Miranda Wood, had spoken to her on several occasions. On this small island, in the dead of winter, only green thumb fanatics braved the icy roads to attend meetings of the local garden club. That's where Miss St. John had met Miranda. They'd sat together during a lecture on triploid marigolds, and again at the talk on gloxinia cultivation. Miranda was polite and deferential, but genuinely so. A lovely girl, not a hint of dishonesty in her eyes. It seemed to Miss St. John that any woman who cared so passionately about flowers, about living, growing things, could simply not be a murderess.

It bothered her, all that cruel talk flying about town these days. Miranda Wood, a killer? It went against Miss St. John's instincts, and her instincts were always, always good.

Ozzie bounded through the last stand of trees and shot off toward Rose Hill Cottage. Miss St. John resignedly followed suit. That's when she saw the light flickering through the trees. It came from the Tremain cottage. Just as quickly, it vanished.

At once she froze as an eerie thought flashed to mind. *Ghosts?* Richard was the only one who ever used that cottage. *But he's dead.*

The rational side of her brain, the side that normally guided Miss St. John's day-to-day existence, took control. It must be one of the family, of course. Evelyn, perhaps, come to wrap up her husband's affairs.

Still, Miss St. John couldn't shake off her uneasiness.

She crossed the driveway and went up the front porch steps. "Hello?" she called. "Evelyn? Cassie?" There was no answer to her knock.

She tried to peer in the window, but it was dark inside. "Hello?" she called again, louder. She thought she heard, from somewhere in the cottage, a soft thud. Then—silence.

Ozzie began to bark. He danced around on the porch, his claws tip-tapping on the wood.

"Oh, hush!" snapped Miss St. John. "Sit!"

The dog whined, sat, and gave her a distinctly wounded look.

Miss St. John stood there a moment, listening for more sounds, but she heard nothing except the whap-whap of Ozzie's tail against the porch.

Perhaps she should call the police. She debated that move all the way back to her cottage. Once there, in her cheery little kitchen, the very idea seemed so silly, so alarmist. It was a good half-hour drive out here to the north shore. The local police would be reluctant to send a man all the way out here, and for what? A will-o'-the-wisp tale? Besides, what could there possibly be in Rose Hill Cottage that would interest any burglars?

"It's just my imagination. Or my failing eyesight. After all, when one's seventy-four, one has to expect the faculties to get a little screwy."

Ozzie walked in a tight circle, lay down and promptly went to sleep.

"Good Lord," said Miss St. John. "I'm talking to my dog now. What part of my brain will rot next?"

Ozzie, as usual, offered no opinion.

THE COURTROOM WAS PACKED. Already, a dozen people had been turned away at the door, and this wasn't even a trial, just a bail review hearing, a formality required by law to be held forty-eight hours after arrest.

Chase, who sat in the second row with Evelyn and her father, suspected the proceedings would be brief. The facts were stark, the suspect's guilt indisputable. A few words by the judge, a bang of the gavel and they'd all be out of there.

And the murderess would slink back to her cell, where she belonged.

"Damned circus, that's what it is," growled Evelyn's father, Noah DeBolt. Silver haired and gravel throated, at sixty-six he was still as formidable as ever. Chase felt the automatic urge to sit up straight and mind his manners. One did not slouch in the presence of Noah DeBolt. One was always courteous and deferential, even if one was an adult.

Even if one was the chief of police, Chase noted, as Lorne Tibbetts stopped and politely tipped his hat at Noah.

The principals were settling in their places. The deputy D.A. from Bass Harbor was seated at his table, flipping through a sheaf of papers. Lorne and Ellis, representing half the local police force, sat off to the left, their uniformed spines ramrod straight, their hair neatly slicked down. They had even parted it on the same side. The defense attorney, a youngster wearing a suit that looked as if it cost twice his annual salary, was fussing with the catch on his leather briefcase.

"They should clear this place out," grunted Noah. "Who the hell let all these spectators in? Invasion of privacy, I call it."

"It's open to the public, Daddy," said Evelyn wearily.

"There's public, and then there's *public*. These people don't belong here. It's none of their damn business." Noah rose and waved for Lorne's attention, but the chief of police's brilliantined head was facing forward. Noah glanced around for the bailiff, but the man had disappeared through a side door. In frustration, Noah sat back down. "Don't know what this town's coming to," he muttered. "All these new people. No sense of what's proper anymore."

"Quiet, Daddy," murmured Evelyn. Then, fuming, she muttered, "Where are the twins? Why aren't they here? I want the judge to see them. Poor kids without a father."

Noah snorted. "They're full-grown adults. They won't impress anyone."

"There. I see them," said Chase, spotting Cassie and Phillip a few rows back. They must have slipped in later, with the other spectators.

So the audience is in place, he thought. *All we need now are the two main players. The judge. And the accused.*

As if on cue, a side door opened. The ape-size bailiff reappeared, his hand gripping the arm of the much smaller prisoner.

At his second glimpse of Miranda Wood, Chase was struck by how much paler she appeared than he remembered. And how much more fragile. The top of her head barely reached the bailiff's shoulder. She was dressed unobtrusively, in a blue skirt and a simple white blouse, an outfit no doubt chosen by her attorney to make her look innocent, which she did. Her hair was gathered back in a neat but trim ponytail. No wanton-woman looks here. Those lush chestnut highlights were carefully restrained by a plain rubber band. She wore no jewelry, no makeup. The pallor of those cheeks came without the artifice of face powder.

On her way to the defendant's table she looked once, and only once, at the crowd. Her gaze swept the room and came to rest on Chase. It was only a few seconds of eye contact, a glimpse of her brittle mask of composure. Pride, that's what he saw in her face. He could read it in her body language: the straight back, the chin held aloft. Everyone else in this room would see it, too, would resent that show of pride. The brazen murderess, they'd think. A woman without repentance, without shame. He wished *he* could feel that way about her. It would make her guilt seem all the more assured, her punishment all the more justified.

But he knew what lay beneath the mask. He'd seen it in those eyes two days before, when they'd gazed out at him through a one-way mirror. Fear, pure and simple. She was terrified.

And she was too proud to show it.

FROM THE INSTANT MIRANDA walked into the courtroom, none of it seemed real. Her feet, her legs felt numb. She was actually grateful for the firm grip of the bailiff's hand around her arm as they stepped in the side door. She caught a kaleidoscopic glimpse of all those faces in the audience—if that's what you called a courtroom full of spectators. What else could you call them? An audience here to watch her performance, an act in the theater of her life. Half of them had come to hang her; the other half were here to watch. As her gaze slowly swept the room she saw familiar faces. There were her colleagues from the *Herald*: Managing Editor Jill Vickery, looking every bit the sleek professional, and staff reporters Annie Berenger and Ty Weingardt, both of them dressed à la classic rumpled writer. It was hard to tell that they were—or had been— friends. They all wore such carefully neutral expressions.

As her gaze shifted, she took in a single friendly face in the crowd—old Mr. Lanzo, her next-door neighbor. He was mouthing the words *I'm with you, sweetie!* She found herself almost smiling back.

Then her gaze shifted again, to settle on Chase Tremain's stony face. The smile instantly died on her lips. Of all the faces in the room, his was the one that most made her feel like shrinking into some dark, unreachable crevice, anywhere to escape his gaze of judgment. The faces beside him were no less condemning. Evelyn Tremain, dressed in widow's black, looked like a pale death's mask. Next to Evelyn was her father, Noah DeBolt, town patriarch, a man who with one steely look could wither the spirit of any who dared offend him. He was now aiming that poisonous gaze at Miranda.

The tug of the bailiff's hand redirected Miranda toward the defendant's table. Meekly she sat beside her attorney, who greeted her with a stiff nod. Randall Pelham was Ivy League and impeccably dressed for the part, but all Miranda could think of when she saw his face was how young he looked. He made her feel, at twenty-nine, positively middle-aged. Still, she'd had little choice in the matter. There were only two attorneys in practice on Shepherd's Island. The other was Les Hardee, a man with experience, a fine reputation and a fee to match. Unfortunately, Hardee's client list happened to include the names DeBolt and Tremain.

Randall Pelham had no such conflict of interest. He didn't have many clients, either. As the new kid in town, he was ready and willing to represent anyone, even the local murderess.

She asked softly, "Are we okay, Mr. Pelham?"

"Just let me do the talking. You sit there and look innocent."

"I am innocent."

To which Randall Pelham offered no response.

"All rise for His Honor Herbert C. Klimenko," said the bailiff.

Everyone stood.

The sound of shuffling feet announced the arrival of Judge Klimenko, who creaked behind the bench and sank like a bag of old bones into his chair. He fumbled around in his pockets and finally managed to perch a pair of bifocals on his nose.

"They brought him out of retirement," someone whispered in the front row. "You know, they say he's senile."

"They also say he's deaf!" shot back Judge Klimenko. With that, he slammed down the gavel. "Court is now in session."

The hearing convened. She followed her attorney's advice and let him do the talking. For forty-five minutes she didn't say a word as two men, one she barely knew, one she knew not at all, argued the question of her freedom. They weren't here to decide guilt or innocence. That was for the trial. The issue to be settled today was more immediate: should she be set free pending that trial?

The deputy D.A. ticked off a list of reasons the accused should remain incarcerated. Weight of evidence. Danger to the community. Undeniable flight risk. The savage nature of the crime, he declared, pointed to the defendant's brutal nature. Miranda could not believe that this monster he kept referring to was *her. Is that what they all think of me?* she wondered, feeling the gaze of the audience on her back. *That I'm evil? That I would kill again?*

Only when she was asked, twice, to stand for Judge Klimenko's decision did her attention shift back to the present. Trembling, she rose to her feet and gazed up at the pair of eyes peering down at her over bifocals.

"Bail is set at one hundred thousand dollars cash or two hundred thousand dollars secured property." The gavel slammed down. "Court dismissed."

Miranda was stunned. Even as the audience milled around behind her, she stood frozen in despair.

"It's the best I could do," Pelham whispered.

It might as well have been a million. She would never be able to raise it.

"Come on, Ms. Wood," said the bailiff. "Time to go back."

In silence she let herself be escorted across the room, past the gazes of all those prying eyes. Only for a second did she pause, to glance back over her shoulder at Chase Tremain.

As their gazes locked she thought she saw, for an instant, a flicker of something she hadn't seen before. Compassion. Just as quickly, it was gone.

Fighting tears, she turned and followed the bailiff through the side door.

Back to jail.

"THAT WILL KEEP HER locked away," said Evelyn.

"A hundred thousand?" Chase shook his head. "It doesn't seem out of reach."

"Not for us, maybe. But for someone like her?" Evelyn snorted. The look of satisfaction on her flawlessly made-up face was not becoming. "No. No, I think Ms. Miranda Wood will be staying right where she belongs. Behind bars."

"SHE HASN'T BUDGED an inch," said Lorne Tibbetts. "We've been questioning her for a week straight now and she sticks to that story like glue."

"It doesn't matter," said Evelyn. "Facts are facts. She can't refute them."

They were sitting outside, on Evelyn's veranda. At midmorning they'd been driven from the house by the heat; the sun streaming in the windows had turned the rooms into ovens. Chase had forgotten about these hot August days. In his memory, Maine was forever cool, forever immune to the miseries of summer. So much for childhood memories. He poured another glass of iced tea and handed the pitcher over to Tibbetts.

"So what do you think, Lorne?" asked Chase. "You have enough to convict?"

"Maybe. There are holes in the evidence."

"What holes?" demanded Evelyn.

Chase thought, *my sister-in-law is back to her old self again. No more hysterics since that day at the police station.* She looked cool and in control, which is how he'd always remembered her from their childhood. Evelyn the ice queen.

"There's the matter of the fingerprints," said Tibbetts.

"What do you mean?" asked Chase. "Weren't they on the knife?"

"That's the problem. The knife handle was wiped clean. Now, that doesn't make a lot of sense to me. Here's this crime of passion, see? She uses her own knife. Pure impulse. So why does she bother to wipe off the fingerprints?"

"She must be brighter than you think," Evelyn said, sniffing. "She's already got you confused."

"Anyway, it doesn't go along with an impulse killing."

"What other problems do you have with the case?" asked Chase.

"The suspect herself. She's a tough nut to crack."

"Of course she is. She's fighting for her life," said Evelyn.

"She passed the polygraph."

"She submitted to one?" asked Chase.

"She insisted on it. Not that it would've hurt her case if she flunked. It's not admissible evidence."

"So why should it change *your* mind?" asked Evelyn.

"It doesn't. It just bothers me."

Chase stared off toward the sea. He, too, was bothered. Not by the facts, but by his own instincts.

Logic, evidence, told him that Miranda Wood was the killer. Why did he have such a hard time believing it?

The doubts had started a week ago, in that police station hallway. He'd watched the whole interrogation. He'd heard her denials, her lame explanations. He hadn't been swayed. But when they'd come face-to-face in the hall, and she'd looked him straight in the eye, he'd felt the first stirrings of doubt. Would a murderess meet his gaze so unflinchingly? Would she face an accuser with such bald courage? Even when Evelyn had appeared, Miranda hadn't ducked for cover. Instead, she'd said the unexpected. *He loved you. I want you to know that.* Of all the things a murderess might have said, that was the most startling. It was an act of kindness, an honest attempt to comfort the widow. It earned her no points, no stars in court. She could simply have walked past, ignoring Evelyn, leaving her to her grief. Instead, Miranda had reached out in pity to the other woman.

Chase did not understand it.

"There's no question but that the weight of the evidence is against her," said Tibbetts. "Obviously, that's what the judge thought. Just look at the bail he set. He knew she'd never come up with that kind of cash. So she won't be walking out anytime soon. Unless she's been hiding a rich uncle somewhere."

"Hardly," said Evelyn. "A woman like that could only come from the wrong side of the tracks."

Wrong side of the tracks, thought Chase. Meaning poor. But not trash. He'd been able to see that through the one-way mirror. Trash was cheap, easily bent, easily bought. Miranda Wood was none of those.

A car marked Shepherd's Island Police pulled up in the driveway.

Tibbetts sighed. "Geez, they just won't leave me alone. Even on my day off."

Ellis Snipe, spindly in his cop's uniform, climbed out. His boots crunched toward them across the gravel. "Hey, Lorne," he called up to the veranda. "I figured you was here."

"It's Saturday, Ellis."

"Yeah, I know. But we sort of got us a problem."

"If it's that washroom again, just call the plumber. I'll okay the work order."

"No, it's that—" Ellis glanced uneasily at Evelyn. "It's that Miranda Wood woman."

Tibbetts rose to his feet and went over to the veranda railing. "What about her?"

"You know that hundred thousand bail they set?"

"Yeah."

"Well, someone paid it."

"*What?*"

"Someone's paid it. We just got the order to release her."

There was a long silence on the veranda. Then, in a low voice laced with venom, Evelyn said, "*Who* paid it?"

"Dunno," said Ellis. "Court says it was anonymous. Came through some Boston lawyer. So what do we do, huh, Lorne?"

Tibbetts let out a deep breath. He rubbed his neck, shifted his weight back and forth a few times. Then he said, "I'm sorry, Evelyn."

"Lorne, you can't do this!" she cried.

"I don't have a choice." He turned back to the other cop. "You got the court order, Ellis. Let her walk."

"I DON'T UNDERSTAND," said Miranda, staring in bewilderment at her attorney. "Who would do this for me?"

"A friend, obviously" was Randall Pelham's dry response. "A very *good* friend."

"But I don't have any friends with that kind of money. No one with a hundred thousand to spare."

"Well, someone's putting up the bail. My advice is, don't look a gift horse in the mouth."

"If I just knew who it was—"

"It's been handled through some Boston attorney who says his client wishes to stay anonymous."

"Why?"

"Maybe the donor's embarrassed."

To be helping a murderess, she thought.

"It's his—or her—right to remain anonymous. I say, take it. The alternative is to stay in jail. Not exactly the most comfortable spot to be in."

She let out a deep breath. "No, it isn't." In fact, it had been horribly bleak in that cell. She'd spent the past week staring at the window, longing for the simple pleasure of a walk by the sea. Or a decent meal. Or just the warmth of the sunshine on her face. Now it was all within reach.

"I wish I knew who to thank," she said softly.

"Not possible, Miranda. I say, just accept the favor." He snapped his briefcase shut.

Suddenly he irritated her, this kid barely out of braces, so smart and snazzy in his gray suit. Randall Pelham, Esquire.

"The arrangements are made. You can leave this afternoon. Will you be staying at your house?"

She paused, shuddering at the memory of Richard's body in her bed. The house had since been cleaned, courtesy of a housekeeping service. Her neighbor Mr. Lanzo had arranged it all, had told her the place looked fine now. It would be as if nothing had happened in that bedroom. There would be no signs of violence at all.

Except in her memory.

But where else could she go?

She nodded. "I—I suppose I'll go home."

"You know the drill, right? Don't leave the county. Bass Harbor's as far as you can go. Stay in touch at all times. And don't, I repeat don't, go around discussing the case. My job's tough enough as it is."

"And we wouldn't want to tax your abilities, would we?" she said under her breath.

He didn't seem to hear the comment. Or maybe he was ignoring her. He strode out of the cell, then turned to gaze at her. "We can still try a plea bargain."

She looked him in the eye. "No."

"That way we could limit the damage. You could walk out of here in ten years instead of twenty-five."

"I didn't kill him."

For a moment Pelham returned her gaze. With a shrug of impatience, he turned. "Plea bargain," he said. "That's my advice. Think about it."

She *did* think about it, all afternoon as she sat in that stark cell waiting for the release papers.

But as soon as she stepped out of the building and walked, as a free woman, into the sunshine, all thoughts of trading away even ten years of her life seemed unimaginable. She stood there on the sidewalk, gazing up at the sky, inhaling the sweetest air she'd ever breathed in her life.

She decided to walk the mile to her house.

By the time she came within sight of her front yard, her cheeks were flushed, her muscles pleasantly tired. The house looked the same as it always had, shingled cottage, trim lawn—which someone had obviously watered in her absence—brick walkway, a hedge of hydrangea bushes sprouting fluffy white clouds of flowers. Not a large house, but it was hers.

She started up the walkway.

Only when she'd mounted the porch steps did she see the vicious words someone had soaped on her front window. She halted, stung by the cruelty of the message.

Killer.

In sudden fury she swiped at the glass with her sleeve. The accusing words dissolved into soapy streaks. Who could have written such a horrible thing? Surely none of her neighbors. Kids. Yes, that's who it must have been. A bunch of punks. Or summer people.

As if that made it easier to dismiss. No one much cared what the summer people thought. The ones who lived on the island year round—those were the ones whose opinions counted. The ones you had to face every day.

She paused at the front door, almost afraid to go in. At last she reached for the knob and entered.

Inside, to her relief, everything seemed orderly, just the way things should be. A bill, made out by the Conscientious Cleaners Company, lay on the end table. "Complete cleaning," read the work order. "Special attention to the master bedroom. Remove stains." The work order was signed by her neighbor, Mr. Lanzo, bless him. Slowly she made a tour of inspection. She glanced in the kitchen, the bathroom, the spare bedroom. Her bedroom she left for last, because it was the most painful to confront. She stood in the doorway, taking in the neatly made bed, the waxed floor, the spotless area rug. No signs of murder, no signs of death. Just a sunny bedroom with plain farmhouse furniture. She stood there, taking it all in, not budging even when the phone rang in the living room. After a while the ringing stopped.

She went into the bedroom and sat on the bed. It seemed like a bad dream now, what she'd seen here. She thought, *If I just concentrate hard enough, I'll wake up. I'll find it was a nightmare.* Then she stared down at the floor and saw, by the foot of the bed, a brown stain in the oak planks.

At once she rose and left the room.

She walked into the living room just as the phone rang again. Automatically she picked up the receiver. "Hello?"

"Lizzie Borden took an ax and gave her mother forty whacks. When she saw what she had done, she gave her father forty-one!"

Miranda dropped the receiver. In horror she backed away, staring at the dangling earpiece. The caller was laughing now. She could hear the giggles, cruel and childlike, emanating from the receiver. She scrambled forward, grabbed the earpiece and slammed it down on the cradle.

The phone rang again.

She picked it up.

"Lizzie Borden took an ax—"

"Stop it!" she screamed. "Leave me alone!"

She hung up and again the phone rang.

This time she didn't answer it. In tears, she ran out the kitchen door and into the garden. There she sank into a heap on the lawn. Birds chirped overhead. The smell of warm soil and flowers drifted sweetly in the afternoon. She buried her face in the grass and cried.

Inside, the phone kept on ringing.

Chapter Four

Miranda stood alone and unnoticed outside the cemetery gates. Through the wrought-iron grillwork she could see the mourners grouped about the freshly dug grave. It was a large gathering, as befitted a respected member of the community. *Respected, perhaps,* she added to herself. *But was he beloved?* Did any among them, including his wife, truly love him? *I thought I did. Once....*

The voice of Reverend Marriner was barely a murmur. Much was lost in the rustle of the lilac branches overhead. She strained to hear the words. "Loving husband... always be missed ... cruel tragedy ... Lord, forgive ..."

Forgive.

She whispered the word, as though it were a prayer that could somehow pull her from the jaws of guilt. But who would forgive her?

Certainly not anyone in that gathering of mourners.

She recognized almost every face there. Among them were her neighbors, her colleagues from the newspaper, her friends. *Make that former friends,* she thought with bitterness. Then there were those too lofty to have made her acquaintance, the ones who moved in social circles to which Miranda had never gained entrance.

She saw the grim but dry-eyed Noah DeBolt, Evelyn's father. There was Forrest Mayhew, president of the local

bank, attired in his regulation gray suit and tie. In a cate-
gory all to herself was Miss Lila St. John, the local flower
and garden nut, looking freeze-dried at the eternal age of
seventy-four. And then, of course, there were the Tremains. They formed a tragic tableau, poised beside the
open grave. Evelyn stood between her son and Chase Tremain, as though she needed both men to steady her. Her
daughter, Cassie, stood apart, almost defiantly so. Her
flowered peach dress was in shocking contrast to the background of grays and blacks.

Yes, Miranda knew them all. And they knew her.

By all rights she should be standing there with them. She
had once been Richard's friend; she owed it to him to say
goodbye. She should follow her heart, consequences be
damned.

But she lacked the courage.

So she remained on the periphery, a lone and voiceless
exile, watching as they laid to rest the man who had once
been her lover.

She was still there when it was over, when the mourners
began to depart in a slow and steady procession through the
gates. She saw their startled glances, heard the gasps, the
murmurs of "Look, it's her." She met their gazes calmly.
To flee would have seemed an act of cowardice. *I may not
be brave,* she thought, *but I am not a coward.* Most of them
quickly passed by, averting their eyes. Only Miss Lila St.
John returned Miranda's gaze, and the look she gave her
was neither friendly nor unfriendly. It was merely
thoughtful. For an instant Miranda thought she saw a
flicker of a smile in those searching eyes, and then Miss St.
John, too, moved on.

A sharp intake of breath made Miranda turn.

The Tremains had halted by the gate. Slowly Evelyn
raised her hand and pointed it at Miranda. "You have no
right," she whispered. "No right to be here."

"Mom, forget it," said Phillip, tugging her arm. "Let's
just go home."

"She doesn't belong here."

"Mom—"

"Get her away from here!" Evelyn lunged toward Miranda, her hands poised to claw.

At once Chase stepped between the two women. He pulled Evelyn against him, trapping her hands in his. "Evelyn, don't! I'll take care of it, okay? I'll talk to her. Just go home. Please." He glanced at the twins. "Phillip, Cassie! Come on, take your mother home. I'll be along later."

The twins each took an arm and Evelyn allowed herself to be led away. But when they reached their car she turned and yelled, "Don't let the bitch fool you, Chase! She'll twist you around, the way she did Richard!"

Miranda stumbled back a step, physically reeling from the impact of those accusing words. She felt the gate against her back swing away, found herself grabbing at it for support. The cold wrought iron felt like the only solid thing she could cling to and she held on for dear life. The squeal of the gate hinges suddenly pierced her cloud of confusion. She found she was standing in a clump of daisies, that the others had gone, and that she and Chase Tremain were the only people remaining in the cemetery.

He was watching her. He stood a few feet away, as though wary of approaching her. As though she was some sort of dangerous animal. She could see the suspicion in his dark eyes, the tension of his pose. How aristocratic he looked today, so remote, so untouchable in that charcoal suit. The jacket showed off to perfection his wide shoulders and narrow waist. Tailored, of course. A real Tremain wouldn't consider any off-the-rack rag.

Still, she had trouble believing this man, with his Gypsy eyes and his jet black hair, was a Tremain.

For a year she had gazed up at those portraits in the newspaper building. They'd hung on the wall opposite her desk, five generations of Tremain men, all of them ruddy faced and blue eyed. Richard's portrait, just as blue eyed, had fit right in. Hang a portrait of Chase Tremain on that same wall and it would look like a mistake.

"Why did you come here, Ms. Wood?" he asked.

She raised her chin. "Why shouldn't I?"

"It's inappropriate, to say the least."

"It's very appropriate. I cared about him. We were—we were friends."

"Friends?" His voice rose in mocking disbelief. "Is that what you call it?"

"You don't know anything about it."

"I know that you were more than friends. What shall we call your relationship, Ms. Wood? An affair? A romance?"

"Stop it."

"A hot little tumble on the boss's couch?"

"Stop it, damn you! It wasn't like that!"

"No, of course not. You were just *friends.*"

"All right! All right...." She looked away, so he wouldn't see her tears. Softly she said, "We were lovers."

"At last. A word for it."

"And friends. Most of all, friends. I wish to God it had stayed that way."

"So do I. At least he'd still be alive."

She stiffened. Turning back to him she said, "I didn't kill him."

He sighed. "Of course you didn't."

"He was already dead. I found him—"

"In your house. In your bed."

"Yes. In my bed."

"Look Ms. Wood. I'm not the judge and jury. Don't waste your breath with me. I'm just here to tell you to stay away from the family. Evelyn's gone though enough hell. She doesn't need constant reminders. If we need to, we'll get a restraining order to keep you away. One false move and you'll be back in jail. Right where you belong."

"You're all alike," she said. "You Tremains and De-Bolts. All cut from the same fancy silk. Not like the rest of us, who can be shoved out of sight. Right where we be-long."

"It's not a matter of which cloth we're cut from. It's a matter of cold-blooded murder." He took a step toward her. She didn't move. She couldn't; her back was against the gate. "What happened, exactly?" he said, moving closer. "Did Richard break some sacred promise? Refuse to leave his wife? Or did he just come to his senses and decide he was walking out on you?"

"That's not what happened."

"So what did happen?"

"I walked out on *him!*"

Chase gazed down at her, skepticism shadowing every line of his face. "Why?"

"Because it was over. Because it was all wrong, every-thing between us. I wanted to get away. I'd already left the paper."

"He fired you?"

"I quit. Look in the files, Mr. Tremain. You'll find my letter of resignation. Dated two weeks ago. I was going to leave the island. Head somewhere I wouldn't have to see him every day. Somewhere I wouldn't be constantly re-minded of what a disaster I'd made of things."

"Where were you planning to go?"

"It didn't matter. Just away." She looked off, past the gravestones. Far beyond the cemetery lay the sea. She could catch glimpses of it through the trees. "I grew up just fifty miles from here. Right across the water. This bay is my home. I've always loved it. Yet all I could think about was getting away."

She turned to look at him. "I was already free of him. Halfway back to happiness. Why should I kill Richard?"

"Why was he in your house?"

"He insisted on meeting me. I didn't want to see him. So I left and went for a walk. When I came back, I found him."

"Yes, I've heard your version. At least your story's consistent."

"It's also the truth."

"Truth, fiction." He shrugged. "In your case it all blends together, doesn't it?" Abruptly he turned and headed up the cemetery drive.

"What if it's *all* truth?" she called after him.

"Stay away from the family, Ms. Wood!" he yelled over his shoulder. "Or I'll have to call in Lorne Tibbetts."

"Just for a moment, consider the possibility that I didn't kill him! That someone else did!"

He was still walking away.

"Maybe it's someone you know!" she shouted. "Think about it! Or do you already know and you want me to take the blame? Tell me, Mr. Tremain! Who *really* killed your brother?"

That brought Chase to a sudden halt. He knew he should keep walking. He knew it was a mistake to engage the woman in any more of this insane dialogue. It *was* insane. Or she was insane. Yet he couldn't break away, not yet. What she'd just said had opened up too many frightening possibilities.

Slowly he turned to face her. She stood absolutely still, her gaze fixed on him. The afternoon sun washed her head with a coppery glow. All that beautiful hair seemed to overwhelm her face. She looked surprisingly fragile in that black dress, as though a strong gust might blow her away.

Was it possible? he wondered. Could this woman really have picked up a knife? Raised the blade over Richard's body? Plunged it down with so much rage, so much strength, that the tip had pierced straight through to his spine?

Slowly he moved toward her. "If you didn't kill him," he said, "who did?"

"I don't know."

"That's a pretty disappointing answer."

"He had enemies—"

"Angry enough to kill him?"

"He ran a newspaper. He knew things about certain people in this town. And he wasn't afraid to print the truth."

"Which people? What sort of scandal are we talking about?"

He saw her hesitate, wondered if she was dredging up some new lie.

"Richard was writing an article," she said. "About a local developer named Tony Graffam. He runs a company called Stone Coast Trust. Richard said he had proof of fraud—"

"My brother had paid reporters on his staff. Why would he bother to do his own writing?"

"It was a personal crusade of his. He was set on ruining Stone Coast. He needed just one last piece of evidence. Then he was going to print."

"And did he?"

"No. The article was supposed to appear two weeks ago. It never did."

"Who stopped it?"

"I don't know. You'd have to talk to Jill Vickery."

"The managing editor?"

Miranda nodded. "She knew the article was in the works and she wasn't crazy about the idea. Richard was the driving force behind the story. He was even willing to risk a libel suit. In fact, Tony Graffam has already threatened to sue."

"So we have one convenient suspect. Tony Graffam. Anyone else?"

She hesitated. "Richard wasn't a popular man."

"*Richard?*" He shook his head. "I doubt that. I was the brother with the popularity problem."

"Two months ago he cut salaries at the *Herald*. Laid off a third of the staff."

"Ah. So we have more suspects."

"He hurt people. Families—"

"Including his own."

"You don't know how hard it is these days! How desperate people are for work. Oh, he talked a good story. About how sorry he was to be laying people off. How it hurt him just as much as it hurt everyone else. It was *garbage*. I heard him talking about it later, to his accountant. He said, 'I cut the deadwood, just as you advised.' Deadwood. Those employees had been with the *Herald* for years. Richard had the money. He could have carried the loss."

"He was a businessman."

"Right. That's exactly what he was." Her hair, tossed by the wind, was like flames dancing. She was a wild and blazing fire, full of anger at him, at Richard, at the Tremains.

"So we've added to the pool of suspects," he said. "All those poor souls who lost their jobs. And their families. Why don't we toss in Richard's children? His father-in-law? His wife?"

"Yes! Why not Evelyn?"

Chase snorted in disgust. "You're very good, you know that? All that smoke and mirrors. But you haven't convinced me. I hope the jury is just as smart. I hope to hell they see through you and make you pay."

She looked at him mutely, all the fire, all the spirit suddenly drained from her body.

"I've already paid," she whispered. "I'll pay for the rest of my life. Because I'm guilty. Not of killing him. I didn't kill him." She swallowed and looked away. He could no longer see her face, but he could hear the anguish in her voice. "I'm guilty of being stupid. And naive. Guilty of having faith in the wrong man. I really thought I loved your brother. But that was before I knew him. And then, when I did know him, I tried to walk away. I wanted to do it while we were still . . . friends."

He saw her hand come up and stroke quickly across her face. It suddenly struck him how very brave she was. Not brazen, as he'd first thought upon seeing her today, but truly, heartbreakingly courageous.

She raised her head again, her gaze drawing level to his. The tears she'd tried to wipe away were still glistening on her lashes. He had a sudden, crazy yearning to touch her face, to wipe away the wetness of those tears. And with that yearning came another, just as insane, a man's hunger to know the taste of her lips, the softness of her hair. At once he took a step back, as though retreating from some dangerous flame. He thought, *I can see why you fell for her, Richard. Under different circumstances I might have fallen for her myself.*

"Oh, hell," she muttered in disgust. "What does it matter now, what I felt? To you or to anyone else?" Without looking back she left him and started up the driveway. Her abrupt departure seemed to leave behind an unfillable vacuum.

"Ms. Wood!" he yelled. She kept walking. He called out, "Miranda!" She stopped. "I have one question for you," he said. "Who bailed you out?"

Slowly she turned and looked at him. "You tell me," she said.

And then she walked away.

IT WAS A LONG WALK to the newspaper building. It took Miranda past familiar streets and storefronts, past people she knew. That was the worst part. She felt them staring at her through the shop windows. She saw them huddle in groups and whisper to each other. No one came right out and said anything to her face. They didn't have to. *All I lack,* she thought, *is a scarlet letter sewn on my chest.* M *for murderess.*

She kept her gaze fixed straight ahead and walked up Limerock Street. The *Herald* building stood before her, a brick-and-slate haven against all those watching eyes. She ducked through the double glass doors, into the newsroom.

Inside, all activity came to a dead halt.

She felt assaulted by all those startled looks.

"Hello, Miranda," said a cool voice.

Miranda turned. Jill Vickery, the managing editor, glided out of the executive office. She hadn't changed clothes since the funeral. On dark-haired, ivory-skinned Jill, the color black looked quite elegant. Her short skirt hissed against her stockings as she clipped across the floor.

"Is there something I can do for you?" Jill asked politely.

"I—I came to get my things."

"Yes, of course." Jill shot a disapproving glance at the other employees, who were still gawking. "Are we all so efficient that we've no more work to do?"

At once everyone redirected their attention to their jobs.

Jill looked at Miranda. "I've already taken the liberty of cleaning out your desk. It's all in a box downstairs."

Miranda was so grateful for Jill's simple civility she scarcely registered annoyance that her desk had been cold-bloodedly emptied of her belongings. She said, "I've also a few things in my locker."

"They should still be there. No one's touched it." There was a silence. "Well," said Jill, a prelude to escape from a socially awkward situation. "I wish you luck. Whatever happens." She started back toward her office.

"Jill?" called Miranda.

"Yes?"

"I was wondering about that article on Tony Graffam. Why it didn't run."

Jill looked at her with frank puzzlement. "Why does it matter?"

"It just does."

Jill shrugged. "It was Richard's decision. He pulled the story."

"Richard's? But he was working on it for months."

"I can't tell you his reasons. I don't know them. He just pulled it. And anyway, I don't think he ever wrote the story."

"But he told me it was nearly finished."

"I've checked his files." Jill turned and walked toward her office. "I doubt he ever got beyond the research stage. You know how he was, Miranda. The master of overstatement."

Miranda stared after her in bewilderment. The master of overstatement. It hurt to admit it, but yes, there was a lot of truth in that label.

People were staring at her again.

She headed down the stairwell and pushed into the women's lounge. There she found Annie Berenger, lacing up running shoes. Annie was dressed in her usual rumpled-reporter attire—baggy drawstring pants, wrinkled cotton shirt. The inside of her locker looked just as disorderly, a mound of wadded-up clothes, towels and books.

Annie glanced up and tossed her head of gray-streaked hair in greeting. "You're back."

"Just to clean out my things." Miranda found the cardboard box with her belongings stuffed under one of the benches. She dragged it out and carried it to her locker.

"I saw you at the funeral," said Annie. "That took guts, Mo."

"I'm not sure guts is the word for it."

Annie shoved her locker door shut and breathed a sigh of relief. "Comfortable at last. I just had to change out of that funeral getup. Can't think in those stupid high heels. Cuts the blood supply to my brain." She finished lacing up her running shoe. "So what's going to happen next? With you, I mean."

"I don't know. I refuse to think beyond a day or two." Miranda opened her locker and began to throw things into the box.

"Rumor has it you have friends in high places."

"What?"

"Someone bailed you out, right?"

"I don't know who it was."

"You must have an idea. Or is this your lawyer's advice, to plead ignorance?"

Miranda gripped the locker door. "Don't, Annie. Please."

Annie cocked her head, revealing all the lines and freckles of too many summers in the sun. "I'm being a jerk, aren't I? Sorry. It's just that Jill assigned me to the trial. I don't like having to drag an old colleague across the front page." She watched as Miranda emptied the locker and shut the door. "So. Can I get a statement from you?"

"I didn't do it."

"I've already heard that one."

"Want to earn a Pulitzer?" Miranda turned, squarely faced her. "Help me find out who killed him."

"You'll have to give me a lead, first."

"I don't have one."

Annie sighed. "That's the problem. Whether or not you did it, you're still the obvious suspect."

Miranda picked up the box and headed up the stairs. Annie trailed behind her.

"I thought real reporters went after the truth," said Miranda.

"This reporter," said Annie, "is basically lazy and angling for early retirement."

"At your age?"

"I turn forty-seven next month. I figure that's a good age to retire. If I can just get Irving to pop the question, it'll be a life of bonbons and TV soaps."

"You'd hate it."

"Oh, yeah." Annie laughed. "I'd be just miserable."

They walked into the newsroom. At once Miranda felt all those gazes turn her way. Annie, oblivious to their audience, went to her desk, threw her locker keys in her drawer and pulled out a pack of cigarettes. "You happen to have a light?" she asked Miranda.

"You always ask me, and I never have one."

Annie turned and yelled, "Miles!"

The summer intern sighed resignedly and tossed her a cigarette lighter. "Just give it back," he said.

"You're too young to smoke, anyway," snapped Annie.

"So were you once, Berenger."

Annie grinned at Miranda. "I love these boy wonders. They're so damn petulant."

Miranda couldn't help smiling. She sat on the desktop and looked at her ex-colleague. As always, Annie wore a wreath of cigarette smoke. It was part addiction, part prop, that cigarette. Annie had earned her reporter's stripes in a Boston newsroom where the floor was said to be an inch deep in cigarette butts.

"You do believe me, don't you?" asked Miranda softly. "You don't really think..."

Annie looked her straight in the eye. "No. I don't. And I was kidding about being lazy," said Annie. "I've been digging. I'll come up with something. It's not like I'm doing it out of friendship or anything. I mean, I could find out things that could hurt you. But it's what I have to do."

Miranda nodded. "Then start with this."

"What?"

"Find out who bailed me out."

Annie nodded. "A reasonable first step."

The back office door swung open. Jill Vickery came out and glanced around the newsroom. "Marine distress call. Sailboat's taking on water. Who wants the story?"

Annie slunk deep in her chair.

Miles sprang to his feet. "I'll take it."

"Coast Guard's already on the way. Hire a launch if you have to. Go on, get going. You don't want to miss the rescue." Jill turned and looked at Annie. "Are you busy at the moment?"

Annie shrugged. "I'm always busy."

Jill nodded toward Miles. "He'll need help. Go with the kid." She turned back to her office.

"I can't."

Jill stopped, turned to confront Annie. "Are you refusing my assignment?"

"Yeah. Sort of."

"On what grounds?"

Annie blew out a long, lazy puff of smoke. "Seasickness."

"I KNEW SHE'D CONFUSE YOU, Chase. I just knew it. You don't understand her the way I do."

Chase looked up from the porch chair where he'd been brooding for the past hour. He saw that Evelyn had changed out of her black dress and was now wearing an obscenely bright lime green. He knew he should feel sorry for his sister-in-law, but at the moment Evelyn looked more in need of a stiff drink than of pity. He couldn't help comparing her to Miranda Wood. Miranda, with her ill-fitting black dress and her windblown hair, so alone on that cemetery hillside. He wondered if Richard ever knew how much damage he'd done to her, or if he'd ever cared.

"You haven't said a word since you got home," complained Evelyn. "What is going on with you?"

"Just how well did you know Miranda Wood?" he asked.

She sat down and fussily arranged the folds of her green dress. "I've heard things. I know she grew up in Bass Harbor. Went to some—some state university. Had to do it all on scholarship. Couldn't afford it otherwise. Really, not a very good family."

"Meaning what?"

"Mill workers."

"Ah. Dregs of the earth."

"What is the matter with you, Chase?"

He rose to his feet. "I need to take a walk."

"Oh. I'll go with you." She jumped to her feet, instantly wreaking havoc on all those nicely arranged folds of her dress.

"No. I'd like to be alone for a while. If you don't mind."

Evelyn looked as if she minded very much, but she managed to cover it gracefully. "I understand, Chase. We all need to mourn in our own way."

He felt a distinct sense of relief as he walked away from that front porch. The house had started to feel oppressive, as though the weight of all those memories had crowded out the breathable air. For a half hour he walked aimlessly. Only as his feet carried him closer to town did he begin to move with a new sense of purpose.

He headed straight for the newspaper building.

He was greeted by Jill Vickery, the sleekly attractive managing editor. It was just like Richard to surround himself with gorgeous women. Chase had met her earlier that day, at the funeral. Then, as now, she played the part of the professional to the hilt.

"Mr. Tremain," she said, offering her hand. "What a pleasure to see you again. May I show you around?"

"I was just wondering..." He glanced around the newsroom, which was currently occupied by only a bare-bones staff: the layout man arranging ads, another one staring at a computer screen, and that sloppy reporter puffing on a cigarette as she talked on the phone.

"Yes?" asked Jill.

"If I could go over some of my brother's files."

"Business or personal files?"

"Both."

She hesitated, then led him into the back office and through a door labeled Richard Tremain, Owner and Publisher. "These aren't all his files, you understand. He kept most of them here, but some he kept at home or at the cottage."

"You mean Rose Hill?"

"Yes. He liked to work out there, on occasion." She pointed to the desk. "The key's in the top drawer. Please let me know if you take anything."

"I wasn't planning to."

She paused, as though uncertain whether to trust him. But what choice did she have? He was, after all, the publisher's brother. At last she turned and left.

Chase waited for the door to shut, then he unlocked the file cabinet. He flipped immediately to the *W*'s.

He found a file on Miranda Wood.

Chase carried it to the desk and spread it open. It appeared to be a routine personnel record. The employment application was dated one year ago, when Miranda was twenty-eight. Her address was listed as 18 Willow Street. In the attached photograph she was smiling; it was the face of a confident young woman with her whole life ahead of her. It almost hurt to see how happy she looked. Her university record was outstanding. If anything, she was overqualified for her job as copy editor. Under the question "Why do you want this job?" she had written, "I grew up near Penobscot Bay. I want, more than anything, to live and work in the place I've always called home." He flipped through the pages and scanned the semiannual employee evaluation, filled out by Jill Vickery. It was excellent. He turned to the last page.

There was a letter of resignation, dated two weeks ago.

To: Richard Tremain, Publisher, *Island Herald.*
Dear Mr. Tremain,
I hereby notify you of my resignation from my position as copy editor. My reasons are personal. I would greatly appreciate a letter of reference, as I plan to seek employment elsewhere.

That was all. No explanations, no regrets. Not even a hint of recrimination.

So she told me the truth, he thought. *She really did walk off the job.*

"Mr. Tremain?" It was Jill Vickery, back again. "Are you looking for anything in particular? Maybe I can help you."

"Maybe you can."

She came in and gracefully settled into the chair across from him. Her gaze at once took in the file on the desk. "I see you have Miranda's employee record."

"Yes. I'm trying to understand what happened. Why she did it."

"I think you should know she was here just a short while ago."

"In the building?"

"She came to collect her things. I'm glad you two avoided a, uh . . . unexpected encounter."

He nodded. "So am I."

"Let me say this, Mr. Tremain. I'm very sorry about your brother. He was a wonderful man, an exceptional writer. He truly believed in the power of the printed word. We're going to miss him."

It was a canned speech, but she delivered it with such sincerity he was almost convinced she meant it. Jill Vickery certainly had the PR down flat.

"I understand Richard had a story in the pipeline," he said. "Something about a company called Stone Coast Trust. You familiar with it?"

Jill sighed. "Why does this particular article keep coming up?"

"Someone else interested?"

"Miranda Wood. She just asked about it. I told her that as far as I know, the story was never written. At least, I never saw it."

"But it was scheduled to run?"

"Until Richard canceled it."

"Why?"

She sat back and smoothly flicked her hair off her face. "I wouldn't know. I suspect he didn't have enough evidence to go to print."

"What, exactly, is the story on Stone Coast Trust?"

"Small-town stuff, really. Not very interesting to outsiders."

"Try me."

"It had to do with developers' rights. Stone Coast has been buying up property on the north shore. Near Rose Hill Cottage, as a matter of fact, so you know how lovely it is up there. Pristine coastline, trees. Tony Graffam—he's president of Stone Coast—claimed he was out to preserve the area. Then we heard rumors of a high-class development in the works. And then, a month ago, the zoning on those lots was abruptly changed from conservation to resort. It's now wide open to development."

"That's all there is to the article?"

"In a nutshell. May I ask the reason for your interest?"

"It was something Miranda Wood told me. About other people having motives to kill my brother."

"In this case, she's stretching the point." Jill rose to her feet. "But one can hardly blame her for trying. She hasn't much else to grab onto."

"You think she'll be convicted?"

"I wouldn't want to hazard a guess. But from what my news staff tells me, it sounds likely."

"You mean that reporter? Annie something?"

"Annie Berenger. Yes, she's assigned to the story."

"Can I talk to her?"

Jill frowned. "Why?"

He shook his head. "I don't know. I guess I'm just trying to understand who this Miranda Wood really is. Why she would kill." He sat back, ran his hand through his hair. "I still can't quite fit the pieces together. I thought, maybe someone who's been watching the case—someone who knew her personally..."

"Of course. I understand." The words were sympathetic but her eyes were indifferent. "I'll send Annie in to talk to you."

She left. A moment later Annie Berenger appeared.

"Come in," said Chase. "Have a seat."

Annie shut the door and sat in the chair across from him. She looked like a reporter: frizzy red hair streaked with gray, sharp eyes, wrinkled slacks. She also reeked of cigarettes. It brought back memories of his father. All she needed was a splash of whiskey on her breath. A good old newsman's smell.

She was watching him with clear suspicion. "Boss lady says you want to talk about Miranda."

"You knew her pretty well?"

"The word is *know*. Present tense. Yes, I do."

"What do you think of her?"

Her mouth twitched into a smile. "This is your own private investigation?"

"Call it my quest for the truth. Miranda Wood denies killing my brother. What do you think?"

Annie lit a cigarette. "You know, I used to cover the police beat in Boston."

"So you're familiar with murder."

"In a manner of speaking." Leaning back, she thoughtfully exhaled a cloud of smoke. "Miranda had the motive. Oh, we all knew about the affair. It's hard to hide something like that in this newsroom. I tried to, well, advise her against it. But she follows her heart, you know? And it got her into trouble. That's not to say she did it. Killed him." Annie flicked off an ash. "I don't think she did."

"Then who did?"

Annie shrugged.

"You think it's tied to the Tony Graffam story?"

Annie's eyebrow shot up. "You dig stuff up fast. Must run in the family, that newsman's nose."

"Miranda Wood says Richard had a story about to break. True?"

"He said he did. I know he was writing it. He had a few more details to check before it went to print."

"What details?"

"Financial data, about Stone Coast Trust. Richard had just got his hands on some account information."

"Why didn't the article get to print?"

"Honest opinion?" Annie snorted. "Because Jill Vickery didn't want to risk a libel suit."

Chase frowned. "But Jill says the article doesn't exist. That Richard never wrote it."

Annie blew out a last breath of smoke and stubbed out her cigarette in the ashtray. "Here's a piece of wisdom for you, Mr. T," she said. She looked him in the eye. "Never trust your editor."

DID THE ARTICLE EXIST or didn't it?

Chase spent the next hour searching the files in Richard's office. He found nothing under *G* for Graffam or *S* for Stone Coast Trust. He tried a few more headings, but none of them panned out. Did Richard keep the file at home?

It was late afternoon when he finally returned to the house. To his relief, Evelyn and the twins were out. He had the place to himself. He went straight into Richard's home office and continued his search for the Graffam file.

He didn't find it. Yet Miranda claimed it existed. So did Annie Berenger.

Something strange was going on, something that added to all his doubts about Miranda's guilt. He mentally played back all the holes in the prosecution's case. The lack of fingerprints on the murder weapon. The fact she had passed the polygraph test. And the woman herself—proud, unyielding in her protestations of innocence.

He gave up trying to talk himself out of his next move. There was no way around it. Not if he wanted to know more. Not if he wanted to shake these doubts.

He had to talk to Miranda Wood.

He pulled on his windbreaker and headed out into the dusk.

Five blocks later he turned onto Willow Street. It was just the way he'd remembered it, a tidy, middle-class neighborhood with inviting front porches and well-tended lawns. Through the fading light he could just make out the address numbers. A few more houses to go....

Farther up the street a screen door slammed shut. He saw a woman come down her porch steps and start toward him along the sidewalk. He recognized her silhouette, the thick cloud of hair, the slim figure clad in jeans. She'd taken only a few steps when she spotted him and stopped dead in her tracks.

"I have to talk to you," he said.

"I made a promise, remember?" she answered. "Not to go near you or your family. Well, I'm keeping that promise." She turned and started to walk away.

"This is different. I have to ask you about Richard."

She kept walking.

"Will you listen to me?"

"That's how I got into this mess!" she shot back over her shoulder. "Listening to a Tremain!"

He watched in frustration as she headed swiftly up the street. It was useless to pursue her. She was already a block away now, and by the set of her shoulders he could tell she wasn't going to change her mind. In fact, she had just stepped off the sidewalk and was crossing the street, as though to put the width of the road between them.

Forget her, he thought. *If she's too stubborn to listen, let her go to jail.*

Chase turned and had started in the opposite direction when a car drove past. He would scarcely have noticed it except for one detail: its headlights were off. A few paces was all it took for Chase to register that fact. He stopped, turned. Far ahead, Miranda's slender figure was crossing the street.

By then the car had moved halfway down the block.

The driver'll see her in time, he thought. *He has to see her.*

The car's engine suddenly revved up in a threatening growl of power. Tires screeched. The car leaped forward in a massive blur of steel and smoke, and roared ahead through the shadows.

It was aiming straight for Miranda.

Chapter Five

The headlights sprang on, trapping its insubstantial victim in a blaze of light.

"Look out!" Chase shouted.

Miranda whirled and found her eyes flooded with a terrible, blinding brightness. Even as the car shot closer and those lights threatened to engulf her, she was paralyzed by disbelief, by the detached sense of certainty that this was not really happening. She had no time to reason it out. An instant before that ton of steel could slam into her body, her reflexes took over. She flung herself sideways, out of the path of the onrushing headlights.

Suddenly she was flying, suspended for an eternity in the summer darkness as death rushed past her in a roar of wind and light.

And then she was lying on the grass.

She didn't know how long she had been there. She knew only that the grass was damp, that her head hurt and that gentle hands were stroking her face. Someone called her name, again and again. It was a voice she knew, a voice she thought, in that confused moment, she must have known all her life. Its very timbre seemed to blanket her with the warmth of safety.

Again he called her name, and this time she heard panic in his voice. *He's afraid. Why?*

She opened her eyes and dazedly focused on his face. That's when she registered exactly who he was. All illusion of safety fell away.

"Don't." She brushed his hand aside. "Don't touch me."

"Lie still."

"I don't need you!" She struggled to sit up, but found herself unable to move under his restraining hands. He had her pinned by her shoulders to the grass.

"Look," he said, his voice maddeningly reasonable. "You took a mean tumble. You might have broken something—"

"I said, don't touch me!" Defiantly she shoved him away and sat up. Pure rage propelled her to her knees. Then, as the night wavered before her eyes, she found herself sinking back to the grass. There she sat and clutched her spinning head. "Oh, God," she groaned. "Why can't you just—just go away and leave me alone."

"Not on your life," came the answer, grim and resolute.

To her amazement she was suddenly, magically lifted up into the air. Through her anger she had to admit it felt good to be carried, good to be held, even if the man holding her was Chase Tremain. She was floating, borne like a featherweight through the darkness. *Toward what?* she wondered with sudden apprehension.

"That's enough," she protested. "Let me down."

"Only a few more steps."

"I hope you get a hernia."

"Keep up the damn wiggling and I will."

He swept her up the porch steps and in the front door. With unerring instinct he carried her straight to the bedroom and managed to flick on the wall switch. The room—the bed—sprang into view. The bed where she'd found Richard. Though the blood was gone, the mattress new and unstained, this room would always remind her of death. She hadn't slept here since that night, would never sleep here again.

She shuddered against him. "Please," she whispered, turning her face against his chest. "Not here. Not this room."

For a moment he paused, not understanding. Then, gently he answered, "Whatever you say, Miranda."

He carried her back to the living room and lowered her onto the couch. She felt the cushions sag as he sat beside her. "Does anything hurt?" he asked. "Your back? Your neck?"

"My shoulder, a little. I think I fell on it."

She flinched at the touch of his hands. Carefully he maneuvered her arm, checking its range of motion. She was scarcely aware of the occasional twinges he evoked from her muscles. Her attention was too acutely focused on the face gazing down at her. Once again she was struck by how unlike Richard he was. It wasn't just the blackness of his hair and eyes. It was his calmness under fire, as though he held any emotions he might be feeling under tight rein. This was not a man who'd easily reveal himself, or his secrets, to anyone.

"It seems all right," he said, straightening. "Still, I'd better call a doctor. Who do you see?"

"Dr. Steiner."

"Steiner? Is that old goat still in practice?"

"Look, I'm okay. I don't need to see him."

"Let's just be on the safe side." He reached for the telephone.

"But Dr. Steiner doesn't make house calls," she protested. "He never has."

"Then tonight," Chase said grimly, dialing the phone, "I guess we're going to make history."

LORNE TIBBETTS POURED himself a cup of coffee and turned to look at Chase. "What I want to know is, what in blazes are you doing here?"

Chase, leaning over Miranda's kitchen table, wearily rubbed his face. "To tell you the truth, Lorne," he muttered, "I don't know."

"Oh."

"I guess I thought I could . . . figure things out. Make sense of what's happened."

"That's our job, Chase. Not yours."

"Yeah, I know. But—"

"You don't think I'm doing a good job?"

"I just get this feeling there's more than meets the eye. Now I know there is."

"You mean that car?" Lorne shrugged. "Doesn't prove a thing."

"He was *aiming* for her. I saw it. As soon as she stepped into the street he hit the gas."

"He?"

"He, she. It was dark. I didn't see the driver. Just the license plate. And the taillights. Big car, American. I'm pretty sure."

"Color?"

"Dark. Black, maybe blue."

Lorne nodded. "You're not a bad witness, Chase."

"What do you mean?"

"I had Ellis check on that license number. Matches a brown '88 Lincoln, registered to an island resident."

"Who?"

"Mr. Eddie Lanzo. Ms. Wood's next-door neighbor."

Chase stared at him. "Her neighbor? Have you brought him in yet?"

"The car was stolen, Chase. You know how it is around here. Folks leave their keys in the ignition. We found the car over by the pier."

Chase sat back, stunned. "So the driver's untraceable," he said. "That makes it even more likely he was trying to kill her."

"It just means it was some crazy kid out for a joyride. Got his hands on that wheel, got a little overwhelmed by all that power, pushed too hard on the gas pedal."

"Lorne, he was out to kill her."

Lorne sat down and looked him in the eye. "And what are you out to do?"

"Learn the truth."

"You don't believe she did it?"

"I've been hearing some things, Lorne. Other names, other motives. Tony Graffam, for instance."

"We've looked into that. Graffam was off the island when your brother was killed. I have half a dozen witnesses who'll say so."

"He could have hired someone."

"Graffam was in big enough trouble with that north shore development. Charges of bribing the land planning commission. That article would've simply been the last nail in the coffin. Anyway, how does this tie in with what happened tonight? Why would he go after Miranda Wood?"

Chase fell silent at that question. He couldn't see a motive, either. Other people in town might dislike Miranda, but who would go to the trouble of killing her?

"Maybe we're looking at this the wrong way," said Chase. "Let's ask a more basic question. Who put up the bail money? Someone wanted her out so badly he put up a hundred thousand dollars."

"A secret admirer?"

"In jail she's safe. Out here she's a sitting duck. You have any idea who bailed her out, Lorne?"

"No."

"The money could be traced."

"A lawyer handled the transfer of funds. All cash. Came from some Boston account. Only the bank knows the account holder's identity. And they aren't talking."

"Subpoena the bank. Get the name on that account."

"It'll take time."

"Do it, Lorne. Before something else happens."

Lorne went to the sink and rinsed his coffee cup. "I still don't see why you're getting into this," he said.

Chase himself didn't know the answer. Just this morning he'd wanted Miranda Wood put behind bars. Now he wasn't sure what he wanted. That innocent face, her heartfelt denials of guilt had him thoroughly confused.

He looked around the kitchen, thinking it didn't *look* like the kitchen of a murderess. Plants hung near the window, obviously well tended and well loved. The wallpaper had dainty wildflowers scattered across an eggshell background. Tacked to the refrigerator were snapshots of two little towheaded boys—nephews, maybe?—a schedule of the local garden club meetings and a shopping list. At the bottom of the list was written "cinnamon tea." Was that the sort of beverage a murderess would drink? He couldn't picture Miranda holding a knife in one hand and a cup of herbal tea in the other.

Chase looked around as Dr. Steiner shuffled into the kitchen. Some things on the island never changed, and this old grouch was one of them. He looked exactly the same as Chase remembered from his boyhood, right down to the wrinkled brown suit and the alligator medical bag. "All this to-do," the doctor said disapprovingly. "For nothin' but a muscle strain."

"You sure about that?" asked Chase. "She was sort of dazed for a minute. Right after it happened."

"I looked her over good. She's fine, neurologically speaking. You just keep an eye on her tonight, young man. Make sure she doesn't get into trouble. You know, headache, double vision, confusion—"

"I can't."

"Can't what?"

"I can't stay and watch her. It's awkward. Considering..."

"No kidding," muttered Lorne.

"She's not my responsibility," said Chase. "What do I do?"

Dr. Steiner grunted and turned for the kitchen door. "You figure it out. By the way," he said, pausing in the doorway, "I don't do house calls." The door slammed shut.

Chase turned to find Lorne looking at him. "What?"

"Nothing," said Lorne. He reached for his hat. "I'm going home."

"And what the hell am I supposed to do?"

"That," said Lorne with an I-told-you-so look, "is your problem."

MIRANDA LAY on the living-room couch and stared at the ceiling. She could hear voices from the kitchen, the sound of the door opening and closing. She wondered what Chase had told them, whether Tibbetts believed any of it. She herself couldn't believe what had happened. But all she had to do was close her eyes and it came back to her: the roar of the car engine, the twin headlights rushing at her.

Who hates me so much they want me dead?

It wasn't hard to come up with an answer. The Tremain family. Evelyn and Phillip and Cassie. . . .

And Chase.

No, that wasn't possible. His shout of warning had saved her life. If not for him, she would be lying right now on a slab in Ben LaPorte's Funeral Home.

That thought made her shudder. Hugging herself, she burrowed deeper into the couch cushions, seeking some safe little nook in which to hide. She heard the kitchen door open and shut again, then footsteps creaked into the living room and approached the couch. She looked up and saw Chase.

Weariness was what she read in his eyes, and uncertainty, as though he hadn't quite made up his mind what should be done next. Or what should be said next. He'd shed his windbreaker. His chambray shirt was the comfortably faded blue of a well-worn, well-loved garment. That shirt reminded her of her father, of how it used to feel to nestle her face against his shoulder, of those wondrous childhood scents of laundry soap and pipe tobacco and safety. That was what she saw in that faded blue shirt, what she longed for.

What she'd never find with this man.

Chase sat in the armchair. A prudent distance away, she noted. *Keeping me at arm's length.*

"Feeling better?" he asked.

"I'll be fine." She kept her voice like his—detached, neutral. She added, "You can leave if you want."

"No. Not yet. I'll wait here awhile, if that's okay. Until Annie gets here."

"Annie?"

"I didn't know who else to call. She said she'd be over to spend the night. You should have someone here to keep an eye on you. Make sure you don't slide into a coma or something."

She gave a tired laugh. "A coma would feel pretty good right now."

"That's not very funny."

She looked up at the ceiling. "You're right. It isn't."

There was a long silence.

Finally he said, "That wasn't an accident, Miranda. He was trying to kill you."

She didn't answer. She lay there fighting back the sob swelling in her throat. *Why should it matter to you?* she thought. *You, of all people.*

"Maybe you haven't heard," he said. "The car belonged to your neighbor. Mr. Lanzo."

She looked at him sharply. "Eddie Lanzo would never hurt me! He's the only one who's stood by me. My one friend in this town."

"I didn't say it was him. Lorne thinks the driver stole Mr. Lanzo's car. They found it abandoned by the pier."

"Poor Eddie," she murmured. "Guess that's the last time he leaves his keys in the car."

"So if it wasn't Eddie, who does want you dead?"

"I can make a wild guess." She looked at him. "So can you."

"Are you referring to Evelyn?"

"She hates me. She has every right to hate me. So do her children." She paused. "So do you."

He was silent.

"You still think I killed him. Don't you?"

Sighing, he raked his fingers through his hair. "I don't know what to think anymore. About you, about anyone. All I can be sure of is what I saw tonight. It's all tied in, this whole bloody mess. It has to be."

He looks so tired, so confused, she thought. *Almost as confused as I am.*

"Maybe you should move out of here for a few days," he said. "Until things get sorted out."

"Where would I go?"

"You must have friends."

"I did." She looked away. "At least, I thought I did. But everything's changed. I pass them on the street and they don't even say hello. Or they cross to the other side. Or they pretend they don't see me. That's the worst of all. Because I begin to think I don't exist." She looked at him. "It's a very small town, Chase. You either fit in, or you don't belong. And there's no way a murderess could ever fit in." She lay back against the cushions and stared at the ceiling. "Besides, this is my house. *My* house. I saved like crazy for the down payment. I won't leave it. It's not much, but at least it's mine."

"I can understand that. It's a nice house."

He sounded sincere enough, but his words struck her as patronizing. The lord of the manor extolling the charms of the shepherd's hovel.

Suddenly annoyed, she sat up. The abrupt movement made the room spin. She clutched her head for a moment, waiting for the spell to pass.

"Look, let's be straight with each other," she muttered through her hands. "It's only a two-bedroom cottage. The basement's damp, the water pipes screech and there's a leak in the kitchen roof. It's not Chestnut Street.''

"To be honest," he said quietly, "I never felt at home on Chestnut Street.''

"Why not? You were raised there.''

"But it wasn't really a home. Not like this house.''

Puzzled, she looked up at him. It struck her then how rough around the edges he seemed, a dark, rumpled stranger hulking in her mauve armchair. No, this man didn't quite fit on Chestnut Street. He belonged on the docks, or on the windswept deck of a schooner, not in some stuffy Victorian parlor.

"I'm supposed to believe you'd prefer a cottage on Willow Street to the family mansion?''

"I guess it does sound—I don't know. Phony. But it's true. Know where I spent most of my time as a kid? In the turret, playing around all the trunks and the old furniture. That was the only place in the house where I felt comfortable. The one room no one else cared to visit.''

"You sound like the family outcast.''

"In a way, I was.''

She laughed. "I thought all Tremains were, by definition, *in.*''

"One can have the family name and still not be part of the family. Or didn't you ever feel that way?''

"No, I was always very much part of my family. What there was of it.'' Her gaze drifted to the spinet piano, where the framed photo of her father was displayed. It was a grainy shot, one of the few she still had of him, taken with her old Kodak Brownie. He was grinning at her over the hood of his Chevy, a bald little gnome of a man dressed in blue overalls. She found herself smiling back at the image.

"Your father?'' asked Chase.

"Yes. Stepfather, really. But he was every bit as wonderful as any real father.''

"I hear he worked for the mill.''

She frowned at him. It disturbed her that Chase was obviously acquainted with that detail of her life. A detail that was none of his business. "Yes," she said. "Both my parents did. What else have you heard about me?"

"It's not that I've been checking up on you."

"But you have, haven't you? You and your family have probably run my name through some computer. Criminal check. Family history. Credit report—"

"We've done no such thing."

"Personal life. All the hot and juicy details."

"Where would I find those?"

"Try my police record." In irritation she rose from the couch and moved to the fireplace. There she stood focused on the clock over the mantelpiece. "It's getting late, Mr. Tremain. Annie should be here any minute. You're free to leave, so why don't you?"

"Why don't you sit back down? It makes me nervous, having you up and about."

"I make *you* nervous?" She turned to him. "You hold all the cards. You know everything about me. What my parents did for a living. Where I went to school. Who I slept with. I don't like that."

"Were there that many?"

His retort struck her like a physical blow. She could think of no response to such a cruel question. She was reduced to staring at him in speechless fury.

"Don't answer," he said. "I don't want to know. Your love life's none of my business."

"You're right. It's none of your damn business." She turned away, angrily clutching the mantelpiece with both hands. "No matter what you learn about me, it'll all fit right in with your image of the mill worker's daughter, won't it? Well, I'm not ashamed of where I came from. My parents made an honest living. They didn't have some trust fund to keep them in caviar. Like some families I know," she added, leaving no doubt by the tone of her voice just which family she was referring to.

He acknowledged the insult with a brief silence.

"I'm surprised you fell for Richard," he said. "Considering your attitude toward trust-funders."

"Before I knew Richard, I didn't *have* an attitude problem." She turned to confront him. "Then I got to know him. I saw what the money did to him. For him. He never had to struggle. He always had that green buffer to protect him. It made him careless. Immune to other people's pain." Her jaw came up in a pose of proud disdain. "Just like you."

"Now you're making the assumptions about me."

"You're a Tremain."

"I'm like you. I have a job, Miranda. I work."

"So did Richard. It kept him amused."

"Okay, maybe you're right about Richard. He didn't need to work. The *Herald* was more of a hobby to him, a reason to get up in the morning. And he got a kick out of telling his friends in Boston that he was a publisher. But that was Richard. You can't slap that rich-boy label on me because it won't stick. I was booted out of the family years ago. I don't have a trust fund and I don't own a mansion. But I do have a job that pays the bills. And, yes, keeps me *amused*."

His anger was tightly controlled but evident all the same. *I've touched a nerve,* she thought. An acutely sensitive one. Chastened, she sat in a chair by the fireplace. "I guess—I guess I assumed a few too many things."

He nodded. "We both did."

In silence they gazed at each other across the room. A truce, however uneasy, had at last settled between them.

"You said you were booted out of the family. Why?" she asked.

"Simple. I got married."

She looked at him in puzzlement. He had said the words without emotion, with the tone of voice one used to describe the weather. "I take it she wasn't a suitable bride."

"Not according to my father."

"The wrong side of the tracks?"

"In a manner of speaking. My father, he was attuned to that sort of thing."

Naturally, she thought. "And was your father right? About those girls from the wrong side of the tracks?"

"That wasn't why we got divorced."

"Why did you?"

"Christine was too...ambitious."

"Hardly a flaw."

"It is when I'm just the rung on the social ladder she's trying to climb."

"Oh."

"And then we had some lean years. I was working all the time, and..." He shrugged. Another silence stretched between them.

"Richard never told me what kind of work you do."

He leaned back, the tension easing away from his face. Unexpectedly he laughed. "Probably because what I do struck him as so damn boring. My partners and I design office buildings."

"You're an architect?"

"Structural engineer. My architect partners do the creative work. I make sure the walls don't come crashing down."

An engineer. Not exactly a fluff career, she thought, but a real, honest job. Like her father had.

She shook her head. "It's strange. When I look at you, I can't quite believe you're his brother. I always assumed..."

"That we'd be a matched set? No, we were definitely different. In more ways than you'll ever know."

Yes, the more she knew about Chase, the less he seemed like a Tremain. And the more she thought she could like him.

"What did you ever see in my brother?" he asked.

His question, voiced so softly, was jarring all the same. It reminded her of the ghosts that still hovered in this house.

She sighed. "I saw what I wanted to see."

"Which was?"

"A man who needed me. A man I could play savior to."

"Richard?"

"Oh, it *seemed* as if he had everything going for him. But he also had this...this vulnerability. This need to be saved. From what, I don't know. Maybe himself."

"And you were going to save him."

She gave a bitter laugh. "I don't know. You don't think about these things. You just feel. And you fall into it...."

"You mean you followed your heart."

She looked up at him. "Yes," she whispered.

"Didn't it seem wrong to you?"

"Of course it did!"

"But?"

Her whole body sagged with the weight of her unhappiness. "I couldn't...see my way out of it. I cared about him. I wanted to be there for him. And he'd string me along. He'd tell me things would work out, as long as we both had faith." She looked down at her hands, clasped together in her lap. "I guess I lost my faith first."

"In him? Or the situation?"

"Him. I began to see the flaws. It came out, after a while. How he manipulated people, used people. If he didn't need you, he'd ignore you. A user, that's what he was. An expert at making people do what he wanted."

"Then you broke it off. How did he react?"

"He couldn't believe it. I don't think anyone ever left *him.* He kept calling me, bothering me. And every day, at work, I'd have to face him. Pretend nothing was going on between us."

"Everyone knew, though."

She shrugged. "Probably. I'm not very good at hiding things. Annie knew, because I told her. And everyone else must have guessed." She sighed. The truth was, she hadn't cared at the time. Love, and then pain, had made her indifferent to public opinion.

They said nothing for a moment. She wondered what he thought of her now, whether any of it made a difference. Suddenly it mattered what he *did* think of her. He was scarcely more than a stranger, and a hostile one, but it mattered very much.

"You're not the first one, you know," he said. "There were other women."

It was a cruel revelation to spring on her, and Chase didn't know why he did it. He only knew that he wanted to give her a good, hard shaking. To shatter any rose-colored illusions she might still harbor about Richard. She might say the feelings were gone, but deep inside, might a few warm memories still linger?

He saw, by the look in her eyes, that his words had had their intended effect. Instantly he regretted the wounds he'd inflicted. Still, shouldn't she know? Shouldn't she be told just how naive she'd been?

"Were there many?" she asked softly.

"Yes."

She looked away, as though to hide the pain from view. "I—I think I knew that. Yes, I must have known that."

"It's just the way he was," said Chase. "He liked being admired. He was like that as a boy, too."

She nodded. And he realized, yes, she did know that about Richard. On some level she must have sensed his unquenchable thirst for admiration. And tried to satisfy it.

Chase had done damage enough. Here she was, demoralized and wounded. *And I pour on the salt.*

I should get out of here, leave her alone.

Where the hell was Annie Berenger?

Miranda seemed to shake herself back to life. She brushed her hair off her face, sat up and looked at him. So much torment in those eyes, he thought. And, at the same time, so much courage.

"You never told me why you're here," she said.

"The doctor thought someone should watch you—"

"No. I mean, why did you come in the first place?"

"Oh." He sat back. "I was at the *Herald* this afternoon. Talked to Jill Vickery, about the Stone Coast Trust article you mentioned. She says it was never written. That Richard never got that far with it."

Miranda shook her head. "I don't understand. I know he had at least a few pages written. I saw them on his desk, at the *Herald.*"

"Well, I couldn't find any article. I thought maybe you'd know where to look. Or maybe you'd have it."

She looked at him in bewilderment. "Why would I?"

"I assume Richard was a frequent visitor here."

"But he didn't bring his work. Have you checked the house?"

"It's not there."

She thought about it a moment. "Sometimes," she said, "he'd drive up to the north shore, to write. He had a cottage..."

"You mean Rose Hill. Yes, I suppose I should check there tomorrow."

Their gazes intersected, held. She said, "You're starting to believe me. Aren't you?"

He heard, in her voice, the stirring of hope—however faint. He found himself wanting to respond, to offer her some small scrap of a chance that he might believe her. It was hard *not* to believe her, especially when she looked at him that way, her gaze unwavering, those gray eyes bright and moist. They could rob a man of his common sense, those eyes, could sweep self-control right out from under him. They awakened other sensations as well, disturbing ones. She was sitting more than half a room away, but even at that distance her presence was like some heady perfume, impossible to ignore.

She asked again, softly, "Do you believe me?"

Abruptly he rose to his feet, determined to shake off the dangerous spell she was weaving around him. "No," he said. "I can't say that I do."

"But don't you see there's something more to this than just a—a crime of passion?"

"I admit, things don't feel quite right. But I'm not ready to believe you. Not by a long shot."

There was a knock on the door. Startled, Chase turned to see the door swing open and Annie Berenger poke her head in.

"Hello, cavalry's here," she called. She came in dressed in an old T-shirt and sweatpants. Blades of wet grass clung to her running shoes. "What's the situation?"

"I'm fine," said Miranda.

"But she needs watching," said Chase. "If there are any problems, Dr. Steiner's number is by the phone."

"Leaving already?" asked Annie.

"They'll be expecting me at home." He went to the door. There he paused and glanced back at Miranda.

She hadn't moved. She just sat there. He had the urge to say something comforting. To tell her that what he'd said earlier wasn't quite true. That he *was* starting to believe her. But he couldn't admit it to her; he could scarcely admit it to himself. And there was Annie, watching everything with her sharp reporter's eyes.

So he merely said, "Good night, Miranda. I hope you're feeling better. And Annie, thanks for the favor." Then he turned and walked out the door.

Outside, it took him a few seconds to accustom his eyes to the darkness. By the time he'd reached the edge of the front yard he could finally make out the walkway under his feet.

He could also see the silhouette of a man standing stoop-shouldered before him on the sidewalk.

Chase halted, instantly tense.

"She okay?" asked the man.

"Who are you?" demanded Chase.

"I could ask the same o' you," came the cranky reply.

"I'm . . . visiting," said Chase.

"So, is Mo gonna be all right, or what?"

"Mo? Oh, you mean Miranda. Yes, she'll be fine, Mr. . . ."

"Eddie Lanzo. Live next door. Like to keep an eye on her, y'know? Not good, a nice young woman livin' all by herself. And all these crazies runnin' around here, peekin' in windows. Not safe to be female these days."

"Someone's staying with her tonight, so you needn't worry."

"Yeah. Okay. Well, I won't bother her none, then." Eddie Lanzo turned to go back to his house. "Whole island's going to pot, I tell ya," he muttered. "Too many crazies. Last time I leave my keys in the car."

"Mr. Lanzo?" called Chase.

"Yeah?"

"Just a question. I was wondering if you were home the night Richard Tremain was killed?"

"Me?" Eddie snorted. "I'm always home."

"Did you happen to see or hear anything?"

"I already tol' Lorne Tibbetts. I go to bed at nine o'clock sharp, and that's it till morning."

"Then you're a sound sleeper? You didn't hear anything?"

"How can I with my hearing aid turned off?"

"Oh." Chase watched as the man shuffled back to his house, still muttering about Peeping Toms and car thieves. It somehow surprised Chase that a grouchy old geezer like Lanzo would show such concern about Miranda Wood. *A nice young woman,* Lanzo had called her.

What the hell does he know? thought Chase. *What do we ever know about anyone? People have their secrets. I have mine, Miranda Wood has hers.*

He turned and headed for Chestnut Street.

It was a twenty-minute walk, made invigorating by the brisk night air. When at last he stepped in the front door he found that, except for the lamp in the foyer, all the lights were out. Had no one else come home?

Then he heard Evelyn call out his name.

He found her sitting all alone in the darkened parlor. He could barely make out her shadow in the rocking chair. The dim glow of the street lamp through the window framed her silhouette.

"At last you're home," she said.

He started toward one of the lamps. "You need some light in here, Evelyn."

"No, Chase. Don't. I like the dark. I always have."

He paused, uncertain of what to say, what to do. He lingered in the shadows, watching her.

"I've been waiting for you," she murmured. "Where did you go, Chase?"

He paused. "To see Miranda Wood."

Her reaction was cold, dead silence. Even the creak of her rocking chair had stilled.

"She has you in her spell. Doesn't she?" Evelyn whispered.

"There's no spell. I just had some questions to ask her, about Richard." He sighed. "Look, Evelyn, it's been a long day for you. Why don't you go up and get some sleep?"

Still the figure did not move. She sat like a black statue against the window. "That night I called you," she said, "the night he died—I was hoping . . ."

"Yes?"

Another silence. Then, "I've always liked you, Chase. Since we were kids. I always hoped you'd be the one to propose. Not Richard, but you." The rocking chair began to creak again, softly. "But you never did."

"I was in love with Christine. Remember?"

"Oh, Christine." She hissed out the name in disgust. "She wasn't good enough for you. But you found that out."

"We were mismatched, that's all."

"So were Richard and I."

He didn't know what to say. He knew what she was leading up to, and he wanted to avoid that particular path of conversation. In all those years of growing up together he had never been able to picture himself and Evelyn DeBolt as a couple. Certainly she was attractive enough. And she was closer to his age than she was to Richard's. But he had seen, early on, that she had a talent for manipulating people, for twisting minds and hearts. The same talent Richard had possessed.

And yet, he felt so very sorry for her.

He said gently, "You're just tired, Evelyn. You've had a terrible week. But the worst of it's over now."

"No. The worst part is just beginning. The loneliness."

"You have your children—"

"You'll be leaving soon, won't you?"

"A few more days. I have to. I have a job in Greenwich."

"You could stay. Take over the *Herald*. Phillip's still too young to run it."

"I'd be a lousy publisher. You know that. And I don't belong here anymore. Not on this island."

For a moment they regarded each other through the shadows.

"So that's it, then," she whispered. "For us."

"I'm afraid so."

He saw the silhouette nod sadly.

"Will you be all right?"

"Fine." She gave a soft laugh. "I'll be just fine."

"Good night, Evelyn."

"Good night."

He left her sitting there by the window. Only as he moved toward the stairwell did he suddenly notice the sour odor lingering in the hall. An empty glass sat on the foyer table, near the telephone. He picked up the glass and sniffed it.

Whiskey.

We all have our secrets. Evelyn does, too.

He set the glass back down. Then, deep in thought, he climbed the stairs to bed.

Chapter Six

"So where were you two last night?" Chase asked.

The twins, busy attacking sausage and eggs, simultaneously looked up at their uncle.

"I was over at Zach Brewer's," said Phillip. "You remember the Brewers, don't you? Over on Pearl Street."

"What little Phil really means is, he was checking out Zach's sister," said Cassie.

"At least I wasn't holed up in some cave, pining for a date."

"I wasn't pining for a date. I was busy."

"Oh, sure," snorted Phillip.

"Busy? Doing what?" asked Chase.

"I was over at the *Herald,* trying to get a handle on things," said Cassie. "You know, Dad left things such a mess. No written plans for succession. Not a clue as to which direction he wanted the paper to go. Editorially speaking."

"Let Jill Vickery take care of it," said Phillip with a shrug. "That's what we pay her for."

"I'd think at least you'd care, Phil. Seeing as you're the heir apparent."

"These transitions need to be handled gradually." Phil nonchalantly shoveled another forkful of eggs into his mouth.

"In the meantime, the *Herald* drifts around rudderless. I don't want it to be just another church and social rag. We should turn it into a muckraking journal. Shake things up along the coast, get people mad. The way Dad got 'em mad a few months ago."

"Got who mad?" asked Chase.

"Those stooges on the planning board. The ones who voted to rezone the north shore. Dad made 'em out to look pretty greasy. I bet Jill was quaking in her shiny Italian shoes, waiting for that libel suit to pop."

"You seem to know a lot about what goes on at the *Herald*," said Chase.

"Of course. Second best tries harder."

She said it lightly, but Chase couldn't miss the note of resentment in her voice. He understood exactly how she felt. He, too, had been the second-best sibling, had spent his childhood trying harder, to no avail. Richard had been the anointed one. Just as Phillip was now.

The doorbell rang. "That'll be Granddad," said Phillip. "He's early."

Chase stood. "I'll get it."

Noah DeBolt was standing on the front porch. "Good morning, Chase. Is Evelyn ready for her appointment?"

"I think so. Come in, sir."

That "sir" was automatic. One simply didn't call this man by his first name. As Noah walked in the door, Chase marveled at the fact that the years hadn't stooped the shoulders in that tailored suit, nor softened the glare of those ice blue eyes.

Noah paused in the foyer and glanced critically around the house. "It's about time we made some changes in here. A new couch, new chairs. Evelyn's put up with this old furniture long enough."

"They're my mother's favorites," said Chase. "Antiques—"

"I know what the hell they are! Junk." Noah's gaze focused on the twins, who were staring at him through the doorway. "What, are you two still eating breakfast? Come on, it's eight-thirty! With the fees lawyers charge, we don't want to be late."

"Really, Mr. DeBolt," said Chase. "I can drive us all to the lawyer. You didn't have to bother—"

"Evelyn asked me to come," said Noah. "What my girl asks for, I deliver." He glanced up the stairs. Evelyn had just appeared on the landing. "Right, sweetheart?"

Head held high, Evelyn came down the stairs. It was the first Chase had seen of her since the night before. No tremor, no effects of whiskey were apparent this morning. She looked cool as aspic. "Hello, Daddy," she said.

Noah gave her a hug. "Now," he said softly, "let's go finish this unpleasant business."

They drove in Noah's Mercedes, Evelyn and her father in the front seat, Chase crammed in the back with the twins. How had Richard tolerated it all these years, he wondered, living in the same town with this bully of a father-in-law? But that was the price one paid for marrying Noah DeBolt's only daughter: eternal criticism, eternal scrutiny.

Now that Richard was dead, Noah was back in control of his daughter's life. He drove them to Les Hardee's office. He escorted Evelyn through the front door. He led her by the arm right up to the reception desk.

"Mrs. Tremain to see Les," said Noah. "We're here to review the will."

The receptionist gave them a strange look—something Chase could only read as panic—and pressed the intercom button. "Mr. Hardee," she said. "They're here."

Instantly Les Hardee popped out of his office. His suit and tie marked him as a dapper man; his sweating brow did not match the image. "Mr. DeBolt, Mrs. Tremain," he said, almost painfully. "I would have called you earlier, but I only just— That is to say, we . . ." He swallowed. "There seems to be a problem with the will."

"Nothing that can't be fixed," said Noah.

"Actually..." Hardee opened the conference-room door. "I think we should all sit down."

There was another man in the room. Hardee introduced them to Vernon FitzHugh, an attorney from Bass Harbor. FitzHugh looked like a working-class version of Hardee, articulate enough, but rough around the edges, the sort of guy who probably had had to sling hash to pay his way through law school. They all sat at the conference table, Hardee and FitzHugh at opposite ends.

"So what's this little problem with Richard's will?" asked Noah. "And what do you have to do with all this, Mr. FitzHugh?"

FitzHugh cleared his throat. "I'm afraid I'm the bearer of bad news. Or, in this case, a new will."

"What?" Noah turned to Hardee. "What's this garbage, Les? *You* were Richard's attorney."

"That's what I thought," said Hardee morosely.

"Then where did this other will come from?"

Everyone looked at FitzHugh.

"A few weeks ago," explained FitzHugh, "Mr. Tremain came to my office. He said he wanted to draw up a new will, superseding the will drawn up previously by Mr. Hardee. I advised him that Mr. Hardee was the one who should do it, but Mr. Tremain insisted I draw it up. So I honored his request. I would have brought it to your attention earlier, but I've been out of town for a few weeks. I didn't hear of Mr. Tremain's death until last night."

"This is bizarre," said Evelyn. "Why would Richard draw up a new will? How do we even know it was really him?"

"It was him," confirmed Hardee. "I recognize his signature."

There was a long silence.

"Well," said Evelyn. "Let's hear it, Les. What's been changed."

Hardee slipped on his glasses and began to read aloud. "I, Richard D. Tremain, being of sound mind and body—"

"Oh, skip the legal gobbledygook!" snapped Noah. "Get to the basics. What's different about the new will?"

Hardee looked up. "Most of it is unchanged. The house, joint accounts, contents therein, all go to Mrs. Tremain. There are generous trust accounts for the children, and a few personal items left to his brother."

"What about Rose Hill Cottage?" asked Noah.

Here Hardee shifted in his chair. "Perhaps I should just read it." He flipped ahead six pages and cleared his throat. "That parcel of land on the north shore comprising approximately forty acres, inclusive of the access road, as well as the structure known as Rose Hill Cottage, I bequeath to..." Here Hardee paused.

"What about Rose Hill?" pressed Evelyn.

Hardee took a deep breath. "I bequeath to my dear friend and companion, Miranda Wood."

"Like hell," said Noah.

ON THE STREET OUTSIDE Hardee's office, Noah and Evelyn sat side by side in the car. Neither one spoke. Neither was comfortable with the silence. The others had chosen to walk home, much to Noah's relief. He needed this time alone with Evelyn.

Noah said softly, "Is there anything you want to tell me, Evelyn?"

"What do you mean, Daddy?"

"Anything at all. About Richard."

She looked at her father. "Am I supposed to say something?"

"You can tell me, you know. We're family, that's what matters. And family stick together. Against the whole world, if they have to."

"I don't know what you're talking about."

Noah looked into his daughter's eyes. They were the same shade of green as his wife's eyes had been. Here was the one link he had left to his darling Susannah. Here was the one person in the world he still cared about. She returned his gaze calmly, without even the tiniest flicker of uneasiness. Good. Good. She could hold her own against anyone. In that way, she truly was a DeBolt.

He said, "I'd do anything for you, Evelyn. Anything. All you have to do is ask."

She looked straight ahead. "Then take me home, Daddy."

He started the engine and turned the car toward Chestnut Street. She didn't say a word during the entire drive. She was a proud girl, his daughter. Though she'd never ask for it, she needed his help. And she'd get it.

Whatever it takes, he thought. *It'll be done.*

After all, Evelyn was his flesh and blood, and he couldn't let flesh and blood go to prison.

Even if she was guilty.

HER GARDEN HAD ALWAYS been her sanctuary. Here Miranda had planted hollyhocks and delphiniums, baby's breath and columbine. She hadn't bothered with color schemes or landscape drawings. She'd simply sunk plants into the earth, scattered seeds and let the jungle of vines and flowers take over her backyard. They'd been neglected this past week, poor things. A few days of no watering had left the blooms bedraggled. But now she was home and her babies looked happier. Strangely enough, *she* was happy, as well. Her back was warmed by the sun, her hands were working the rich loam. This was all she needed. Fresh air and freedom. *How long will I have it?*

She put that thought firmly aside and swung the pickax into the hardened earth. She'd turn a little more soil, expand the perennial bed another two feet. She leaned the pickax against the house and knelt to loosen up the clods, sift out the stones.

The sun was making her drowsy.

At last, unable to resist the promise of a nap, she stretched out on the lawn. There she lay, her hands and knees caked with soil, the grass cushioning her bare legs. A perfect summer day, just like the days she remembered from her childhood. She closed her eyes and thought about all those afternoons when her mother was still alive, when her father would stand at the barbecue, singing as he grilled hamburgers....

"What a sharp game you play," said a voice.

Miranda sat up with a start and saw Chase standing at her white picket fence. He shoved open the gate and came into the yard. As he approached, it occurred to her how filthy she must look in her gardening shorts and T-shirt. Framed against the glare of sun and blue sky, Chase looked immaculate, untouchable. She squinted to see his expression, but all she could make out was a dark oval, the flutter of his windblown hair.

"You knew, didn't you?" he said.

She rose to her feet and clapped the dirt from her hands. "Knew what?"

"How did you manage it, Miranda? A few sweet whispers? Write me into the will and I'll be yours forever?"

"I don't know what you're talking about."

"I just came from our family attorney. We found a nasty surprise waiting for us. Two weeks ago Richard made out a new will. He left Rose Hill Cottage to you."

Her immediate reaction was stunned silence. In disbelief she stared at him.

"Nothing to say? No denials?"

"I never expected—"

"I think it's exactly what you expected."

"No!" She turned away, confused. "I never wanted a thing—"

"Oh, come on!" He reached for her arm and pulled her around to face him. "What was it, blackmail? A way to keep you quiet about the affair?"

"I don't know anything about a will! Or the cottage! Besides, how could he leave it to me? Doesn't it go to his wife? Evelyn owns half—"

"No, she doesn't."

"Why not?"

"Rose Hill came through my mother's family. An inheritance that went directly to Richard, so Evelyn had no claim on it. It was Richard's to pass on any way he chose. And he chose to give it to you."

She shook her head. "I don't know why."

"That cottage was the one place on this island he really cared about. The one place we both cared about."

"All right, then!" she cried. "*You* take it! It's yours. I'll sign a statement today, handing it over. I don't want it. All I want is to be left *alone*." She stared straight up at his coldly immobile face. "And to never, ever see another Tremain for as long as I live."

She broke away and ran up the back porch steps, into the house. The screen door slammed shut behind her. She headed straight into the kitchen, where she suddenly halted. There was nowhere else to run. In agitation she went to the sink and turned on the faucet. There, surrounded by her beloved ferns, she scrubbed furiously at the dirt caked on her hands.

She was still scrubbing when the screen door opened, then softly swung shut again. For a long time he didn't say a word. She knew he was standing behind her, watching her.

"Miranda," he said.

Angrily she turned off the faucet. "Go away."

"I want to hear your side of it."

"Why? You wouldn't believe me. You don't *want* to believe me. But you know what? I don't care anymore." She grabbed a dish towel and blotted her hands. "I'll go to the lawyer's this afternoon. Sign a statement of refusal, or whatever it's called. I would never accept it. Anything I received from him would be tainted. Just like I'm tainted."

"You're wrong, Miranda. I do want to believe you."

She stood very still, afraid to turn, to look at him. She sensed his approach as he moved toward her across the kitchen. And still she couldn't turn, couldn't face him. She could only stare down at the clumps of wet garden dirt in the sink.

"But you can't, can you?" she said.

"The facts argue against it."

"And if I tell you the facts are misleading?" Slowly she turned and found he was right there, so close she could reach up and touch his face. "What then?"

"Then I'd be forced to trust my instincts. But in this particular case, my instincts are shot all to hell."

She stared at him, suddenly confused by the signals he was sending. By the signals her body was sending. He had her closed off from all retreat, her back pinned against the kitchen sink. She had to tilt her head up just to meet his gaze, and the view she had of him, towering above her, was more than a little frightening. Yet it wasn't fear that seemed to be pumping through her veins. It was the warm and unexpected pulse of desire.

She slid away and paced across the kitchen, as far as she could get from him and still be in the same room. "I meant what I said. About refusing all rights to Rose Hill Cottage. In fact, I think we should do it right now. Go to the lawyer."

"Is that really what you want?"

"I know I don't want anything of his. Anything to remind me of him."

"You'd give up the cottage, just like that?"

"It doesn't mean a thing to me. I've never even seen the place."

Chase looked surprised. "He never took you to Rose Hill?"

"No. Oh, he told me about it. But it was his own private retreat. Not the sort of place he'd share with me."

"You could be handing back a fortune in real estate, sight unseen."

"It's not my fortune. It never was."

He regarded her with narrowed eyes. "I can't figure you out. Every time I think I have, you throw me a curve ball."

"I'm not all that complicated."

"You managed to intrigue Richard."

"I was hardly the first woman to do that."

"But you're the first one who ever left him."

"And look where it got me." She gave a bitter laugh. "You may not believe this, but I used to think of myself as a person with high morals. I paid my taxes. Stopped at every red light. Followed all the rules." She turned and stared out the window. Softly she said, "Then I fell for your brother. Suddenly I didn't know what the rules were anymore. I was slipping around in strange territory. God, it scared me. At the same time I felt...exhilarated. And that scared me even more." She turned to him. "I'd give anything to turn back the clock. To feel ... innocent again."

Slowly he came toward her. "Some things we can't recapture, Miranda."

"No." She stared down, her cheeks flushed with guilt. "Some things we lose forever."

His touch, so unexpected, made her flinch. It was the gentlest of strokes, just his hand tracing the curve of her cheek. Startled, she looked up to find a gaze so searching it left her nowhere to hide. She hated feeling so nakedly exposed but she found she could not break away. The hand cupping her face was warm and so very compelling.

Here I am, falling into the same old trap, she thought. *With Richard I lost my innocence. What will I lose to this man? My soul?*

She said, "I learned my lesson from your brother, Chase. I'm no longer fair game." She turned and walked away, into the living room.

"I'm not Richard."

She looked back. "It doesn't matter who you are. What matters is that I'm not the same dumb, trusting soul I used to be."

"He really hurt you, didn't he?" He was watching her from the kitchen threshold. His shoulders seemed to fill the doorway.

She didn't answer. She sank into an armchair and stared at her dirt-stained knees.

Chase studied her from across the room. All his anger toward her, which had built up since that morning in Les Hardee's office, suddenly evaporated. In its place was a fury toward Richard. Golden boy Richard, who had always gotten what he wanted. Richard the firstborn, the one with the classic Tremain fair hair and blue eyes, had bought everything he ever coveted with the coin of wit and charm. But once he'd attained his goal, he'd lose interest.

That was his pattern with women. Once, Richard had wanted Evelyn DeBolt, and he'd won her. He'd had to marry her, of course. You didn't play games with the only child of Noah DeBolt. But after the prize was his he'd grown bored with his wife. That was Richard, always coveting, never satisfied.

And here was the one woman, the one prize, he hadn't been able to keep. Such an unassuming female, thought Chase, feeling a strange ache in his throat. Was it pity or sympathy? He couldn't tell the difference.

He sat in the chair across from her. "You...seem to have recovered from last night."

"Just some sore muscles. That's all." She shrugged, as though she knew he couldn't possibly be interested. Whatever turmoil was swirling in her head, she kept it carefully concealed. "I sent Annie home this morning. I couldn't see the point of her staying."

"Safety's sake?"

"Safety from what?"

"What if it wasn't an accident?"

She looked up. "At the moment I'm not terrifically popular in this town. But I can't see one of our upstanding citizens turning hit-and-run driver."

"Still, one of our upstanding citizens did steal Mr. Lanzo's car."

"Poor Eddie." She shook her head. "It'll just reinforce his paranoia. Now he'll add car thieves to that list of crazies he imagines cruising the street."

"Yes, he mentioned that last night. Something about Peeping Toms."

She smiled. "Eddie grew up in Chicago. He never did shake those big-city jitters. He swears he spotted some mob car watching my..." She suddenly paused, frowning. "You know, I never paid much attention to his stories. But now that I think about it..."

"When did he tell you about that car?"

"Maybe a month or two ago."

"Before Richard's murder, then."

"Yes. So it's probably not related." She sighed. "It's just poor, crazy Eddie." She stood. "I'll change clothes. I can't go to the lawyer looking like this."

"You really want to go right now?"

"I have to. Until I do, I won't feel clean. Or free of him."

"I'll call ahead, then." He glanced at his watch. "We can just make the ferry to Bass Harbor."

"Bass Harbor? I thought Les Hardee was Richard's lawyer."

"He is. But this last will was drawn up by some lawyer named Vernon FitzHugh. Do you know him?"

"No, thank God." She turned and headed up the hall. "Or you'd probably accuse Mr. FitzHugh and me of fraud." She vanished into the bedroom.

Chase watched the door swing shut behind her. "As a matter of fact," he muttered, "the thought did cross my mind."

VERNON FITZHUGH WAS expecting them. What he didn't anticipate was the purpose of their visit.

"Have you really thought this through, Ms. Wood? This is prime real estate we're talking about. The north shore has just been rezoned for development. I expect your piece of property, in a few years, will be worth well over—"

"It should never have come to me," said Miranda. "It belongs to the Tremain family."

FitzHugh glanced uneasily at Chase, one of those sidelong looks that reveal so much. "Perhaps we should discuss this in private, Ms. Wood. If Mr. Tremain would care to wait outside..."

"No, I want him to stay. I want him to hear every word." She looked meaningfully at FitzHugh. "So he can't accuse us of collusion."

"Collusion?" FitzHugh, alarmed, sat up straight. "Mr. Tremain, you don't think I wanted to get involved in this, do you? It's a messy situation. Two lawyers, two wills. And then, the complicating circumstances of the client's death." He assiduously avoided looking at Miranda. "I'm just trying to carry out Mr. Tremain's instructions. Which are to ensure that Rose Hill Cottage goes to Ms. Wood."

"I don't want it," said Miranda. "I want to give it back."

FitzHugh looked troubled. He removed his glasses and set them on the desk. It seemed, with that one gesture, he simultaneously shed the role of the detached professional. Now he was speaking to her as a friend, an adviser. The flat accent of a working-class Mainer slipped into his voice. This man knew only too well what it was like to be poor. And here was this stubborn young woman, throwing away the promise of security.

"Richard Tremain," he began, "came to me with a request. I'm bound to honor it. It's not my job to decide whether you're innocent or guilty. I just want to see that the intent of the will is carried out. I made very sure that this was what he wanted, and he wanted that land to go to you.

If you're convicted, then the point will be moot—you can't inherit. But let's say you're found innocent. Then Rose Hill goes to you, no question about it. Wait a few days, Ms. Wood. If this is really what you want, come back and I'll draw up the papers. But I won't do it today. I have to think of Mr. Tremain's last request. After all, he was my client.''

"Why *did* he come to you?" Chase asked. "Mr. Hardee has been Richard's attorney for years.''

FitzHugh studied Chase for a moment, weighing the man's motives. Coercion was what he suspected, the wealthy Tremain family putting pressure on this woman, this outsider, to surrender her inheritance. It wasn't right. Someone had to take the woman's side, even if she refused to stand up for herself.

"Richard Tremain came to me," FitzHugh said, "because he *didn't* want Les Hardee involved.''

"Why not?''

"Mr. Hardee is also Noah DeBolt's attorney. I think Mr. Tremain was worried this would leak out to his father-in-law.''

"And what a riot that would have caused," said Chase.

"Having met Mr. DeBolt this morning, yes, I can imagine there would've been fireworks.''

Chase leaned forward, his gaze narrowing on the attorney. "The day Richard was here to change his will, how did he seem to you? I mean, his state of mind. People don't just walk in and change their wills for no good reason.''

FitzHugh frowned. "Well, he seemed...upset. He didn't mention any fear of dying. Said he just wanted to straighten out his affairs....'' He glanced at Miranda and reddened at the unintentional double entendre.

Miranda flushed, as well, but she refused to shrink from his gaze. *I'm through with being punished,* she thought. *Through with cringing at the looks people give me.*

"You said he was upset. What do you mean?" asked Chase.

"He seemed angry.''

"At whom?"

"We didn't discuss it. He just came in and said he didn't want the cottage to go to Mrs. Tremain."

"He was specific about Evelyn?"

"Yes. And he was concerned only about Rose Hill Cottage. Not the bank account or the other assets. I assumed it was because those other assets were joint marital property, and he couldn't redirect those. But Rose Hill was his, through inheritance. He could dispose of it as he wished." FitzHugh looked at Miranda. "And he wanted you to have it."

She shook her head. "Why?"

"I assume, because he cared about you. Giving you Rose Hill was his way of telling you how much."

In silence Miranda bowed her head. She knew both men were watching her. She wondered what expression she'd see in Chase's eyes. Cynicism? Disbelief? *You can't imagine that your brother would feel love, not just lust, for a woman like me?*

"So, Ms. Wood?" asked FitzHugh. "You agree this isn't a move you should make?"

She raised her head and looked across the desk at the attorney. "Draw up the papers. I want to do it now."

"Maybe you don't," said Chase quietly.

Miranda looked at him in disbelief. "What?"

"Mr. FitzHugh has brought up some points I hadn't considered. You should think about it, just for a few days." His gaze met Miranda's. She could see that he was baffled by something he'd heard here today.

"Are you saying I should keep Rose Hill Cottage?"

"All I'm saying is this. Richard had a reason for changing the will. Before we go changing things back, let's find out why he did it."

Vernon FitzHugh nodded. "My thoughts exactly," he said.

THEY EXCHANGED SCARCELY a word on the ferry back to Shepherd's Island. Only when they'd driven off the pier and turned onto Shore Circle Road did Miranda stir from her silence. "Where are we going?" she asked.

"The north shore."

"Why?"

"I want you to see Rose Hill. It's only fair you know exactly what you're handing back to Evelyn."

"You enjoy this, don't you?" she said. "Running me around in circles. Playing your little mind games. One minute you say I'm stealing Tremain property. The next, you're trying to talk me into playing thief. What's the point of it all, Chase?"

"I'm bothered by what FitzHugh told us. That Richard wanted to keep the cottage away from Evelyn."

"But it *should* go to her."

"Rose Hill came from my mother's side. The Pruitts. Evelyn has no claim to it."

"He could have left it to you."

Chase laughed. "Not likely."

"Why not?"

"We weren't exactly the closest of brothers. I was lucky just to get his collection of rusty Civil War swords. No, he wanted Rose Hill to go to someone he loved. You were his first choice. Maybe his only choice."

"He didn't love me, Chase," she said softly. "Not really."

They drove north, winding past summer cottages, past granite cliffs jagged with pines, past stony beaches where waves broke into white foam. Gulls circled and swooped at the blue-gray sea.

"Why did you say that?" he asked. "About Richard not loving you?"

"Because I knew. I think I always knew. Oh, maybe he *thought* he loved me. But for Richard, love was a lot of moonlight and madness. A fever that eventually breaks. It was just a matter of time."

"That sounds like Richard. As a kid, he was always in pursuit of the never-ending high."

"Are all you Tremains like that?"

"Hardly. My father was married to his work."

"And what are you married to?"

He glanced at her. She was struck by the intensity of his gaze, the gaze of a man who's not afraid to tell the truth. "Nothing and no one. At least, not anymore. Not since Christine."

"Your wife?"

He nodded. "It didn't last very long. I was just a kid, really, only twenty. Doing my share of wild and crazy things. It was a handy way to get back at my father, and it worked."

"What happened to Christine?"

"She found out I wasn't going to inherit the Tremain fortune and she walked out. Smart girl. She, at least, was using her head."

He focused on the road, which he obviously knew well. Miranda noticed how easily he handled the curves, guiding the car skillfully around each treacherous bend. Whatever wildness he'd displayed in his youth had since been reined in. Here was a man in tight control of his life, his emotions, not a man in pursuit of the ephemeral moonlight and madness.

A twenty-minute drive brought them to the last stretch of paved road. The asphalt gave way to a dirt access road flanked by birch and pine. Rustic signs proclaimed the different camps hidden among the tress. Mom and Pop's. Brandywine Cottage. Sanity Camp. Here and there, dirt tracks led off to the dozen or so summer retreats of prominent island families, most of whom had held their cottages for generations.

The access road began to climb, winding a half mile up the contours of the hillside. They passed a stone marker labeled St. John's Wood. Then they came to the last sign, every bit as rustic as the others: Rose Hill. A final bend in the road took them through the last stand of trees, and then a broad, sloping field lay before them. It sat at the very crest of the hill—a weathered cottage facing north, to the sea. Vines of purple clematis clung lovingly about the veranda railings. Rosebushes, overgrown with weeds but still valiantly blooming, crouched like thorny sentinels beside the porch steps.

They parked in the gravel turnaround and stepped out into an afternoon fragrant with the scent of flowers and sun-warmed grass. For a moment Miranda stood motionless, her face turned to the sky. Not a cloud marred that perfect blue. A single gull, riding the wind off the hillside, drifted overhead.

"Come on," said Chase. "Let me show you inside."

He led her up the porch steps. "I haven't seen the place in at least ten years. I'm almost afraid to go in."

"Afraid of what?"

"The changes. Of what they might've done to it. But I guess that's how it is with your childhood home."

"Especially if you were happy there."

He smiled. "Exactly."

For a moment they stood and regarded the old porch swing, creaking back and forth in the breeze.

"Do you have a key?" she asked.

"There should be one under here." He crouched down beneath one of the windowsills. "There's this little crack in the wood where Mom always kept a spare key...." He sighed and straightened. "Not anymore. Well, if the door's locked, maybe we can find a window open somewhere." Tentatively he reached for the knob. "How do you like that?" He laughed, pushing open the door. "It's not even locked."

As the door creaked open, the front room swung into view—a faded Oriental carpet stretched across the threshold, a stone fireplace, wide pine floors. Miranda stepped inside and suddenly halted in surprise.

At her feet lay a jumble of papers. A rolltop desk stood in the corner, its drawers wide open, their contents strewn across the floor. Books had been pulled off a nearby shelf and tossed haphazardly among the papers.

Chase stepped inside and came to a halt beside her. The screen door slammed shut.

"What the hell?" he said.

Chapter Seven

In silence they took in the ransacked desk, the scattered papers. Without a word Chase moved quickly toward the next room.

Miranda followed him into the kitchen. There were no signs of disturbance here. The pots and pans were hung on a beam rack, the flour and sugar canisters lined up neatly on the butcher block counters.

She was right on his heels as he headed for the stairs. They ran up the steps and looked first in the small guest bedroom. Everything appeared in order. Quickly Chase circled the room, opening closets, glancing in drawers.

"What are you looking for?" she asked.

He didn't answer. He moved across the hall, into the master bedroom.

Here double windows, flanked by lace curtains, faced the sea. A cream coverlet draped the four-poster bed. Motes of dust drifted in the sun-warmed stillness.

"Doesn't look like they touched this room, either," said Miranda.

Chase went to the dresser, picked up a silver hairbrush, and set it back down. "Obviously not."

"What on earth is going on here, Chase?"

He turned and glanced in frustration about the room. "This is crazy. They left the paintings on the walls. The furniture..."

"Nothing's missing?"

"Nothing valuable. At least, nothing your ordinary thief would go after." He opened a dresser drawer and glanced through the contents. He opened a second drawer and paused, staring inside. Slowly he withdrew a pair of women's panties. It was scarcely more than a few strips of black lace and silk. He pulled out a matching bra, equally skimpy, equally seductive.

He looked at Miranda, his gaze flat and unreadable. "Yours?" he asked quietly.

"I told you, I've never been here. They must belong to Evelyn."

He shook his head. "I don't think so."

"How would you know?"

"She never comes out here. Despises the rustic life, or so she claims."

"Well, they're not mine. I don't own anything like—like that."

"There's more inside here. Maybe you'll recognize something else."

She went to the dresser and pulled out an emerald-and-cream bra. "Well, it's obvious this isn't mine."

"How so?"

"This is a 36C. I'm..." She cleared her throat. "Not that big."

"Oh."

Quickly she turned away, before he could confirm her statement. Not that he hadn't had the chance to look. He had eyes, didn't he?

And he sees too damn much, she thought. She turned toward the window and stood with her back to Chase, all the while struggling to regain her composure. Outside, the fading light of day slanted across the treetops. A long summer dusk. In the field below there would be fireflies and the hum of insects in the grass. And the chill. Even on these August evenings there was always the chill that rose from the sea. She hugged herself and shivered.

His approach was gentle, silent. She couldn't hear him, but she knew, without looking, that he was right behind her.

Chase was standing so close, in fact, that he could smell the scent of her hair—clean and sweet and intoxicating. The fading daylight from the window brought out its glorious chestnut hues. He wanted to reach out and run his fingers through those shimmering strands, to bury his face in the tangled silk. A mistake, a mistake. He knew it before it happened, and yet he couldn't help himself.

She shivered at his touch. Just the tiniest tremble, the softest sigh. He ran his hands down her shoulders, down the cool smoothness of her bare arms. She didn't pull away. No, she leaned back, as though melting against him. He wrapped his arms around her, enfolding her in their warmth.

"When I was a boy," he whispered, "I used to think there were magical creatures in that field down there. Elves and fairies hiding among the toadstools. I'd see their lights flitting about at night. It was only fireflies, of course. But to a kid, they might have been anything. Elvish lanterns, Dragon lights. I wish..."

"What do you wish, Chase?"

He sighed. "That I still had some of that child inside me. That we could have known each other then. Before all this happened. Before..."

"Richard."

Chase fell silent. His brother would always be there, his life and his death like a darkness hovering over them. What could possibly thrive in such shadow? Not friendship; certainly not love. *Love?* No, what Chase felt, standing there behind her, hugging her slim, warm body to his, had far more to do with lust. *Well, what the hell. Maybe it runs in my family,* he thought, *in my tainted bloodline. This propensity for reckless, hopeless affairs. Richard had it. My mother had it. Is it my turn to succumb?*

Miranda shifted in his embrace, turned to face him. One look at that soft, upturned mouth and he was lost.

She tasted of summer and warmth and sweet amber honey. At the first touch of their lips he wanted more, more. He felt like a man who has fallen drunk at his first sip of nectar and now craves nothing else. His hands found their way into that silken mass of hair, were buried in it, lost in it. He heard her murmur, "please," and was too fevered to think it anything but a request for more. Only when she said it again, and then, "Chase, no," did he finally pull away.

They stared at each other. The confusion he felt was mirrored in her eyes. She retreated a step, nervously shoving back her hair.

"I shouldn't have let you do that," she said. "It was a mistake."

"Why?"

"Because you—you'll say I led you on. That's what you'll tell Evelyn, isn't it? You think it's how I got hold of Richard. Temptation. Seduction. It's what everyone else believes."

"But is it true?"

"You've just proved it. Get me alone in a room and look what happens! Another Tremain male bites the dust." Her voice took on a cold edge. "What I want to know is, who's really seducing whom?"

She's all motion, all skittishness, he thought. In another moment she would shatter and fly into pieces.

"Neither of us did any seducing, any tempting. It just happened, Miranda. The way it usually happens. Nature tugs on our strings and we can't always resist."

"This time I will. This time I know better. Your brother taught me a few things. The most important thing is not to be so damn gullible when it comes to men."

That last word was still hanging in the air between them when they heard footsteps thump onto the porch below. Someone rapped on the front door.

Chase turned and left the room.

Miranda, suddenly weak, leaned against the windowsill. She clutched it tightly, as though drawing strength from the wood. *Too close,* she thought. *I let down my guard, let him slip right past my defenses.*

She would have to be more careful. She would have to remind herself that Chase and Richard were variations on a theme, a theme that had already wreaked havoc on her life. She took a deep breath and slowly let it out, willing the turmoil, the confusion, to flow out of her body. *Back in control,* she thought. She released the sill. She stood straight. Then, with a new semblance of calmness, she followed Chase down the stairs.

He was in the front room with the visitor. Miranda recognized her old acquaintance from the garden club, Miss Lila St. John, local expert on flowering perennials. Miss St. John was dressed in her signature black dress. Summer or winter, she always wore black, set off with a touch of white lace here and there. Today it was a black walking dress of crinkled linen. It did not quite match her brown boots or her straw hat, but on Miss St. John it all seemed to look just right.

She turned at the sound of Miranda's footsteps. If she was surprised to see Miranda she didn't show it. She simply nodded, then turned her sharp gray eyes back to the ransacked desk. On the front porch a dog whined. Through the screen door Miranda saw what looked like a large black fur ball with a red tongue.

"It's all my fault, you know," said Miss St. John. "I can't believe I was such an imbecile."

"How is it your fault?" asked Chase.

"I sensed something was wrong last week. We were taking our walk, you see, Ozzie and I. We walk every evening around dusk. That's when the deer come out, the pests, though I do love to see them. Anyway, I saw a light through the trees, somewhere in this direction. I came up to the cottage and knocked on the door. No one answered, so I left.'' She shook her head. ''I shouldn't have, you know. I should have looked into it. I *knew* it didn't feel right.''

''Did you see a car?''

''If you were coming to loot the joint, would *you* park your car out front? Of course not. I know I'd park down the road a bit, in the trees. Then I'd sneak up here on foot.''

It was hard to imagine Miss St. John doing any such thing.

''It's a good thing you didn't get involved,'' said Chase. ''You could have gotten yourself killed.''

''At my age, Chase, getting killed is not a major concern.'' She used her walking stick, a knobby affair with a duck's head handle, to prod among the papers on the floor. ''Any idea what he was after?''

''Not a clue.''

''Not valuables, obviously. That's a Limoges on that shelf over there, isn't it?''

Chase glanced sheepishly at the hand-painted vase. ''If you say so.''

Miss St. John turned to Miranda. ''Have you any thoughts on the matter?''

Miranda found herself under the gaze of two very intense gray eyes. Miss St. John might be dismissed by many as little more than a charming eccentric, but Miranda could see the intelligence in that gaze. While their previous conversations had tended more toward delphiniums and daffodils, even then, Miss St. John had made her feel like some sort of new plant species under a magnifying glass. ''I'm not sure I know what to think, Miss St. John,'' she said.

''Take a look at the mess. What does it tell you?''

Miranda glanced at the papers, the scattered books. Then her gaze shifted to the bookcases. Only a top shelf had been emptied. Two full bookcases were undisturbed. ''He didn't look through all the books. So whoever broke in here must have been interrupted. By you, maybe.''

''Or he found what he was looking for,'' said Chase.

Miss St. John turned to him. ''And what might that be?''

"A guess?" Chase and Miranda glanced at each other. "The file on Stone Coast Trust," Chase ventured.

"Ah." Miss St. John's eyes took on a gleam of interest. "Your brother's little campaign against Tony Graffam. Yes, Richard seemed to do quite a bit of writing out here. At that desk, in fact. On my evening walks I'd see him through the window."

"Did you ever stop to talk to him? About what he was working on?"

"Oh, no. That's why we come out here, isn't it? To get away from all those prying townies." She glanced at Miranda. "I never saw *you* out here."

"I've never been here," she said, shifting uneasily under that thoughtful gaze. This matter-of-fact reference to her link with Richard had taken her by surprise. And yet, Miss St. John's bluntness was far preferable to the delicate avoidance with which so many others treated the subject.

Miss St. John bent down for a closer look at the papers. "He must have done a prodigious amount of work here, judging by this mess. What is all this, anyway?"

Chase bent and sifted through the papers. "Looks like a lot of old article files. . . . Financial records from the *Herald . . .* And here we've got a collection of local personality profiles. Why, here's one of you, Miss St. John."

"Me? But I was never interviewed for anything."

Chase grinned. "Must be the unauthorized version, then."

"Does it mention all my sexy secrets?"

"Well, let's just take a good look here—"

"Oh, *give* me the damn thing." Miss St. John snatched the page out of his hands and scanned the typewritten notes. She read them aloud. "Age seventy-four. . .holds title to lot number two, St. John's Wood, and cottage thereon . . . rabid member of local garden club." Here she glanced up huffily. *"Rabid?"* She continued reading. "Eccentric recluse, never married. Engaged once, to an Arthur Simoneau, killed in action . . . Normandy. . . ." Her voice trailed off. Slowly she sat down, still clutching the piece of paper in both hands.

"Oh, Miss St. John," said Miranda. "I'm sorry."

The elderly woman looked up, still shaken. "It . . . was a very long time ago."

"I can't believe he went digging into your personal life, without you even knowing about it. Why would he do that?"

"You're saying it was Richard?" asked Miss St. John.

"Well, these are his papers."

Miss St. John frowned at the page for a moment. "No," she said slowly. "I don't believe he wrote this. There's an error in here. It says my cottage lies in St. John's Wood. But it lies three feet over the line, on Tremain property. A surveyor's mistake from seventy years past. Richard knew that."

Chase frowned. "I never heard that, about your cottage."

"Yes, your family land goes past the second stone wall. It includes the entire access road. So, technically, all the rest of us are trespassers on your private road. Not that it ever mattered. It always felt like a giant family out here. But now . . ." She shook her head. "So many strangers on the island. All those tourists from *Massachusetts*." She made it sound like an invasion from hell.

"Did Stone Coast Trust approach you?" Miranda asked her. "About selling St. John's Wood?"

"They approached everyone on this road. I, of course, refused. So did Richard. That effectively squelched the project. Without Rose Hill, Stone Coast would own a disconnected patchwork of little lots. But now . . ." Sadly she sighed. "I imagine Evelyn, at this very moment, has her pen poised over the sales contract."

"Actually, she does not," said Chase. "Rose Hill didn't go to Evelyn. Richard left the property to Miranda."

Miss St. John stared at them. "Now that," she said after a long pause, "is an entirely unexpected development."

"For me, as well," said Miranda.

While Miss St. John sat back in thought, Miranda and Chase gathered up the rest of the papers. They found more article files, a few miscellaneous clippings, an old financial report from the *Herald*. Obviously Richard had used the cottage as another office. Was this where he had stored his most sensitive papers? Miranda wondered about this when she came across a whole bundle of personality profiles. Like the page on Miss St. John, the information contained in these files was highly private.

In some cases it was downright shocking. She was startled to read that Forrest Mayhew, the local bank president, had been arrested for drunk driving in Boston. That town selectman George LaPierre, married thirty years, had been treated last year for syphilis. That Dr. Steiner—*her* doctor—was under investigation for medicare fraud.

She handed the papers to Chase. "Look at these! Richard was collecting dirt on everyone in town!"

"Here, what's this?" he asked. There was a yellow adhesive note attached to the back cover of the folder. On it was the handwritten scrawl, "Mr. T., do you want more? Let me know." It was signed "W.B.R."

"So Richard *didn't* write these," said Miranda. "This person W.B.R.—whoever he was—must've done the reporting."

"You have anyone on staff with those initials?"

"No. At least, not at the moment." She reached for a manila folder lying on the floor. "Look, there's another note from W.B.R." This time the note was paper-clipped to the top cover. "All I could get. Sorry—W.B.R."

"What's inside?" asked Miss St. John.

Miranda opened the file and stared. "This is it! The file on Stone Coast Trust!"

"Jackpot," said Chase.

"There's no profile of Tony Graffam. But here's his tax return. A list of bank account numbers and assets..." She nodded. "We hit pay dirt."

"I think not," said Miss St. John.

They both looked at her.

"If that file is so important, why did the burglar leave it here?"

In silence they considered that question.

"Maybe our burglar wasn't interested in Stone Coast Trust at all," said Miss St. John. "I mean, look at all this nasty information Richard's been gathering. Snoopy reports on drunk driving. Medicare fraud. Syphilis. George LaPierre, of all people! And at his age, too. These files could destroy some fine reputations. Now, I tell you, isn't that a motive for burglary?"

Or murder, thought Miranda. Why had Richard gathered such information in the first place? Was he planning an exposé on island residents? Or was there some darker reason? Coercion, for instance. Blackmail.

"If someone broke in to steal his own file, then we can assume it's now gone," said Chase. "Which means George LaPierre, Dr. Steiner, all the others in this pile didn't do it."

"Not necessarily," said Miss St. John. "What if he broke in and simply substituted a milder version? Mine, for instance. There's not a thing in my profile that qualifies as scandalous. How do you know I didn't come in here and destroy a far more venomous version?"

Chase smiled. "I will duly place you on the list of suspects, Miss St. John."

"Don't you discount me, Chase Tremain. Age alone does not take one out of the running. I have more up here—" she tapped her head "—than that imbecile George La-Pierre had in his prime. If he ever *had* a prime."

"What you're saying, Miss St. John," said Miranda, "is that we can't count out any name in this pile. Or any name *not* in this pile."

"Correct."

Miranda frowned at the books. "One thing doesn't make sense. First, our burglar searches the desk. He throws around some papers, looking for some incriminating file.

Why would he then search the bookcase? That's not the sort of place Richard would keep papers.''

After a pause Miss St. John said, "You're right, of course. That doesn't make sense."

"Well," said Chase, "I guess we should call Lorne. Though I'm not sure he'd be much help at this point." He turned to the phone.

He'd already picked up the receiver when Miss St. John suddenly said, "Wait. Perhaps you should hold off on that call." She was staring at a loose page near her feet. Thoughtfully she picked up the paper and smoothed it across her knee.

Frowning, Chase hung up the receiver. "Why?"

"This is a profile of Valerie Everhard. You remember her, Chase. Our local librarian. And a married lady. According to this, Valerie has taken on a lover."

"So?"

"The man she's seeing is our chief of police." Miss St. John looked up and her eyes had lost all trace of humor. "Lorne Tibbetts."

"WHY DID HE HAVE THESE awful reports?" asked Miranda. "What was he planning to do with them?"

They were driving through darkness back to town. The fog had rolled in from the sea and curtained off all view beyond the dim haze of their headlights. Nothing seemed real in this mist, nothing seemed familiar. They were driving through a strange land, through a swirling cloud that seemed as if it would never lift.

"It doesn't sound like Richard," said Chase. "Snooping around in his neighbors' private lives. He committed enough sins of his own. If anyone was vulnerable to blackmail, it was Richard. Besides, who cares if Lorne is having a little fling with the librarian?"

"The librarian's husband?"

"Okay, but why would Richard care?"

She shook her head, unable to come up with an answer. "I wonder if any of these people knew about these files. Miss St. John didn't." She looked down at the papers on her lap and thought of the terrible secrets they contained. She had the sudden urge to shove the pile away, to throw off that unclean burden. "Chase?" she asked. "How do we know any of this is true?"

"We don't." He gave a short laugh. "And we can't exactly knock on George LaPierre's door and ask if he's had syphilis."

Miranda frowned at the note clipped to the folder. "I wonder who this is. This W.B.R. who got the information."

"The initials don't ring any bells?"

"None at all."

As the darkness flew past their windshield, Miranda thought of all the secrets revealed in these files. The banker's weakness for whiskey. The doctor's white-collar fraud. The husband and wife who conversed with their fists. All of it concealed beneath the glaze of respectability. *What private pains we nurse in silence.*

"Why *these* particular people?" she asked suddenly.

"Because they have the most to lose?" Chase suggested. "We're talking old island families here. LaPierre, Everhard, St. John. All of them respected names."

"Except for Tony Graffam."

"That's true. I guess he has a file in there, too..." He paused. "Wait. There's our link."

"What?"

"The north shore. You haven't lived here long enough to know all these families. But I grew up with them. I remember the summers I used to play with Toby LaPierre. And Daniel Steiner. And Valerie Everhard. Their families all have summer cottages out there."

"It could be coincidental."

"Or it could mean everything."

Chase frowned at the highway. The fog was thinning. "When we get back to your house," he said, "let's take a good look at those names. See if my hunch holds up."

An hour and a half later they sat at Miranda's dining table, the pages spread out before them. The remains of a hastily prepared supper—mushroom omelets and toast—had been pushed aside and they were now on their second cup of coffee. It was such a domestic scene, she thought with a twinge of longing, almost like newlyweds lingering at the dinner table. Except that the man sitting across from her could never, would never, fit into the picture. He was a temporary apparition, a visitor passing through her dining room.

She forced herself to focus on the sheet of paper, where he'd just checked off the final name.

"Okay, here's the list," said Chase. "Everyone in Richard's file. I'm almost certain they all own property on the north shore."

"Are any names missing?"

Chase sat back and mentally ticked off the camps along the access road. "There's Richard, of course. Then there's old man Sulaway's property, down the road. He's a retired lobsterman, sort of a recluse. And then there's Frenchman's Cottage. I think it was sold some years back. To hippies, I heard. They come up for the summers."

"So they'd be living there now."

"If they still own the place. But they're not from this area. I can't see Richard bothering to dig up information on them. And as for old Sully, well, an eighty-five-year-old sounds like a pretty unlikely victim for blackmail."

Blackmail. Miranda gazed at the papers on the table. "What was Richard thinking of?" she wondered. "What did he have against these people?"

"Something to do with the rezoning? Were any of these names on the land commission?"

"They couldn't have voted, anyway. They would've been disqualified. You know, conflict of interest." She sat back.

"Maybe our burglar was looking for something entirely different."

"Then the question is, did he—or she—find it?"

From somewhere in the house came a sound that made them both glance up. It was the soft tinkle of breaking glass.

Miranda jerked to her feet in alarm. At once Chase grabbed her hand, signaled her to be silent. Together they moved from the dining room into the living room. A quick glance around told them the windows were all intact. They paused for a moment, listening, but heard no other sounds. Chase started toward the bedrooms.

They were moving up the hall when they heard, louder this time, the distinct crash of shattering glass.

"That came from the cellar!" said Miranda.

Chase wheeled and headed back into the kitchen. He flicked on a wall switch and yanked open the cellar door. A single bare bulb shone over the narrow stairway. A strange mist seemed to swirl in the shadows, obscuring the bottom of the stairs. They had taken only two steps down when they both smelled smoke.

"You've got a fire in here!" said Chase, moving down the steps. "Where's your extinguisher?"

"I'll get it!" Miranda scrambled into the kitchen, pulled the extinguisher from the pantry shelf and dashed back down the cellar steps.

By now the smoke was thick enough to make her eyes burn. Through the whirling haze she saw the source: a bundle of flaming rags. Nearby, just beneath a shattered basement window, lay a red brick. At once she understood what had happened, and her panic gave way to fury. *How dare they smash my window? How dare they attack me in my own home?*

"Stay back!" Chase yelled, plunging forward through the smoke. His shoes crunched over broken glass as he crossed the concrete floor. He aimed the extinguisher; a stream of white shot out and hissed over the flames. A few sweeps of the nozzle and the fire faltered and died under a smothering blanket of powder. Only the smoke remained, a stinking pall that hung like a cloud around the bare light bulb.

"It's out!" said Chase. He was prowling the basement now, searching for new flames. He didn't notice that Miranda had gone rigid with fury, didn't see that she was staring, white-faced, at the broken glass on the floor.

"Why can't they leave me *alone?*" she cried.

Chase turned and looked at her with sudden intensity. He said, dead quiet, "You mean this has happened before?"

"Not—not this. But phone calls, really cruel ones. Again and again. And messages, written on my window."

"What sort of messages?"

"What you'd expect." She swallowed and looked away. "You know, to the local murderess."

He took a step toward her. "You know who's doing it?"

"I told myself it was just—just some kids. But kids, they wouldn't set fire to my house...."

Chase glanced down at the brick, then up at the shattered window. "It's a crazy way to burn down a house," he said. He went to her, took her by the shoulders, gently rubbed her arms. She felt warmth in his touch, and strength. Courage. He framed her face with his hands and said quietly, "I'm going to call the police."

She nodded. Together they started up the steps to the kitchen. They were halfway up the stairs when the door above them suddenly slammed shut. An instant later the bolt squealed home.

"They've shut us in!" cried Miranda.

He dashed past her up the stairs and began pounding on the door. In frustration he threw himself against it. His shoulder slammed into the wood.

"It's solid!" said Miranda. "You can't break it down."

Chase groaned. "I think I just found that out."

Footsteps creaked across the floor overhead. Miranda froze, tracing with her gaze the intruder's movements.

"What's he doing?" she whispered.

As if in answer to her question, the single light bulb suddenly went out. The basement was plunged into darkness.

"Chase?" she cried.

"I'm here! Right here. Give me your hand."

She reached up blindly toward him; at once he found her wrist. "It's all right," he murmured, pulling her toward him, gathering her tightly against his chest. Just the unyielding support of that embrace was enough to take the edge off her panic. "We'll be okay," he murmured. "We just have to find a way out. We can't make it through the window. You have a cellar door? A coal hatch?"

"There's—there's an old loading hatch near the furnace. It opens to the side yard."

"All right. Let's see if we can get it open. Just move us in the right direction."

Together they felt their way down the steps, to the cellar floor. Shards of glass skittered before their feet as they inched their way through the darkness. It seemed like a journey across eternity, through a blackness so thick it might have been firm to the touch. At last Miranda's extended hand touched pipes, then the cold, damp granite of the cellar wall.

"Which way to the hatch?" asked Chase.

"I think it's to the left."

Upstairs, the creaking moved across the floor, then a door slammed shut. *They've left the house,* Miranda thought in relief. *They're not going to hurt us.*

"I found the oil tank!" said Chase.

"Then the coal hatch should be just above. There are some steps—"

"Right here." He released her hand. Though she knew he was right beside her, that break in contact left her hovering at the edge of panic. If only she could see something, anything! She could hear Chase shoving up against the wood, could hear the crack and groan of the hatch as he struggled to swing it open. Straining to see through the

darkness, she could make out, little by little, the vague
outline of his head, then the gleam of sweat on his face.
More details seemed to emerge out of darkness: the hulking shadow of the furnace, the oil tank, the reddish glint of
the copper pipes. It was all visible now.

Too visible. Where was the light coming from?

With new apprehension she turned and stared up at the
basement window. Reflected in the shattered glass was a
flickering dance of orange light. Firelight. "Oh, my God,"
she whispered. "Chase..."

He turned and stared.

Even as they watched, the glow in the window shards
leaped to a new and horrifying brilliance.

"We have to get out of here!" she cried.

He shoved against the hatch. "I can't get it open!"

"Here, let me help you!"

They both pushed up against the wood, pounded it with
their bare fists. Already, smoke was swirling in through the
broken window. Overhead, through the cracks in the
floorboards, they could see the terrible glow of flames
consuming the house above. Most of the heat was fun-
neled up, toward the roof, but soon the timbers would give
way. They would be trapped beneath falling debris.

The hatch was immovable.

Chase snatched up the fire extinguisher and began to
pound it against the wood. "I'll keep trying to break
through!" he yelled. "You get to the window—yell for
help!"

Miranda scrambled over to the window. Smoke was bil-
lowing in, a thick, suffocating black cloud. She could
barely reach the opening. She glanced around in panic for
a crate, a chair, something to stand on. Nothing was in
sight.

She screamed louder than she had ever screamed in her
life.

Even then, she knew help wouldn't reach them in time.
The basement window faced the back of the house, to-

ward the garden. She was too far below the opening for her voice to carry any distance. She glanced up, at the floor beams. Already, the evil glow of heat shone through. She could hear the groan of the wood as it sagged. How long before those beams gave way? How long before she and Chase collapsed under that smothering blackness of smoke? The air had grown unbearably close.

It's already an oven, she thought. *And it will only get hotter....*

Chapter Eight

Chase pounded desperately at the hatch. A board splintered, but the barrier held. "Someone's nailed it shut!" he yelled. "Keep calling for help!"

She screamed, again and again, until her voice cracked, until she had almost no voice left.

She heard, in the distance, the sound of a dog barking, and Mr. Lanzo's far-off shouts. She tried to shout back. All she could manage was a pitifully weak cry. There was no answering call. Had she imagined the voice? Or couldn't he hear her?

Even if he did, would he track her screams to this small opening facing the garden? Safety lay so close, yet was so unreachable. If she stood on tiptoe she could actually poke her hand through the shards of broken glass, could feel the soil beneath her fingertips. Just inches away would be her beloved delphiniums, her newly planted violas....

An image of her garden, of rich, moist earth and a freshly tilled flower bed suddenly flashed into her mind. Hadn't she just expanded that bed? Hadn't she used a pickax to break up the sod? The pickax—where did she leave it? She remembered laying it against the side of the house—

Near the cellar window.

With her bare fist she broke away the last shards of glass. Something warm ran down her arm. Blood, she thought with a strange sense of detachment. But no pain—she was too panicked to feel anything but the desperate need to escape the flames. She reached through the open window and ran her fingers along the outside wall. Nothing on the right, just the rough clapboard shingles above a granite foundation. She shifted to the left side of the window, swept her hand along the outside frame and touched warm metal. The pickax head!

She gripped it so tightly her fingers cramped. Painfully she managed to slide the heavy iron head sideways, in front of the window. With a little wriggling she maneuvered first the sharp point, then the blade end, through the window opening.

The pick landed with a hard clang on the concrete floor.

Coughing and gasping, she dragged the tool into the blinding smoke. Already, flames were engulfing the floorboards above her head. "Chase!" she cried. "Where are you?"

"I'm here!"

She started toward the sound of Chase's voice but halfway across she lost her bearings. The whole room seemed to be moving around her like some crazy circus ride. *I can't faint now,* she thought. *If I do, I'll never wake up.* Already her knees were giving way. How she needed a breath of fresh air, just one! She sank to the floor. The concrete felt blessedly damp and cool against her face.

"Miranda!"

The sound of Chase's voice seemed to jump-start some last internal surge of strength. She struggled back to her knees. "I can't—can't see you...."

"I'll find you! Keep talking!"

"No, we'll both get lost! Stay by the hatch!" She began to crawl, moving in the direction of his voice, dragging the pickax behind her. The sound of the fire above them had grown to a roar. Fallen embers lay scattered and glowing on the concrete. Blinded by smoke, she put her hand on one and the pain that seared her skin brought a sob to her throat.

"I'm coming for you!" Chase shouted.

His voice seemed far away, as though he were calling from some distant room. She realized she was fading, and that the room had grown dark, and that this inferno was where she would die. She clawed her way forward, dragging herself and the pickax a few more precious inches.

"Miranda!" His voice seemed even more distant now, another world, another universe. And that seemed most terrible of all—that she would die without the comfort of his touch.

She reached out to drag herself one last time—

And found his hand. Instantly his fingers closed around her wrist and he hauled her close. His touch was like some wondrous restorative. She found the strength to rise once again to her knees.

"Here," she said with a cough, dragging the pickax toward him. "Will this work?"

"It has to!" He staggered to his feet. "Stay low," he commanded. "Keep your head down!"

She heard him grunt as he swung the pickax, heard the thunk of the metal slamming into the wood. Another swing, another blow. Splinters flew, raining into her hair. He was coughing, weaving. Against the backlight of flames she could see him struggle to stay on his feet.

He swung again.

The hatch gave way. A blast of cool air flew in through the jagged opening. The inrush of fresh oxygen was like throwing fuel on the fire. Everywhere, timbers seemed to explode into flame. Miranda dropped to the ground, her face buried in her arms. An ember fell hissing onto her head. She brushed it away, shuddering at the smell of her own burning hair.

Chase gasped in one last breath of air, then, grunting from the effort, he heaved the pickax against the wood.

The hatch flew apart.

Miranda felt herself yanked upward, through some long, dark tunnel. She could see no light at the other end, could see no end at all. There was just that black passage, the dizzying sense of motion, the clawlike grasp of fingers against her flesh.

Then, suddenly, there was the grass.

And there was Chase, cradling her in his arms, stroking her face, her hair.

She took in a breath. The rush of air into her lungs was almost painful. She coughed, drew in more air, more! She felt drunk on its sweetness.

The night was a whirlwind of noise, sirens, shouting voices and the crackle of fire. She gazed up in horror at the flames; they seemed to fill the heavens.

"Oh, God," she whispered. "My house..."

"We made it out," said Chase. "That's all that matters. We're alive."

She focused on his face. It was a mask of soot, lit by the hellish glow of the fire. They stared at each other, a look of shared wonder that they were both still breathing.

"Miranda," he murmured. He bent and pressed his lips to her forehead, her eyelids, her mouth. He tasted of smoke and sweat and desperation. All at once, they were both shaking and clutching each other in wild relief.

"Mo! Honey! You all right?"

Mr. Lanzo, dressed in his pajamas, scuttled toward them across the lawn. "I was afraid you were inside! Kept tellin' those idiot firemen I heard you screaming!"

"We're okay," Chase said. He took Miranda's face in his hands and kissed her. "We're fine."

Somewhere, a window shattered in the heat of the flames.

"Hey! You people move back!" a fireman yelled. "Everyone get back!"

Chase pulled Miranda to her feet. Together they retreated across Mr. Lanzo's lawn and onto the street. They watched as the fire hoses unleashed a torrent of spray. Water hissed onto the flames.

"Aw, honey," said Mr. Lanzo sadly. "It's too late. She's gone."

Even as he said it, the roof collapsed. Miranda watched in despair as a sheet of flame shot up, turning the night sky into a blazing dawn. *It's all gone,* she thought. *Everything I owned. I've lost it all.*

She wanted to scream out her fury, her anguish, but the violence of those flames held her in a trance. She could only watch as a strange numbness took hold.

"Ms. Wood?"

Slowly she turned.

Lorne Tibbetts was standing beside her. "What happened here?" he asked.

"What the hell do you *think* happened?" Chase shot back. "Someone torched her house. While we were in it."

Lorne looked at Miranda, who stared back at him with dazed eyes. He looked at the burning house, which had already collapsed into little more than a heap of firewood.

"You'd better come with me," he said. "I'll need a statement. From both of you."

"Now do you believe it?" asked Chase. "Someone's trying to kill her."

Lorne Tibbetts's gaze, in the best poker player tradition, revealed absolutely nothing. He began to doodle in the margin of his notepad. Nothing artistic there, not even a few healthy free-form loops. These were tight little triangles linked together like crystals. The geometric creation of a geometric mind. He clicked his pen a few times, then he turned and yelled, "Ellis?"

Ellis poked his head in the door. "Yo, Lorne."

"You finished with Ms. Wood?"

"Got it all down."

"Okay." Lorne rose to his feet and started out of the room.

"Wait," said Chase. "What happens now?"

"I talk to her. Ellis talks to you."

"You mean I have to tell it all over again?"

"It's the way we do things around here. Independent questioning. Routine police procedure." He tucked his shirt into his trousers, smoothed back his hair and walked out the door.

Ellis Snipe sat in Lorne's vacated seat and grinned at Chase. "Hey, Mr. T. How ya doing?"

Chase looked at that moronic, gap-toothed smile and wondered, *Was Mayberry ever this bad?*

"Why don't we start at the beginning," said Ellis.

"Which beginning?" Chase shot back.

Ellis looked confused. "Uh, you choose."

Chase sighed. He glanced at the door, wondering how Miranda was holding up. No matter what Dr. Steiner had said, a hospital bed was where she belonged. But the old quack had simply dressed her glass cuts, examined her lungs and declared hospitalization unnecessary. What Dr. Steiner had neglected to consider was her emotional state. She'd lost her house, her possessions; she was left with no sense of order to her life. What she needed was a safe place, a cocoon where no one could hurt her....

"Uh, Mr. Tremain? You think you could maybe try and cooperate?"

Chase looked at Ellis. What was the point of fighting? he thought wearily. Ellis Snipe looked like the kind of robot who'd follow orders to the letter. If he had to, he'd sit there all night, waiting for Chase to talk.

For the second time that night Chase told the story. He took it back to the cottage, the evidence of a break-in, the secret files. This time he left out the information about Lorne Tibbetts and his fling with the librarian. Some things, he thought, should remain private.

Ellis wrote it all down in a weird, spidery script that couldn't possibly be produced by a normal personality.

When Chase was finished, Ellis asked one and only one question. "Was there anything in those secret files about me?"

"Not a thing," said Chase.

Ellis looked disappointed.

After Ellis had left, Chase sat alone at the table, wondering what came next. A third cop, another go-around with the story? The whole affair had taken on a surreal quality, like some never-ending nightmare. For ten minutes he waited for something to happen. Then, fed up with being ignored, he shoved his chair back and went in search of Miranda.

He found her in the same interrogation room where he'd first laid eyes on her over a week before. She was sitting alone. A smudge of soot blackened her cheek, and her hair was dusted with ash.

She gazed at him with a look of utter exhaustion. "The cop station from hell," she murmured.

He smiled. Then he saw her hand. It was encased in bandages. "Is it as serious as it looks?"

"The doctor just believes in doing a thorough job." She looked in wonder at the free-form sculpture of surgical gauze and tape. "I was afraid he'd amputate."

"A hand as nice as yours? I wouldn't have let him."

She tried to return the smile, but couldn't quite manage it.

"You have to leave the island," he said.

"I can't. The terms of my bail—"

"To hell with the bail terms! You can't wait around for the next accident, the next fire."

"I can't leave the county."

"This time you were lucky. Next time—"

"What am I *supposed* to do?" She looked at him in sudden anger. "Run and hide?"

"Yes."

"From *what?* I don't even know who's trying to kill me!" Her cry echoed in the stark room. At once she flushed, as though shamed by the sound of her own hysteria.

"If I leave, I'll never know what I'm running from," she said quietly. "Or if I'm still being hunted. What kind of life is that, Chase? Never knowing if I'm safe. Always waking up at night, listening for footsteps. Wondering if that creak on the stairs is someone coming for me...." She shuddered and stared down at the table.

Lord, he thought. *How did I ever get involved with this woman? She's not my problem. I'm not her white knight. I should get up and walk right out of this room. Who would blame me?*

And then a voice inside him said, *I would.*

He pulled out a chair and sat across from her. She didn't look up. She just kept staring at the ugly tabletop.

"If you won't leave, then what are you going to do?"

She shrugged. It hurt him to see the hopelessness in that gesture. "Does it matter?"

"It matters to me."

"Why?" The look she gave him made him want to say things he knew he'd regret. That he cared whether she lived or died. He cared what happened to her. He cared too much.

He said, with unassailable logic, "Because what happened tonight is somehow tied in with Richard. The break-in at Rose Hill. The fire. And you."

She gave a dispirited laugh. "Yes, somewhere in all this mess, I seem to fit in. And I haven't the faintest idea why."

The door opened. Ellis said, "There you are, Mr. T. Lorne says you both can go. Says he can't think of any more questions."

I hope I never see this place again, thought Chase as they followed Ellis down the hall, into the front office. Lorne was sitting at one of the desks, talking on the phone. He glanced up as Chase and Miranda walked past, and motioned to them to wait.

"Oh, hell." Chase sighed. "He just thought of another question."

Lorne hung up and said to Ellis, "Bring the car around. We got us another call."

"Man, oh, man," Ellis whined as he headed out to the garage. "This is one heck of a Thursday night."

Lorne looked at Miranda. "You got a place to stay?"

"I'll drive her to the hotel," said Chase.

"I was thinking along the lines of someplace safer," Lorne said. "A friend's house, maybe?"

"There's always Mr. Lanzo," said Miranda.

"No, I'll take you over to Annie's house," said Chase. "At least *her* faculties are still intact."

"Yeah, that'd be better," said Lorne, reaching for his hat. "Considering."

"Considering what?" said Chase.

"The two empty gas cans we found over by Ms. Wood's house. Plus the two-by-fours nailed over the cellar hatch."

Miranda stared at him. There it was. Undeniable proof someone was trying to kill her. Her body seemed to sag against Chase. "Then you believe me," she whispered.

Lorne reached for his hat. "Well, I'll tell you what I believe, Ms. Wood. I do believe this is one of the weirdest nights we've ever had here on this island. And I do not like the trend."

"What else is going on?" asked Chase.

"An assault. On Miss Lila St. John, if you can believe it. She just called in the report."

"Someone attacked her?" said Chase, shocked. "Why?"

"She claims she tried to stop a break-in." Lorne, obviously skeptical, started for the door. "At Rose Hill Cottage."

"SO," SAID ANNIE BERENGER, pouring out three tall whiskeys. "Do I get to write all about the juicy details? Or is this baby-sitting job another gratis deal?"

"I thought you and Miranda were friends," said Chase.

"Oh, we are. But I'm a reporter, too." She handed Chase a glass. "It's my job to take advantage of the situation." She glanced at the closed door to the bathroom, where Miranda was showering. "You know, Chase, she looked pretty beat-up. Shouldn't she be in a hospital or something?"

"She'll be fine right here, Annie. As long as you keep your eagle eye on her."

"Terrific. What I always wanted to be. A mommy." She tossed back a quick slug of whiskey. "Oh, don't get me wrong. I like Miranda. I used to be a lot like her. About a century ago." She poured herself a second glass. "But women grow up fast these days. We have to. It's the men who age us. Take my boyfriend, Irving. Please. I've been waiting a year for him to pop the question. It's giving me gray hairs." She took a sip of whiskey, then turned and looked at Chase. "So how much trouble is she in?"

"It could get dangerous. Are you ready for that?"

"Ready?" She went to an end table and opened the drawer. Casually she pulled out a revolver. "Little souvenir I picked up in Boston. I'm a lousy shot, but sometimes I get lucky." She tossed the gun back into the drawer. "Good enough?"

"I'm impressed."

Annie laughed. "Men always are when they see my pistol's bigger than theirs." She glanced over her shoulder as the bathroom door opened. "Hi. Feeling better?"

"Just cleaner," said Miranda, walking barefoot into the living room. She was wearing one of Annie's huge T-shirts. It hung like a dress over her slim hips.

Annie held out a glass of whiskey. "Join us in a toast."

"To what?"

"Just drink it. We'll think of something."

Miranda came toward them and took the glass. She brought with her those fresh shower smells, the scent of flowers and soap and feminine warmth. Her hair, still damp, was a mass of unruly waves. The sight of her sent Chase's head swimming. Or was it the whiskey?

"So what happens now?" asked Annie.

Chase turned away and set his glass on the nearest table. "The police are handling it."

"Look, I've been covering that beat for five years. I wouldn't be too optimistic."

"Lorne's a bright guy. He can figure it out."

"But whose side is he on? I'm not saying Lorne's corrupt, or anything. But you did find that page about him and Valerie Everhard."

"A fling with the local librarian?" Chase shrugged. "I'd consider that only a minor scandal."

"Did you ask Lorne about it?"

"Yes. He didn't deny it. And he didn't seem bothered by it."

"Annie, did you know Richard had those files?" Miranda asked.

Annie shrugged. "We had a number of files on local personalities. Jill did the interviews, wrote the pieces. Every summer we'd run a few profiles. But nothing that'd make tongues twitter." She set her glass down. "Well, whatever was in those files, it's all up in smoke now. A pity you didn't have copies. You've lost your only clues."

"I don't think so," said Chase. "Those were the papers the burglar left behind. Whatever he's really after is still at Rose Hill."

"How do you know?"

"Because he went back there tonight."

"What he didn't count on," said Miranda, "was tangling with Miss Lila St. John. Again."

Annie shook her head and laughed. "That is one poor, unfortunate burglar."

MISS LILA ST. JOHN WAS, at that moment, holding a bag of ice to a nasty-looking goose egg on the back of her head. "What do you mean, did I get a good look at him?" she snapped. "Does it seem likely I got a look at him? Considering where he whacked me?"

"It was just a routine question, ma'am," whimpered Ellis.

"That is the problem with you police people. You are so tied up with your routine questions you never bother to think."

"Miss St. John," Lorne politely interjected, "allow me to rephrase Ellis's question. What, exactly, *did* you see?"

"Precious little."

"A figure? A face?"

"Just a light. I told you, I was sitting here reading. *Death Becomes You.*

"Excuse me?"

"The name of the book. It features a police detective with a genius IQ." She paused. "Obviously, a novel with no basis in reality."

Lorne let that one slide by. Miss St. John deserved a little leeway tonight. After all, a blow on the head—even a head as hard as hers—would make anyone cranky. "Go on," he said.

"Well, I put the book aside to make tea. And as I did, I happened to look out that window. It faces south, toward Rose Hill Cottage. That's when I saw the light."

"A car headlight?"

"No, much dimmer. A flashlight, I think. Moving through the woods. I knew it was headed for Rose Hill. That's all that lies in that direction. So I decided to check on it."

"Why didn't you call us?"

"Because it might simply have been one of the Tremains. Now, how would it look if I dragged you men all the way out here, just to confront the rightful owner?"

"The rightful owner seems to be in doubt."

"Let's not confuse ourselves with that issue. Anyway, I went out—"

"Alone?"

"If only! I would have been just fine if Ozzie hadn't followed me."

"Ozzie?" inquired Ellis.

As if on cue, an enormous black dog sauntered across the room and eyed Ellis.

"Yes, you certainly made a racket," said Miss St. John to the dog. "All that yowling and thrashing in the bushes. No wonder you never catch anything." She looked at Lorne. "It's *his* fault. He followed me up the road. Somewhere along the way I lost track of the light. I was trying to see through the dark and shoo off Ozzie at the same time. He was making such unattractive noises. I turned around and gave him a slap. And that's when he whacked me."

"Ozzie?" asked Ellis.

"No! The man. Or woman. It was dark, so I couldn't tell you which."

"Did you black out?"

"I'm not sure. Things got a little confused at that point. I remember being on my knees in the bushes. Hearing footsteps run away. And feeling mad as hell." She glared at Ozzie. "Yes, and I do mean at *you.*"

The dog, unperturbed, began to lick Lorne's brand-new boot. Gingerly, Lorne gave the dog a little shove. Ozzie, looking insulted, redirected his affectionate overtures toward a more agreeable target—Ellis's leg.

"Then you never saw your attacker?" Lorne asked.

"No, I can't say I did."

"What happened then?"

"I came back here. Oh, I got a little turned around in the dark, but I found my way back, eventually. And I called you."

"So the attack happened—when?"

"It would be about two hours ago."

About the same time the flames were consuming the last of Miranda Wood's house, thought Lorne. It seemed unlikely that the same culprit could have set fire to the house, then raced out here in time to knock Miss St. John on the head. Two crimes, two criminals. Too bad.

Lorne preferred simple solutions.

"Are you certain your attacker was headed for Rose Hill?" he asked.

"I know he was. And he'll be back."

"Why?"

"Because he didn't get what he wanted."

"You're referring to the scandal sheets?"

Miss St. John gave him a look of pure innocence. "Oh. You know about that?"

"Yes. And for your information, Miss St. John, I didn't come on to Valerie Everhard. She came on to me."

Ellis looked up from the dog now nuzzling his knee. "What was that about Valerie Everhard?"

"Never mind," snapped Lorne and Miss St. John simultaneously.

"There was a report on me, too," said Miss St. John with a faint note of pride. "As well as almost everyone on this road. I had no idea Richard Tremain was such a busybody."

"Any idea why?"

"I'll give the man the benefit of the doubt and attribute it to mere curiosity. As opposed to less benign motives."

Blackmail was what she meant. Lorne couldn't see that such a scheme made much sense. First of all, none of those secrets was particularly nasty. Embarrassing, perhaps, but nothing that couldn't be lived down. And that included his own penchant for married librarians. Second, the would-be victims ranged from the moderately well-to-do Forrest Mayhew to the outright cash-strapped Gordimers. Why blackmail a family that can scarcely pay their grocery bills?

Unless money was not the sought-after payment.

He wondered about this all the way back to town. Wondered why Richard Tremain would want those secrets. Wondered if he was even the one who'd collected them in the first place. The cottage, after all, had been open to others in the family. Cassie. Phillip.

Evelyn.

No, not Evelyn, he thought. She wouldn't dirty her hands in this filth.

"You and Valerie Everhard," Ellis muttered as he drove. "I never woulda guessed."

"Look, I felt sorry for her," said Lorne. "She needed some male attention."

"Oh." Ellis kept staring straight ahead at the road and nodding to himself.

"What the hell's that supposed to mean?" Lorne demanded.

"Oh, I was just thinking."

"About what?"

"How awful sorry you must be feeling for that woman right now."

"Valerie Everhard?"

"No." said Ellis. "The widow Tremain."

"IT'S A MATTER OF LOYALTY, Chase," said Noah. "To the family. To your brother. To the people who *matter.*"

Chase said nothing. He simply continued slicing his ham, albeit with more concentrated vigor than usual. He knew they were all watching him. Noah and Evelyn. The twins. They were waiting for him to respond. But he kept on slicing that meat, mangling it, really, into smaller and smaller pieces.

"Never mind, Daddy," said Evelyn. "Can't you see? He's so wrapped up with that witch, he can't see the trap he's—"

"Please, Evelyn." Chase set down his knife.

"She's twisted you around, Chase! She has a talent for that! Among other things. But you can't be bothered with the facts anymore. No, all you want to believe are her lies."

"I want to believe the truth," he said quietly.

"The truth is, she's a whore."

"Evelyn," cut in Noah. "That is quite enough."

Evelyn turned on her father. "Whose side are you on?"

"You know damn well I'm on your side. I always have been."

"Then why don't you back me up?"

"Because this conversation doesn't become you. You've forgotten all I taught you about dignity. Pride."

"Well, *excuse me,* Daddy. It's not every day one's husband gets murdered." She glanced around at the sideboard. "Where's that wine? It's not too early for a drink."

"You will get over the murder. You'll get beyond it. And you will remember who you are."

"Who I am?" She rose to her feet. "Who I am is more of an embarrassment every day." She shoved her chair back against the table and left the room.

There was a long silence.

"She does have a point, Chase," said Noah, sounding quite reasonable. "The family should stick together. No matter what attractions this Miranda Wood person offers, don't you think it's best you stand by us?"

"What attraction *does* she offer?" asked Cassie.

"That's irrelevant," snapped Chase.

Noah raised an eyebrow. "Is it?"

Chase met Noah's gaze with a look of sheer indifference. Which, at that moment, wasn't at all what he was feeling. He had plenty of feelings when it came to Miranda Wood, and indifference wasn't one of them. All night he'd dreamt about her. He'd awakened sweating, remembering the fire, feeling once again the panic of not being able to find her in that well of smoke and flames. He'd drop back to sleep, only to sink yet again into the same nightmare. Some time during his fitful tossing and turning, he'd come to several realizations. That he was incapable of logical thought where Miranda Wood was concerned. That the attraction he felt for her was growing more dangerous every day.

And that, no matter what his instincts told him, the weight of evidence still pointed to her guilt.

This morning he'd risen from bed exhausted but absolutely clearheaded. He knew what he had to do. He had to put some distance between them. As he should have done from the very beginning.

He said, "You don't have to worry, Noah. I don't plan to see her again."

"I always thought you were the smarter Tremain," said Noah. "I was right."

Chase shrugged. "Not really a flattering comment. Considering how little you thought of Richard."

Noah glanced at the twins. "You two! Don't you have something better to do?"

"Not really," said Phillip.

"Well, clear the table, then. Go on."

"It's not as if we didn't know," said Cassie.

Noah frowned at her. "Know what?"

"That you and Dad didn't get along."

"For that matter, young lady, he didn't get along with you, either."

"Normal father-daughter disagreements. Not like you two, always at each other's throats. All that yelling and name-calling—"

"That's enough!" Noah's face had turned an ugly red. He rose partway out of his chair, his gaze targeted on his insolent granddaughter. "The day you were born, Cassandra, I took one look at you and I said, 'Watch out for that one. She's going to be trouble.'"

"Yes, it runs in our family, doesn't it?"

Instantly Phillip was on his feet, tugging at Noah's arm. "Come on, Granddad. Let's go outside, you and me. Walk around the block. I wanted to tell you about my year at Harvard—"

"Damn nursery for snooty rich boys."

"Just a walk, Granddad. It'll do you good."

Noah harrumphed and shoved his chair against the table. "Let's go, then. Hell, I could use the fresh air."

The two men walked out, slamming the front door behind them.

Cassie looked at Chase and smiled ironically. "One big happy family."

"What was that you said? About Noah and Richard."

"They despised each other. You knew that."

"*Despised* wasn't the word that came to mind. Disliked, maybe. You know, the usual rivalry between father and son-in-law."

"This wasn't just your usual rivalry." Cassie began to slice her ham into dainty pieces. For the first time Chase found himself actually seeing his niece. Before, she'd always seemed lost from view, the colorless sister skulking in the shadow of her brother. Now he took a new and closer look, and what he saw was a young woman with a square jaw and eyes like a ferret's. The resemblance to Noah was startling. No wonder the old man didn't get along with her. He probably saw too much of himself in that face. She looked him straight in the eye. No squirming, no discomfort, just that steady gaze.

"What did they argue about? Noah and your father?"

"Anything. Everything. Oh, they never let it get beyond these walls. Dad was weird that way. We could all be screaming at each other in this house, but once we stepped out the door he insisted we look like the perfect family. It was so phony. In public Dad and Noah would make like old buddies. And all the time there was that rivalry between them."

"Over your mother?"

"Of course. Noah's darling. And Dad could never be a good enough husband." She snorted. "Not that he tried very hard."

Chase paused, wondering how to phrase his next question. "Did you know your father was having...affairs?"

"He's been at it for years," Cassie said with a wave of er hand. "Lots of women."

"Which ones?"

She shrugged. "I figured that was his business."

"You two weren't very close, were you?"

"Daughters just weren't his thing, Uncle Chase. While I as working my butt off, getting straight A's, he was planing for Phillip's Harvard education. Grooming him to ke over the *Herald.*"

"Phillip doesn't seem exactly thrilled by the prospect."

"You noticed that? Dad never did." She took a few bites f ham, then gave Chase a thoughtful look. "And what as the problem between *you* two?"

"Problem?" He resisted the urge to look away, to avoid er gaze. She would probably know immediately that he as hiding something. As it was, she'd probably already etected the flicker of discomfort in his eyes.

"The last time I saw you, Uncle Chase, I was ten years ld. That was at Grandpa Tremain's funeral. Now, Greenich isn't that far away. But you never came back for a isit, not once."

"Lives get complicated. You know how it is, Cassie."

She gave him a searching look, then said, "It's not easy, it? Being the ignored sibling in the family?"

Damn this sharp-eyed brat, he thought. He gathered up is empty dishes and rose to his feet.

"You don't think she did it. Do you?" Cassie asked. hey didn't have to mention names. They both knew exctly what they were talking about.

"I haven't decided," he said. He carried the dishes toard the kitchen. In the doorway he stopped. "By the way, assie," he said. "I called here last night about seven, to y I wouldn't be home for dinner. No one answered the hone. Where was your mother?"

"I really wouldn't know." Cassie picked up a slice of ast and calmly began to spread marmalade on it. "You'd ave to ask her."

CHASE DROVE DIRECTLY to Rose Hill. No detours, no little side trips to pick up suspected murderesses. He had no intention of being distracted by Miranda Wood today. What he needed was a dose of coolheaded logic, and that meant keeping his distance. Today he had other things on his mind, the first item being: Who kept trying to break in to the cottage, and what was he searching for?

The answer lay somewhere in Rose Hill.

So that was where he headed. He drove with the window rolled down, the salt air whistling past his cheek. It brought back all those summer days of his childhood, riding with his mother along this very road, the smell of the sea in his face, the cry of the gulls echoing off the cliffs. How she had loved this drive! His mother had been a daredevil behind the wheel, screeching around these curves, laughing as the wind tangled her dark hair. They'd both laughed a lot those days, and he'd wondered if anyone else in the world had a mother so wild, so beautiful. So free.

Her death had left him devastated.

If only, before she'd died, she'd told him the truth.

He turned onto the access road and bumped along past all the old camp signs, past the cottages of families whose kids he'd once played with. Good memories, bad memories—they all returned as he drove up that road. He remembered twirling in the tire swing until he was so dizzy he threw up. Kissing buck-toothed Lucy Baylor behind the water tower. Hearing that awful crash of a breaking window and knowing it was *his* baseball they'd find lying in the shattered glass. The memories were so vivid he didn't notice that he'd already rounded the last bend and was just now turning onto the gravel driveway.

There was a car parked in front of the cottage.

He pulled up beside it and climbed out. He saw no sign of the driver. Could their burglar have turned desperate enough to pay a visit in broad daylight?

He hurried up the porch steps and was startled to hear the whistling of a kettle from the kitchen. Who the hell would

e brazen enough to not only break in, but also make him-
:lf right at home? He shoved open the door and came face-
)-face with the guilty party.

"I've just made some tea," said Miranda. She gave him
 tight smile, not unfriendly, just nervous. Perhaps afraid.
he nodded down at the tea tray she was carrying. "Would
ou like some?"

Chase glanced around the room, at the books arranged
 neat piles on the floor. The desk had been cleared, the
rawers' contents emptied into a series of cardboard boxes.
lowly his gaze shifted and took in the three bookcases.
)ne was already two-thirds empty.

"We spent the morning going through Richard's pa-
:rs," Miranda explained. "I'm afraid we haven't turned
p anything yet, but—"

He shook his head. "We?"

"Miss St. John and I."

"Is she here?"

"She went back to her house, to feed Ozzie."

Their gazes met. *I try to stay away from you,* he thought,
nd damn it, here you are. Here we are, alone in this house.
The possibilities flooded his mind. Temptation, enemy
f reason, danced its devil dance, the way it did every time
e was in the same room with her. He thought of Richard,
ought of her, thought of the two of them together. It
urt. Maybe that's why he chose to think of it. To quell the
sing need he felt when he looked at her now.

"She—Miss St. John—thought it made sense to get
:arted without you," Miranda said in a rush, as though
iddenly frantic to fill the silence. "We didn't know when
ou'd get here, and we didn't want to call the house. I sup-
ose we're trespassing, in a way, but . . ." Her voice trailed
ff.

"Technically speaking," he said after a pause, "you
re."

She set down the tea tray, then straightened to face him.
Ier nervousness was gone. In its place was calm determi-

nation. "Maybe so. But it's what I have to do. We ca
search together. Or we can search separately. But I am go
ing to search." She raised her chin, met his gaze withou
flinching. "So, Chase. Which way shall it be?"

Chapter Nine

His gaze was neutral, as unrevealing as that blank wall behind him. More revealing to Miranda was her acute sense of disappointment. She'd hoped to see at least a trace of gladness in his eyes, that he'd be pleased to find her here today. What she hadn't expected was this . . . indifference. *So that's how it is between us,* she thought. *What's happened since I saw you last? What did Evelyn say to you? That's it, isn't it? They've gotten to you. Richard's family. Your family.*

He shrugged. "It does make sense, I suppose. Working together."

"Of course it does."

"And you've already gotten off to a good start, I see."

In silence she poured a cup of tea, then carried it to the bookcase. There she calmly continued the task she'd been working on earlier—pulling down the books, riffling through the pages for any loose papers. She felt him watching her, sensed his gaze like a prickling in her back. "You can start on the other bookcase," she said without looking at him.

"What have you found so far?"

"No surprises." She reached for another book. "Unless you count Richard's rather weird taste in reading material." She looked at a book jacket. *The Advanced Physics of Ocean Waves.* "This one, for instance. I never knew he was interested in physics."

"He wasn't. When it came to science, he was functionally illiterate."

She opened the cover. "Well, this *is* his book. I see someone's written him a dedication in the front...." Glancing at the title page, she suddenly flushed.

"What is it?"

"You know the old saying?" Miranda murmured. "About not judging a book by its cover?"

Chase moved behind her and read over her shoulder. "*One Hundred and One Sexual Positions.* Fully illustrated?"

Miranda flipped open to a random page and instantly flushed. "They meant what they said about fully illustrated."

He reached around her to take the book. His breath grazed her neck; it left her skin tingling.

"Obviously a dummy jacket," said Chase. "I wonder how many other disguised books are in that stack?"

"I didn't really check," Miranda admitted. "I was looking for loose papers. I wasn't paying much attention to the books themselves."

Chase flipped to the title page and read aloud the hand-written dedication. "To my darling Richard. Can we try number forty-eight again? Love, M." Chase glanced at Miranda.

"I didn't give him that thing!" she protested.

"Then who's M?"

"Someone else. Not me."

He frowned at the dedication. "I wonder what number forty-eight is." He flipped to the page.

"Well?"

Chase took a discreet peek. "You don't want to know," he muttered and let the page riffle shut.

A slip of paper flew out and landed on the floor. They both stared at it in surprise. Chase was the first to snatch it up.

"Dearest love," he read aloud. "I'm thinking of you every day, every hour. I've given up caring about propriety or reputation or hellfire. There's only you and me and the time we have together. That, my darling, is my new definition of heaven." Chase glanced at her, one eyebrow raised in a cynical slant.

Miranda looked straight at him. "In case you're wondering," she said evenly, "I didn't write that note, either." In irritation she took the book and set it down on the nearest pile.

"Then I guess we'll just file it under 'interesting stuff,'" said Chase. "And continue with the rest of these books."

Miranda settled onto the rug. Chase sat in front of the other bookcase. They didn't touch, didn't look at each other. *Safer that way,* she thought. *For both of us.*

For half an hour they flipped through books, slapped them shut, threw clouds of dust in the air. Miranda was the one who found the next piece of the puzzle. It was tucked away in a financial ledger, in an envelope labeled Deductible Expenses.

"It's a receipt," she said, frowning at the slip of paper. "A month ago Richard paid four hundred dollars to this company."

"For what services?" asked Chase.

"It doesn't say. It's just made out to the Alamo Detective Agency in Bass Harbor."

"A detective agency? I wonder what Richard was after."

"Chase." She handed him the slip of paper. "Look at the name of the payee."

"William B. Rodell?" He glanced at her quizzically.

At least you're looking at me again, she thought. *At least we're connecting.* "Don't you remember?" she said. "That note attached to Richard's files."

Chase stared at the receipt, revelation suddenly brightening his dark features.

"Of course," he said softly. "William B. Rodell..."

W.B.R.

IT WAS EASY TO SEE HOW the Alamo Detective Agency got its name. Willie Rodell was a good ol' boy transplant from San Antonio who split his time between Maine and Florida. Summertime was for Maine, and here he was, sitting behind his old steel desk, books and papers piled up in front of him like the battlements of a fort. The office was strictly a solo affair—one phone, one desk, one man. But what a man. Willie Rodell had enough flesh on his bones to fill the suits of two six-footers. *This must be what they mean by Texas-size,* thought Miranda.

"Yeah, I mighta done some work for Mr. Tremain now and again," said Rodell, leaning back in his equally Texas-size chair.

"Meaning you did or you didn't?" asked Chase.

"Well, you're holdin' one of my receipts there, so I guess it means I did."

"What sort of job?"

Willie shrugged. "Routine stuff."

"What *is* your routine stuff?"

"Mostly I do domestic affairs, if you catch my drift. Who's doin' what to whom, that sorta thing." His smirk rearranged the folds of his face into something vaguely obscene.

"But that's not the sort of thing you did for Richard, was it?"

"Nope. Though I hear tell there was more than enough dirt to dig in his particular case."

Cheeks burning, Miranda stared down fixedly at Willie's desk, a battle zone of broken pencils and twisted paper clips scattered among a bizarre assortment of magazines. *Hot Ladies. National Locksmith. Car and Driver.*

Chase got right to the point. "He hired you to compile files on his neighbors. Didn't he?"

Willie looked at him blandly. "Files?"

"We saw them, Mr. Rodell. They were among Richard's papers. Detailed reports on almost every resident along the access road. Each one containing sensitive information."

"Dirt sheets."

"That's right."

Willie shrugged. "I didn't write 'em."

"There was a note attached to one of the reports. It said, 'Want more? Let me know.' It was signed with the initials W.B.R." Chase reached over and plucked one of Willie's business cards from the desk. "Which just happens to be your initials."

"Helluva coincidence, hey?"

"He wanted dirt on his neighbors. Why?"

"He was snoopy?"

"So he paid you to write those reports."

"I told you, I didn't write 'em." Willie held up one fat hand. "Scout's honor."

"Then who did?"

"Dunno. But I admire his work."

Miranda, who'd been sitting quietly, focused on one of the magazines on the desk. *National Locksmith.* "You stole them," she said. She looked up at Willie's moonlike face. "That's what Richard hired you for. To steal those files from someone else."

Willie reached up and smoothed back a nonexistent strand of hair.

"You were paid to be a burglar," said Miranda. "What else were you paid for?"

"Look," said Willie, holding up both fat hands in a gesture of mock surrender. "Folks pay me to gather info, okay? That's all I do. Clients don't care how I get it, long as I get it."

"And where did you get those dirt sheets?" asked Chase.

"They were part of a bunch o' papers I sorta picked up."

"What else did you sort of pick up?"

"Financial records, bank statements. Hey, I didn't exactly *steal* 'em. I just, well, borrowed 'em for a few minutes. Long enough to run 'em through ol' man Xerox. Then I put 'em right back where I found 'em."

"The office of Stone Coast Trust," said Miranda.

Willie gave her a man-in-the-moon grin. "Betcha you're real good at Twenty Questions."

"So those were Tony Graffam's files," said Chase. "Not Richard's."

"Mr. T. didn't even know they existed till I handed 'em over. Thought for sure he was gonna want more. You know how it is. Get a taste of appetizer, you want the main course. Well, those papers were just the appetizer. I coulda got more."

"Why didn't you?"

"He fired me."

They frowned at him. "What?" said Miranda.

"That's right," said Willie. "Two days after I hand him those papers, he calls and says, thanks, he won't be needin' my services no more and how much do I owe you? That was that."

"Did he say why he fired you?"

"Nope. Just told me to keep it under my hat, and that he wasn't interested in Stone Coast no more."

"When was this?"

"Oh, about a week before he died."

"The same time he told Jill to kill the article," said Miranda. She looked at Chase. "Maybe he saw what Tony Graffam had on him. And decided to drop the whole investigation."

"But I looked over those papers, 'fore I handed 'em over," said Willie. "There wasn't any report on Tremain. Far as I could tell, wasn't nothin' in there to blackmail him with."

"Did you keep copies?"

"Mr. T. took it all. Didn't want loose papers floatin' round." Willie folded his hands behind his neck and stretched. Blots of sweat showed in his cavernous armpits. "Naw, I don't think it was the files. I think someone went and offered him a little, you know, incentive payment to forget the whole thing. So that's what he did."

"But Richard didn't need the money," said Miranda. "They couldn't bribe him."

"Sweetie, you can bribe just about anyone," said Willie, obviously an authority on such matters. "All it takes is the right price. And even a fella as rich as Tremain had his price."

"THE LAZY MAN'S METHOD of investigative journalism," said Chase. "Hire a thug to steal the evidence."

"I had no idea he'd do such a thing," said Miranda, gazing ahead in quiet disbelief. It was just after noon, a time when Main Street in Bass Harbor should have been bustling with tourists. Today, though, a cold summer drizzle had cooled the ardor of even the most inveterate sightseers. Miranda and Chase, hunched in their jackets, walked alone.

"And I thought it was just talent," she said softly. "The way he could pull a story together. Come up with evidence that surprised everyone. All that time he was paying someone to do the dirty work."

"It was just Richard's way," said Chase. "Meaning the easy way."

She looked at him. His hair, dampened by mist, was a cap of black, unruly waves. He stared straight ahead, his profile unrevealing. "Is that how he was as a boy?" she asked.

"He was good at finding shortcuts. For a few bucks he'd get someone to write his book report. Or help him cram for tests. He even found some idiot to finish his math homework for him." Chase grinned sheepishly. "Me."

"He bribed you into doing his homework?"

"It was more like, well, blackmail."

"What did he have on you?"

"Lots. Broken windows. Trampled flower beds. I was a pretty bad kid."

"But good at math, obviously."

Chase laughed. "When someone threatened exposure, I was good at a lot of things."

"And Richard took advantage of it."

"He was older. In a lot of ways, smarter. Everyone liked him, wanted to believe the best of him. And the worst of me." He shook his head. "I can see the same thing happening with his kids now. Phillip's the golden boy. And Cassie, she'll be trying all her life to match up."

"Will you be trying all *your* life to match up?"

He looked at her, then looked away. "No. I don't particularly care to make the same mistakes Richard did."

Meaning me, she thought.

The day suddenly seemed colder, darker. It was more than just her sagging spirits. The drizzle had turned to rain.

"Let's duck in someplace and get lunch," said Chase. "We've got another hour and a half till the ferry leaves."

They found a café tucked into an alley off Main Street. From the outside it seemed an unassuming little place with a name to match: Mary Jane's. It was the whiff of rich coffee and grilled meat that finally drew them in. Nothing fancy served here, just good plain food, roast chicken and red potatoes and crisp green beans, accompanied by freshly brewed coffee. Miranda's spirits might be sagging, but her appetite was in fine shape. She moved on to a slice of peach pie and a third round of coffee. A good thing she didn't normally react to stress by overeating. By now she'd be twenty pounds overweight.

"In a way," said Chase, "I'm relieved to learn the truth about those files."

"Relieved to learn Richard paid for an out-and-out burglary?"

"At least he wasn't the one snooping on his neighbors. The one planning blackmail."

She set down her fork. "Yes, I suppose you could talk yourself into thinking that breaking into Stone Coast Trust was somehow, well, morally correct."

"I'm not saying it was. But I can see how Richard might justify it. He's seen the coast eaten away by development. Then it hits close to home and he figures it's time to play dirty. Find out what you can about the developer. Steal a few files, financial records. Throw it back in the other guy's face."

"But he didn't. That's the strange part. He paid Rodell to steal those files. Then, after he gets hold of them, he drops the whole crusade. Kills the article, fires Rodell." She paused, and added softly, "And changes his will."

Chase frowned. "I don't see how that's related."

"The timing fits. Maybe he found something in those papers that got him angry at Evelyn. Made him decide to keep her from ever getting Rose Hill."

"You think there was a file on Evelyn? We didn't see one."

"He might've destroyed it. Or it could have been taken from the cottage. After his death."

They both fell silent at the implications of that statement. Who but Evelyn herself would bother to take such a file?

"This is crazy," said Chase. "Why would Evelyn steal it? It was her own damn cottage. She could walk in and out without anyone raising an eyebrow." He reached for his coffee cup, took a deliberate sip. "I can't see her breaking in and trashing the place."

You can't see her killing anyone, either. Can you? she thought. She wondered about Chase and his sister-in-law. Was their relationship merely cordial? Or did it run deeper than that? He'd stubbornly resisted the possibility that Evelyn might be guilty of wrongdoing, be it theft or murder.

Miranda could understand why. Evelyn was a beautiful woman.

Now a free woman.

There was, after all, an appealing tidiness to a match between Chase and Evelyn. It would keep the money in the family, the same last name on the checkbook. Everyone would slip into their new roles with a minimum of muss and fuss. Chase had spent his boyhood trying to live up to his brother's image. Now he could slip right into Richard's place. Much as Miranda hated to admit it, such a mating would have a certain symmetry, a social correctness.

Something I'd never be able to give him.

The waitress came by with the check. Miranda reached for it, but Chase snatched it up first. "I'll take care of it," he said.

Miranda took a few bills from her pocket and laid them on the table.

"What's that for?" asked Chase.

"Call it pride," she said, rising to her feet, "but I always pay my way."

"With me you don't have to."

"I have to," she said flatly. "Especially with you." She grabbed her jacket and headed out the door.

He caught up with her outside. The rain had stopped but the sun had not yet emerged and the sky was a cold monochrome of gray. They walked side by side for a moment, not quite friends, not quite strangers.

"I'll be honest," he said. "I wasn't planning to see you today. Or ever again."

"It's a small town, Chase. It's hard to avoid a person here."

"I was going to drive back to Greenwich tomorrow."

"Oh." She lowered her eyes, willing herself not to feel disappointment. Or hurt. All those emotions she'd vowed never to feel for another Tremain. The emotions she was feeling now.

"But I've been thinking," he said.

Those four words made her halt and look up at him. *He's watching me, waiting for me to reveal myself. Give myself away as beguiled and bedazzled.*

Which, damn it, I am.

"I've been thinking," he said, "of staying a few more days. Just to clear up those questions about Richard."

She said nothing.

"Anyway, that's why I'm staying in town. It's the only reason."

Her chin came up. "Did I imply otherwise?"

"No." He let out a breath. "No, you didn't."

They walked on, another block, another silence.

"You'll be looking for the same answers, I expect," he said.

"I don't have much choice, do I? It's my future. My freedom."

"Look, I know it makes sense, in a way, for you and I to work together. But it's not exactly..."

"Seemly," she finished for him. "That's what you mean, isn't it? That it's embarrassing for you to be consorting with a woman like me."

"I didn't say that."

"Never mind, Chase." In irritation she turned and continued walking. "You're right, of course. We can't work together. Because we don't really trust each other. Do we?"

He didn't answer. He simply walked beside her, his hands thrust deep in his pockets. And that, more than anything he could have said, was what hurt her most.

THEY MIGHT NOT TRUST each other. They might not want anything to do with each other. But the simple fact was, if they wanted answers, the cottage was where they both had to look. So when Miranda pulled into the gravel driveway of Rose Hill the next morning she was not surprised to see Chase's car already parked there. Ozzie was sprawled on the front porch, looking dejected. He managed a few half-hearted wags of his tail as she came up the steps, but when he saw she wasn't going to invite him inside he flopped back down into a whimpering imitation of a shag rug.

Miss St. John and Chase had already gone through the second bookcase. The place was looking more and more like a disaster zone, with cardboard boxes filled with papers, books precariously stacked in towers, empty coffee cups and dirty spoons littering the end tables.

"I see you started without me," said Miranda, careful to avoid looking at Chase. He was just as carefully avoiding her gaze. "What have you found?"

"Odds and ends," said Miss St. John, thoughtfully eyeing them both. "Shopping lists, receipts. Another love note from M. And a few quite literate college term papers."

"Phillip's?"

"Cassandra's. She must have done some writing out here. A few of the books are hers, as well."

Miranda picked up a bundle of papers and glanced through the titles. "A political analysis of the Boer conflict." "Doom foretold: the French colonialists in Vietnam." "The media and presidential politics." All were authored by Cassandra Tremain.

"A smart cookie," said Miss St. John. "A pity that slick brother of hers always steals the spotlight."

Miranda dug deeper in the box and pulled out the latest note from M. It was typewritten.

I waited till midnight—you never came. Did you forget? I wanted to call, but I'm always afraid she'll pick up the phone. She has you every weekend, every night, every holiday. I get the dregs.

How can you say you love me, when you leave me here, waiting for you? I'm worth more than this. I really am.

Quietly Miranda let the note flutter back into the box. Then she went to the window and stood staring out, to-

ward the sea. Pity stirred inside her, for the woman who
had written that note, for the pain she'd suffered. *The price
we both paid for loving the wrong man.*

"Miranda?" Chase asked. "Is something wrong?"

"No." She cleared her throat and turned to him. "I'm
fine. So... where should I start looking?"

"You could help me finish with this shelf. I'm finding
papers here and there, so it's going slower than I expected."

"Yes, of course." She went to the shelf, pulled out a
book and sat on the floor beside him. Not too close, not too
far. *Neither friends nor enemies,* she thought. Just two
people sharing the same rug, the same purpose. *For that,
we don't even have to like each other.*

For an hour they flipped through pages, brushed away
dust. Most of the books, it seemed, hadn't been opened in
ages. There were old postcards dated twenty years earlier,
addressed to Chase's mother. There was a hand-scrawled
list of bird species sighted at Rose Hill, and a library notice from twelve years before, still stuck in the overdue
book. Over the years, so many bits and pieces of the Tremain and Pruitt families had ended up on these shelves. It
took time to sort out the vital from the trivial.

An oversize atlas of the state of Maine provided the next
clue. Chase pulled it off the shelf and glanced in the front
cover. Then he turned and called, "Miss St. John? You ever
heard of a place called Hemlock Heights?"

"No. Why?"

"There's a map of it tucked in here." Chase pulled the
document out of the atlas and spread it out on the rug. It
was a collection of six photocopied pages taped together to
form a site map. The pages looked fairly fresh. Property
lines had been sketched in, and the lots were labeled by
number. At the top was the development's name: Hemlock Heights. "I wonder if Richard was thinking of invest-
ing in real estate."

Miss St. John crouched down for a closer look. "Wait. This looks rather familiar. Isn't this our access road? And this lot at the end—lot number one. That's Rose Hill. I recognized that little jag up the mountain."

Chase nodded. "You're right. That's exactly what this is. Here's St. John's Wood. And the stone wall."

"It's the Stone Coast Trust map," said Miranda. "See? Most of the lots are labeled Sold."

"Good heavens," said Miss St. John. "I had no idea so many of the camps have changed hands. There are only four of us who haven't sold out to Tony Graffam."

"What kind of offer did he make for St. John's Wood?" asked Miranda.

"It was a very good price at the time. When I refused to sell he bumped it up even higher. That was a year ago. I couldn't understand why the offer was so generous. You see, this was all conservation land. These old camps were grandfathered in, built before the days of land commissions. The cottages were allowed to stand, but you couldn't develop any of it. From a commercial standpoint the land was worthless. Then suddenly it's all been rezoned for development. And now I'm sitting on a gold mine." She looked at the other unsold lots on the map. "So is old Sulaway. And the hippies in Frenchman's Cottage."

"And Tony Graffam," said Miranda.

"But what if the zoning decision was a sham?" said Chase. "What if there were payoffs? If that fact became public knowledge..."

"My guess is, there'd be such protest, the zoning would be reversed," said Miss St. John. "And Mr. Graffam would be the proud owner of a lot of worthless property."

"But it's worthless to him right now, Miss St. John," said Miranda, studying the map. "Graffam needs that access road to get to his lots. And you said the road belongs—belonged—to Richard."

"Yes, we keep coming back to that, don't we?" said Chase softly. "That link between Richard and Stone Coast

Trust. The link that refuses to go away...." He stood, clapping the dust from his trousers. "Maybe it's time we paid a visit to our neighbors."

"Which ones?" asked Miranda.

"Sulaway and the hippies. The other two on this road who didn't sell. Let's find out if Graffam put any pressure to bear. Like a blackmail note or two."

"He didn't try to blackmail Miss St. John," pointed out Miranda. "And she didn't sell."

"Ah, but my property's scarcely worth the effort," said Miss St. John. "I'm just a tiny patch off to the side. And as for trying to blackmail me, well, you saw for yourself he doesn't have a thing on me worth mentioning. Not that I wouldn't mind generating a whiff of scandal at my age."

"The others could be more vulnerable," said Chase. "Old Sulaway, for instance. We should at least talk to him."

"A good idea," said Miss St. John. "Since you thought of it, Chase, *you* do it."

Chase laughed. "You are a coward, Miss St. John."

"No, I'm just too old for the aggravation."

Without warning, Chase reached for Miranda's hand and with one smooth motion pulled her up in an arc that almost, but not quite, ended in his arms. She reached out to steady herself and found her palms pressing against his chest. At once she stepped back.

"Is this a request for me to come along?" she said.

"It's more along the lines of a plea. To help me soften up old Sulaway."

"Does he need softening up?"

"Let's just say he hasn't taken kindly to me since I batted a baseball through his window. And that was twenty-five years ago."

Miranda laughed in disbelief. "You sound like you're afraid of him. Both of you."

"Obviously she's never met old Sulaway," said Miss St. John.

"Is there something I should know about him?"

Chase and Miss St. John glanced at each other.

"Just be careful when you walk into his front yard," said Miss St. John. "Give him lots of warning. And be ready to get out of there fast."

"Why? Does he have a dog or something?"

"No. But he does have a shotgun."

Chapter Ten

"You're that boy who broke my window!" yelled Homer Sulaway. "Yeah, I recognize you." He stood on the front porch, his skinny arms looped around a rifle, his lobsterman's dungarees rolled up at the ankles. Chase had told Miranda the man was eighty-five. The toothless, prunefaced apparition on that porch looked about a century older. "You two go on, now! Leave me alone. Can't afford to fix no more broken windows."

"But I paid for it, remember?" said Chase. "Had to mow lawns for six months, but I did pay for it."

"Damn right," said Sully. "Or I'd 'a got it outta your old man's hide."

"Can we talk to you, Mr. Sulaway?"

"What about?"

"Stone Coast Trust. I wanted to know if—"

"Not interested." Sully turned and shuffled back across the porch.

"Mr. Sulaway, I have a young lady here who'd like to ask—"

"Don't have no use for young ladies. Or old ladies, either." The screen door slammed shut behind him.

There was a silence. "Well," muttered Chase. "The old boy's definitely mellowed."

"I think he's afraid," said Miranda. "That's why he's not talking to us."

"Afraid of what?"

"Let's find out." She approached the cottage and called, "Mr. Sulaway? All we want to know is, are they trying to blackmail you? Has Stone Coast threatened you in some way?"

"Those are lies they're spreading!" Sulaway yelled through the screen door. "Vicious lies! Not true, any of it!"

"That's not what Tony Graffam says."

The door flew open and Sully stormed out onto the porch. "What's Graffam got to say about me? What's he tellin' people now?"

"We could stand out here and yell about it. Or we could talk in private. Which do you prefer?"

Sulaway glanced around, as though searching for watchers in the woods. Then he snapped, "Well? You two need an engraved invitation, or what?"

They followed him inside. Sully's kitchen was a dark little space, the windows closed in by trees, every shelf and countertop crammed full with junk and knickknacks. Newspapers were stacked in piles about the floor. The kitchen table was about the only unoccupied surface. They sat around it, in old ladder-back chairs that look dangerously close to collapse.

"Your brother's the one they was really pressurin'," Sully told Chase. "But Richard, he wasn't about to give in, no sir. He tells us, we gotta stick together. Says we can't sell, no matter how many letters they send us, how many lies they tell." Sully shook his head. "Didn't do no good. Just about everybody on this road went and signed on Graffam's dotted line, just like that. And Richard, look what went and happened to him. Hear he got himself poked with a knife."

Miranda saw Chase glance in her direction. Old Sully was so out of touch he didn't realize he was sitting with the very woman accused of plunging that knife into Richard Tremain.

"You said something about a letter," said Chase. "Telling you to sell. Did Graffam send it?"

"Wasn't signed. I hear none of 'em were."

"So Richard got a letter, as well?"

"I figure. So did Barretts down the way. Maybe everyone did. People wouldn't talk about 'em."

"What did the letter say? The one you got?"

"Lies. Mean, wicked lies...."

"And the one they sent Richard?"

Sully shrugged. "I wasn't privy to that."

Miranda glanced around the kitchen with its overflowing shelves. A pack rat, this Mr. Sulaway was. He kept things, junk and treasure both. She said, "Do you still have that letter?"

Sully hunched his shoulders, like a hermit crab about to retreat into its shell. He grunted. "Maybe."

"May we see it?"

"I dunno." He sighed, rubbed his face. "I dunno."

"We know they're lies, Mr. Sulaway. We just want to see what tactics they're using. We have to stop Graffam before he does any more damage."

For a moment Sully sat hunched and silent. Miranda thought he might not have heard what she said. But then he creaked to his feet and shuffled over to the kitchen counter. From the flour canister he pulled out a folded sheet of paper. He handed it to Miranda.

She laid it flat on the table.

"What really happened to Stanley? The Lula M knows. So do we."

Below those cryptic words was a handwritten note, penciled in. "Sell, Sully."

"Who's Stanley?" asked Miranda.

Sully had shrunk into his chair and was staring down at his leathery hands.

"Mr. Sulaway?"

The answer came out in a whisper. "My brother."

"What does that note refer to?"

"It was a long time ago...." Sully wiped his eyes, as though to clear away some mist clouding his vision. "Just an accident," he murmured. "Happens all the time out there. The sea, you can't trust her. Can't turn yer back on her...."

"What happened to Stanley?" asked Miranda gently.

"Got...got his boot caught in the trap line. Pulled him clean over the side. Water's cold in December. It'll freeze yer blood. I was aboard the *Sally M,* didn't see it." He turned, stared at the window. The trees outside seemed to close in upon the house, shutting it off from light, from warmth.

They waited.

He said softly. "I was the one found him. Draggin' in the water off *Lula*'s stern. I cut him loose...hauled him aboard...brought him to port." He shuddered. "That was it. Long time ago, fifty years. Maybe more...."

"And this note?"

"It's a lie, got spread around after..."

"After what?"

"After I married Jessie." He paused. "Stanley's wife."

There it is, thought Miranda. The secret. The shame.

"Mr. Sulaway?" asked Chase quietly. "What did they have on Richard?"

Sully shook his head. "Didn't tell me."

"But they did have something?"

"Whatever it was, it didn't make him sell. Had a hard head, your brother. That's what got him in the end."

"Why didn't *you* sell, Mr. Sulaway?" Miranda asked.

The old man turned to her. "Because I won't," he said. She saw in his eyes the look of a man who's been backed into the last corner of his life. "Ain't no way they can scare me. Not now."

"Can't they?"

He shook his head. "I got cancer."

"DO YOU THINK HE KILLED his brother?" asked Miranda.

They were walking along the road, through the dappled

shade of pine and birch. Chase had his hands in his pockets, a frown on his brow. "What does it matter now, whether he did it or not?"

Yes, what did it matter? she wondered. The old man was about to face his final judgment. Innocent or guilty, he'd already lived fifty years with the consequences.

"It's hard to believe Graffam was able to dig up that story," said Miranda. "He's a newcomer to the island. What he had on Sully was fifty years old. How did Graffam find out about it?"

"Hired investigator?"

"And he used the name 'Sully' in that note. Remember? Only a local person would use that nickname."

"So he had a local informant. Someone with his finger on the island's pulse."

"Or someone in the business of knowing what goes on in this town," she added, thinking of Willie B. Rodell and the Alamo Detective Agency.

They came to a sign that read Harmony House.

"Used to be called Frenchman's Cottage," said Chase. "Until the hippies bought it." Down a rutted road they walked. They heard the tinkle of wind chimes before they saw the cottage. The sound floated through the trees, dancing on the breeze. The chimes were of iridescent glass, sparkling as they swayed from the porch overhang. The cottage door hung wide open.

"Anyone home?" called Chase.

At first only the wind chimes answered. Then, faintly, they heard the sound of laughter, approaching voices. Through the trees they saw them—two men and a woman, walking toward them.

None of the three was wearing a stitch.

The trio, spotting unexpected visitors, didn't seem in the least perturbed. The woman had wild hair generously streaked with gray, and an expression of placid indifference. The two men flanking her were equally shaggy and serene. One of the men, silver haired and weathered, seemed to be the official spokesperson. As his two companions went into the cottage, he came forward with his hand held out in greeting.

"You've found Harmony House," he said. "Or is this just a fortunate accident?"

"It's on purpose," said Chase, shaking the man's hand. "I'm Chase Tremain, Richard's brother. He owned Rose Hill Cottage, up the road."

"Ah, yes. The place with the weird vibes."

"Weird?"

"Vanna feels it whenever she gets close. Disharmonic waves. Tremors of dissonance."

"I must have missed it."

"Meat eaters usually do." The man looked at Miranda. He had pale blue eyes and a gaze that was far too direct for comfort. "Does my natural state bother you?"

"No," she said. "It's just that I'm not used to..." Her gaze drifted downward, then snapped back to his face.

The man looked at her as though she were a creature to be pitied. "How far we've fallen from Eden," he said, sighing. He went to the porch railing and grabbed a sarong that had been hanging out to dry. "But the first rule of hospitality," he said, wrapping the cloth around his waist, "is to make your guests comfortable. So we'll just cover the family jewels." He motioned them into the cottage.

Inside, the woman, Vanna, now also draped in a sarong, sat cross-legged beneath a stained glass window. Her eyes were closed; her hands lay palm up on her knees. The other man knelt at a low table, rolling what appeared to be brown rice sushi. Potted plans were everywhere, thick as weeds. They blended right in with the Indonesian hangings, the dangling crystals, the smell of incense. The whole effect was jarred only by the fax machine in the corner.

Their host, who went by the surprisingly mundane name of Fred, poured rose hip tea and offered them carob cookies. They came to Maine every summer, he said, to reconnect with the earth. New York was purgatory, a place with one foot in hell. False people, false values. They worked there only because it kept them in touch with the common folk. Plus, they needed the income. For most of the year they tolerated the sickness of city life, breathing in the toxins, poisoning their bodies with refined sugars. Summers were for cleansing. And that was why they came here, why they left their jobs for two months every year.

"What *are* your jobs?" asked Miranda.

"We own the accounting firm of Nickels, Fay and Bledsoe. I'm Nickels."

"I'm Fay," said the man rolling sushi.

The woman, undoubtedly Bledsoe, continued to meditate in silence.

"So you see," said Fred Nickels, "there is no way we can be persuaded to sell. This land is a connection to our mother."

"Was it hers?" asked Chase.

"Mother Earth owns everything."

Chase cleared his throat. "Oh."

"We refuse to sell. No matter how many of those ridiculous letters they send us—"

Both Miranda and Chase sat up straight. "Letters?" they said simultaneously.

"We three have lived together for fifteen years. Perfect sexual harmony. No jealousy, no friction. All our friends know it. So it would hardly upset us to have our arrangement announced to the world."

"Is that what the letters threatened to do?" asked Miranda.

"Yes. 'Expose your deviant life-style' was the phrase, I think."

"You're not the only ones to get a letter," said Chase. "My hunch is, everyone on this road—everyone who didn't want to sell—got one in the mail."

"Well, they threatened the wrong people here. Deviant life-styles are exactly what we wish to promote. Am I right, friends?"

The man with the sushi looked up and said, "Ho."

"He agrees," said Fred.

"Was the letter signed?" asked Miranda.

"No. It was postmarked Bass Harbor, and it came to our house in New York."

"When?"

"Three, four months ago. It advised us to sell the camp. It didn't say to whom, specifically. But then we got the offer from Mr. Graffam, so I assumed he was behind it. I had Stone Coast Trust checked out. A few inquiries here and there, just to find out what I was dealing with. My sources say there's money involved. Graffam's just a front for a silent investor. My bet is it's organized crime."

"What would they want with Shepherd's Island?" asked Chase.

"New York's getting uncomfortable for 'em. Hotdog D.A.'s and all that. I think they're moving up the coast. And the north shore's just the foothold they'd want. Tourist industry's already booming up here. And look at this place! Ocean. Forest. No crime. Tell me some poor schlump from the city wouldn't pay good money to stay at a resort right here."

"Did you ever meet Graffam?"

"He paid us a visit, to talk land deal. And we told him, in no uncertain terms, to—" Fred stopped, grinned "—fornicate with himself. I'm not sure he knew the meaning of the word."

"What kind of man is he?" asked Miranda.

Fred snorted. "Slick. Dumb. I mean, we're talking *really* stupid. The IQ of an eggplant. What idiot names a development Hemlock Heights? Might as well call it Poison Oak Estates." He shook his head. "I can't believe he got those other suckers to sell." He laughed. "You should meet

him, Tremain. Tell me if you don't agree he's a throwback
to our paramecium ancestors.''

"A paramecium," said the woman, Bledsoe, briefly
opening her eyes, "is far more advanced."

"Unfortunately," said Fred, "I'm afraid the rezoning is
a fait accompli. Soon we'll be surrounded. Condos here, a
Dunkin' Donuts there. The Cape Codification of Shepherd's Island." He paused. "And you know what? *That's*
when we'll sell! My God, what a profit! We could buy a
whole damn county up in the Allagash."

"The project could still be stopped," said Miranda.
"They won't get their hands on Rose Hill. And the zoning
could be reversed."

"Not a chance," said Fred. "We're talking tax income
here. Conservation land brings in zilch for the island. But
a nice little tourist resort? Hey, I'm a CPA. I know the
powers of the almighty buck."

"There are people who'll fight it."

"Makes no difference." Fred sniffed appreciatively at his
rose hip tea. The edges of his sarong had slipped apart and
he sat with thighs naked. Incense smoke wafted about his
grizzled head. "They can scream, protest. Lay their bodies
before the bulldozers. But it's hopeless. There are things
people just can't stop."

"A cynical answer," said Miranda.

"For cynical times."

"Well, they can't buy Rose Hill," said Miranda, rising
to her feet. "And if organized crime's behind these pur-
chases, you can bet the island will fight back. People here
don't take well to mobsters. They don't take to outsiders,
period."

Fred gazed up at her with a smile. "But *you* are an outsider, aren't you, Ms. Wood?"

"I'm not from this island. I came here a year ago."

"Yet they accepted *you.*"

"No, they didn't." Miranda turned toward the door. She
stood there for a moment, staring through the screen. Out-

side, the trees were swaying under a canopy of blue sky. "They never accepted me," she said softly. "And you know what?" She let out a long sigh of resignation. "I've only now come to realize it. They never will."

THERE WAS A THIRD CAR parked in the driveway at Rose Hill.

They saw it as they walked up the last bend of the road— a late-model Saab with a gleaming burgundy finish. A glance through the car window revealed a spotless interior, not even a loose business card or candy wrapper on the leather upholstery.

The screen door squealed open and Miss St. John came out on the porch. "There you are," she said. "We have a visitor. Jill Vickery."

Of course, thought Miranda. Who else would manage to keep such an immaculate car?

Jill was standing amidst all the books, holding a box in her arms. She glanced at Miranda with a look of obvious surprise, but made no comment about her presence. "Sorry to pop in unannounced," she said. "I had to get a few records. Phillip and I are meeting the accountant tomorrow. You know, working out any tax problems for the transfer of the *Herald.*"

Chase frowned. "You found the financial records here?"

"Just last month's worth. I couldn't find them back in the office, so I figured he'd brought them out here to work on. I was right."

"Where were they?" asked Chase. "We've combed all through his files. I never saw them."

"They were upstairs. The nightstand drawer." How she knew where to look was something she didn't bother to explain. She glanced around the front room. "You've certainly torn the place apart. What are you looking for? Hidden treasure?"

"Any and all files on Stone Coast Trust," said Chase.

"Yes, Annie mentioned you were dogging that angle. Personally, I think it's a dead end." Coolly she turned to look at Miranda. "And how are things going for you?" It was merely a polite question, carrying neither warmth nor concern.

"Things are...difficult," said Miranda.

"I can imagine. I hear you're staying with Annie these days."

"Only temporarily."

Jill flashed her one of those ironic smiles. "It's rather inconvenient, actually. The trial was going to be Annie's story. And now you're living with her. I'll have to pull her off it. Objective reporting and all."

"No one at the *Herald* could possibly be objective," Chase pointed out.

"I suppose not." Jill shifted the box in her arms. "Well, I'd better be going. Let you get on with your search."

"Ms. Vickery?" called Miss St. John. "I wonder if you could shed some light on an item we found here."

"Yes?"

"It's a note, from someone named M." Miss St. John handed her the slip of paper. "Miranda here didn't write it. Do you know who did?"

Jill read the note without any apparent emotion, not even a twitch of her perfect eyebrow. Miranda thought, *If only I had an ounce of her style, her poise.*

"It's not dated. So..." Jill looked up. "I can think of several possibilities. None of them had that particular initial. But M could stand for a nickname. Or just the word *me.*"

"Several possibilities?"

"Yes." Jill glanced uneasily at Miranda. "Richard, he...had his attractions. Especially for the female summer interns. There was that one we had last year. Before you were hired, Miranda. Her name was Chloe something or other. Couldn't write worth a damn, but she was good decoration. And she picked up interviews no one else could get, which drove poor Annie up a wall." Jill looked again at the note. "This was typed on a manual typewriter. See? The *e* loop's smudged, key needs to be cleaned. If I remember right, Chloe always worked on an old manual. The only one in the office who couldn't compose on a computer keyboard." She gave the note back to Miss St. John. "It could have been her."

"Whatever happened to Chloe?" asked Chase.

"What you'd expect to happen. Some hot and heavy flirting. A few fireworks. And then, just another broken heart."

Miranda felt her throat tighten, her face flush. None of them was looking directly at her, but she knew she was the focus of their attention, as surely as if they were staring. She went to the window and found herself gripping the curtain, fighting to keep her head erect, her spine straight. Another broken heart. It made her feel like some object on an assembly line, just another stupid, gullible woman. It's what they thought of her.

It's what she thought of herself.

Jill again shifted her box of papers. "I'd better get back to the office or the mice will play." She went to the door, then stopped. "Oh, I almost forgot to tell you, Chase. Annie just heard the news."

"What news?" asked Chase.

"Tony Graffam's back in town."

Miranda didn't react. She heard Jill go down the porch steps, heard the Saab's engine roar to life, the tires crunch away across the gravel. She felt Chase and Miss St. John's gaze on her back. They were watching her in silence, an unbearable, pitying silence.

She pushed open the screen door and fled from the cottage.

Halfway across the field Chase caught up to her. He grabbed her arm and pulled her around to face him. "Miranda—"

"Leave me alone!"

"You can't run away from it—"

"If only I could!" she cried. "Jill said it! I'm just another broken heart. Another dumb woman who got exactly what she deserved."

"You didn't deserve it."

"Damn you, Chase, don't feel sorry for me! I can't stand that, either." She broke free and started to turn away. He pulled her back. This time he held on, got a tight grip on each wrist. She found herself staring into his dark, inescapable eyes.

"I don't feel sorry for you," he shot back. "You don't get my pity, Miranda. Because you're too good for it. You've got more going for you than any woman I've met. Okay, you're naive. And gullible. We all start out that way. You've learned from it, fine. You should. You want to kick yourself, and maybe it's well deserved. But don't overdo it. Because I think Richard fell just as hard for you as you fell for him."

"Is that supposed to make me feel better?"

"I'm not trying to make you feel better. I'm just telling you what I think."

"Right." Her laughter was self-mocking. "That I'm one notch above a bimbo?" Again she tried to pull free. Again he held her tight.

"No," he said quietly. "What I'm saying is this. I know you're not the first. I know Richard had a lot of women. I've met a few of them through the years. Some of them were gorgeous. Some of them were talented, even brilliant. But out of all those women—and they were, each and every one of them, exceptional—you're the only one I could see him really falling for."

"Out of all those *gorgeous* women?" She shook her head and laughed. "Why me?"

Quietly he said, "Because you're the one *I'd* fall for."

At once she went still. He stared down at her, his dark hair stirring in the wind, his face awash in sunlight. She heard her own quick breaths, heard her heartbeat pound-

ing in her ears. He released her wrists. She didn't move
even when his arms circled behind her, even as he drew her
hard against him. She scarcely had the breath to whimper
before he settled his mouth firmly on hers.

At the first touch of his lips she was lost. The sun seemed
to spin overhead, a dizzying view of brightness against a
field of blue. And then there was only him, all rough edges
and shadows, his dark head blotting out the sky, his mouth
stealing away her breath. She wavered for an instant between resistance and surrender. Then she found herself
reaching up and around his neck, opening her lips to his
eager assault, pressing more eagerly against the bite of his
teeth. She drank him in, his taste, his warmth. Through the
roaring in her ears she heard his low groans of satisfaction
and need, ever more need. How quickly she had yielded,
how easily she had fallen—the woman mastered first by one
brother, and now the other.

The day's unbearable brightness seemed to flood her eyes
as she pulled away. Her cheeks were blazing. The buzz of
insects in the field and the rustle of grass in the wind were
almost lost in the harsh sound of her own breathing.

"I won't be passed around, Chase," she said. "I won't."

Then she turned and stalked across the field. She headed
back to the cottage, her feet stirring the perfume of sun-
warmed grass. She knew he was following somewhere behind, but this time he made no attempt to catch up. She
walked alone, and the brightness of the afternoon, the
dancing wildflowers, the floating haze of dandelion fuzz
only seemed to emphasize her own wretchedness.

Miss St. John was standing on the porch. With scarcely
a nod to the other woman, Miranda walked right past her
and into the cottage. Inside, she went straight to the bookcase, grabbed another armful of books from the shelf and
sat on the floor. She was single-mindedly flipping through
the pages when she heard footsteps come up the porch.

"It's not a good time for an argument, Chase," she
heard Miss St. John say.

"I'm not planning to argue."

"You have that look in your eye. For heaven's sake, cool own. Stop. Take a deep breath."

"With all due respect, Miss St. John, you're *not* my other."

"All right, I'm not your mother!" Miss St. John napped. As she stomped away down the steps, she mut-red, "But I can see when a man sorely needs my ad-ice!"

The screen door slapped shut. Chase stood just inside the reshold, gazing at Miranda. "You took it the wrong ay," he said.

Miranda looked up at him. "Did I?"

"What happened between you and Richard is a separate ssue. A dead issue. It has nothing to do with you and me."

She snapped the book shut. "It has everything to do with ou and me."

"But you make it sound like I'm just—just picking up he affair where he left off."

"Okay, maybe it's not that bald. Maybe you're not even ware you're doing it." She reached for another book and tubbornly focused on the pages as she flipped through it. But we both know Richard was the golden boy of the amily. The one who had it all, inherited everything. You vere the Tremain who didn't even get a decent trust fund. Vell, if you can't inherit a newspaper or a fortune, at least ou can inherit your brother's cast-off mistress. Or, gee, naybe even his wife. Just think. Evelyn wouldn't even have o go to the trouble of changing her last name."

"Are you finished?"

"Definitely."

"Good. Because I don't think I can stand here and lis-en to that garbage any longer. First of all, I'm not in the east bit interested in my sister-in-law. I never was. When Richard married her, I had to stop myself from sending him ny condolences. Second, I don't give a damn who gets the *Herald*. I sure as hell never wanted the job. The paper was

Richard's baby, from the start. And third—" He paused and took a deep breath, as though drawing the courage to say what had to be said. "Third," he said quietly, "I'm not a Tremain."

She looked up at him sharply. "What are you saying? You're Richard's brother, aren't you?"

"His half brother."

"You mean..." She stared into those Gypsy eyes, saw herself reflected in irises dark as coals.

Chase nodded. "My father knew. I don't think Mother ever told him, exactly. She didn't have to. He could just look at me and see it." He smiled, a bitter, ironic smile. "Funny that I myself never did. All the time I was growing up, I didn't understand why I couldn't match up to Richard. No matter how hard I tried, he was the one who got Dad's attention. My mother tried to make up for it. She was my very best friend, right up until she died. And then it was just the three of us." He sank into a chair and rubbed his forehead, as though trying to massage away the memories.

"When did you learn?" Miranda asked softly. "That he wasn't your father?"

"Not until years later, when Dad was dying. He had one of those cliché deathbed confessions. Only he didn't tell *me*. He told Richard. Even at the very end, Richard was the privileged one." Wearily Chase leaned back, his head pressed against the cushions, his gaze focused on the ceiling. "Later they read the will. I couldn't understand why I'd been essentially cut out. Oh, he left me enough to get me started in business. But that was it. I thought it had to do with my marriage, the fact Dad had opposed it from the start. I was hurt, but I accepted it. My wife didn't. She got in a shouting match with Richard, started yelling that it wasn't fair. Richard lost his cool and let it all out. The big secret. The fact his brother was a bastard."

"Is that when you left the island?"

He nodded. "I came back once or twice, to humor my wife. After we got divorced it seemed like my last link to this place had been cut. So I stayed away. Until now."

They fell silent. He seemed lost in bad memories, old hurts. *No wonder I could never find any hint of Richard in his face,* she thought. *He's not a Tremain at all. He's his own man, the sort of man Richard could never be.*

The sort of man I could love.

He felt her studying him, sensed she was reaching out to him. Abruptly he rose to his feet and moved with studied indifference toward the screen door. There he stood looking out at the field. "Maybe you were right," he said.

"About what?"

"That what happened between you and Richard is still hanging over us."

"And if it is?"

"Then this is a mistake. You, me. It's the wrong reason to get involved."

She looked down, unwilling to reveal, even to the stiffly turned back, the hurt in her eyes. "Then we shouldn't, should we?" she murmured.

"No." He turned to face her. She found her gaze drawn, almost against her will, to meet his. "The truth is, Miranda, we have too many reasons not to. What's happened between us has been . . ." He shrugged. "It was an attraction, that's all."

That's all. Nothing, really, in the larger context of life. Not something you risked your heart on.

"Still . . ." he said.

"Yes?" She looked up with a sudden, insane leap of hope.

"We can't walk away from each other. Not with all that's happened. Richard's death. The fire." He gestured about the book-strewn room. "And this."

"You don't trust me. Yet you want my help?"

"You're the only one with stakes high enough to see this through."

She gave a tired laugh. "You got that part right." She wrapped her arms around herself. "So, what comes next?"

"I'll go have a talk with Tony Graffam."

"Shall I come?"

"No. I want to check him out on my own. In the meantime, you can finish up here. There's still the upstairs."

Miranda gazed around the room, at the dusty piles of books, the stacks of papers, and she shook her head. "If I just knew what I was looking for. What the burglar was looking for."

"I have a hunch it's still here somewhere."

"Whatever *it* is."

Turning, Chase pushed open the door. "When you find it, you'll know."

Chapter Eleven

Fred Nickels had said Tony Graffam was slick and dumb. He was right on both counts. Graffam wore a silk suit, a tie in blinding red paisley and a gold pinkie ring. The office, like the man, was all flash, little substance: plush carpet, spanking new leather chairs, but no secretary, no books on the shelves, no papers on the desk. The wall had only one decoration—a map of the north shore of Shepherd's Island. It was not labeled as such, but Chase needed only a glance at the broad, curving bay to recognize the coastline.

"I tell you, it's a witch-hunt!" Graffam complained. "First the police, now you." He stayed behind his desk, refusing to emerge even to shake hands, as though clinging to the polished barrier for protection. In agitation he slid his fingers through his tightly permed hair. "You think I'd go and waste someone? Just like that? And for what, a piece of property? Do I look dumb?"

Chase politely declined to answer that question. He said, "You were pressing an offer for Rose Hill Cottage, weren't you?"

"Well, of course. It's the prime lot up there."

"And my brother refused to sell."

"Look, I'm sorry about your brother. Tragedy, a real tragedy. Not that he and I were on good terms, you understand. I couldn't deal with him. He had a closed mind when it came to the project. I mean, he actually went and got hostile. I don't know why. It's only business, right?''

"But I was under the impression this wasn't a business deal, at all. Stone Coast Trust is billed as a conservation project."

"And that's exactly what it is. I offered your brother top dollar for that land, more than Nature Conservancy would've paid. Plus, he would've retained lifetime use of the family cottage. An incredible deal."

"Incredible."

"With the addition of Rose Hill, we could extend the park all the way back to the hillside. It would add elevation. Views. Access."

"Access?"

"For maintenance, of course. You know, for the hiking trails. Decent footpaths, so everyone could enjoy a taste of nature. Even the handicapped. I mean, mobility impaired."

"You thought of everything."

Graffam smiled. "Yes. We did."

"Where does Hemlock Heights come in?"

Graffam paused. "Excuse me?"

"Hemlock Heights. That is, I believe, the name of your planned development."

"Well, nothing was *planned*—"

"Then why did you apply for rezoning? And how much did you pay to bribe the land commission?''

Graffam's face had gone rigid. "Let me repeat myself, Mr. Tremain. Stone Coast Trust was formed to protect the north shore. I admit, we might have to develop a parcel here and there, just to maintain the trust. But sometimes we have to compromise. We have to do things we'd rather not."

"Does that include blackmail?"

Graffam sat up sharply. "What?"

"I'm talking about Fred Nickels. And Homer Sulaway. The names should be familiar to you."

"Yes, of course. Two of the property owners. They declined my offer."

"Someone sent them nasty letters, telling them to sell."

"You think I sent them?"

"Who else? Four people turned you down. Two of them got threatening letters. And a third—my brother—winds up dead."

"That's what you're leading up to, isn't it? Trying to make it look like I had something to do with his death."

"Is that what I said?"

"Look, I've taken enough heat on this deal. A year of putting up with this—this small-town crap. I've turned handsprings to make this project work, but I'm not going to be his fall guy."

Chase stared at Graffam in confusion. What was the man babbling about? Whose fall guy?

"I was out of state when it happened. I have witnesses who'll swear to that."

"Who are you working for?" Chase cut in.

Graffam's jaw suddenly snapped shut. Slowly he sat back, his expression hardening to stone.

"So you have a backer," said Chase. "Someone who's put up the money. Someone who's doing the dirty work. Who are you fronting for? The mob?"

Graffam said nothing.

"You're scared, Graffam. I can tell."

"I don't have to answer any of your questions."

Chase pressed the attack. "My brother was set to blow the whistle on Stone Coast, wasn't he? So you sent him one of your threatening letters. But then you found out he couldn't be blackmailed. Or bought off. So what did you do? Pay someone to take care of the problem?"

"Meaning murder?" Graffam burst out laughing. "Come on, Tremain. A broad killed him. We both know that. Dangerous creatures, broads. Tick 'em off and they get ideas. They see red, grab a kitchen knife and that's it. Even the cops agree. It was a broad. She had the motive."

"And you had a lot of money to lose. So did your backer. Richard already had his hands on your account numbers. He traced your invisible partner. He could have exposed the deal—"

"But he didn't. He killed the article, remember? I had it on good authority it was gonna stay dead. So why should we go after him?"

Chase fell silent. That's what Jill had said, that Richard was the one who'd canceled the article, called off the crusade. It was the one detail that didn't make sense. Why had Richard backed down?

Did he back down? Or had Jill Vickery lied?

He brooded over that last possibility as he left Graffam's office and walked to the car. What did he know about Jill, really? Only that she'd been with the *Herald* for five years, that she kept it running smoothly. That she was bright, stylish and underpaid. She could land a better job anywhere on the East Coast. Why had she chosen to stay with this Podunk paper and work for slave wages?

He'd planned to return at once to Rose Hill Cottage. Instead, he drove to the *Herald*.

He found the office manned only by a skeleton crew: the summer intern, tapping at a computer keyboard, and the layout tech, stooped over a drawing table. Chase walked past them, into Richard's office, and went straight to the file cabinet.

He found Jill Vickery's employment file right where it should be. He sat at the desk and opened the folder.

Inside was a neatly typed résumé, three pages, all the right names and jobs. B.A., Bowdoin, 1977. Masters, Columbia, 1979. Stints on the city desk, *San Francisco Chronicle;* then obits, *San Diego Union;* police beat, *San Jose Times;* op-ed editor, *Portland Press Herald.* A solid résumé.

So why does she end up here?

Something about that résumé bothered him. Something that didn't seem quite right. It was enough to make him reach for the phone and dial the *Portland Press Herald,* her previous employer. He spoke to the current op-ed editor, a woman who vaguely recalled a Jill Vickery. It had been a while back, though.

Chase next called the *San Jose Times.* This time there was some uncertainty, a lot of yelling around the city room, asking if anyone remembered a reporter named Jill Vickery from seven years before. Someone yelled, wasn't there a Jill on the police beat years back? That was good enough for Chase. He hung up and considered letting it drop.

Still, that résumé. What was it that bothered him?

The obits. *San Diego Union.* That didn't make sense. Obits was the coal mine equivalent of the newspaper business. You worked your way up from there. Why had she gone from the city desk in San Francisco to a bottom-of-the-barrel position?

He dialed the *San Diego Union.* No one named Jill Vickery had ever worked there.

Ditto for San Francisco.

Half the résumé was a fraud. Was it just a case of padding a thin work history? And what was she doing during those eight years between college and her job with the *San Jose Times?*

Once again he reached for the phone. This time he called Columbia University, Department of Journalism. In any given year, how many students could possibly graduate with a master's degree? And how many of these students would have the first name Jill?

There was only one in 1979, they told him. But it wasn't a Jill Vickery who'd graduated. It was a Jill Westcott.

Once again, he called the *San Diego Union.* This time he asked about a Jill Westcott. This time they remembered the name. We'll fax you the article, they said.

A few minutes later it slid out of the fax machine, sharp and clear.

A photo of Jill Westcott, now named Jill Vickery. And with it was a tale of cold-blooded murder.

MIRANDA SAT IN THE FADING light of day and stared list-lessly at her surroundings. She'd spent the afternoon rum-maging through the bathroom and two bedrooms. Now she was hot, dusty and discouraged. Nothing of substance had turned up, only innocuous bits of paper—store receipts, a ten-year-old postcard from Spain, another typewritten note from M.

> . . . I am not the weak little nothing I used to be. I can live without you quite nicely, and I intend to do so. I don't need your pity. I am not like the others, those women with minds the size of walnut shells. What I want to know, what I don't understand, is what at-tracts you to creatures like that? Is it the jiggling flesh? The cow-eyed worship? Well, it doesn't mean a thing. It's empty devotion. Without your money, you wouldn't rate a second glance from those bimbos. I'm the only one who doesn't give a damn how much you have in the bank. And now you've lost me.

The bitterness, the pain of that letter seemed to rub off on her own mood. She put it back in the drawer, buried it among the silky underclothes. Another woman's lingerie. Another woman's anguish.

By the time she'd straightened up the room again the af-ternoon had slid toward twilight. She didn't turn on the lamp. It was soothing, the veil of semidarkness, the chirp of crickets through the open window. From the field came that indefinable scent of evening—the mist from the sea, the cooling grasses. She went to a chair by the window, sat down and leaned her head back to rest. So many doubts, so many worries weighed upon her. Always, looming over every tentative moment of joy, was that threat of prison. There were times, during these past few days of freedom, that she had almost been able to push the thought from mind. But in the moments like this, when the silence was deep and she was alone in her fears, the image of prison bars seemed to close around her. *How many years will they keep me? Ten, twenty, a lifetime?*

I would rather die.

She shuddered back to alertness.

Downstairs, the screen door had softly squealed open.

"Chase?" she called. "Is that you?" There was silence. She rose from the chair and went to the top of the stairs. "Chase?"

She heard the screen door softly tap shut, then there was nothing, only the distant chirp of crickets from the fields.

Her first instinct was to reach for the light switch. Just in time she stopped herself. Darkness was her friend. It would hide her, protect her.

She shrank away from the stairs. Trembling, she stood with her back pressed against the wall and listened. No new sounds drifted up from the first floor. All she heard was the hammering of her own heartbeat. Her palms were slick. Every nerve ending was scraped raw with fear.

There it was—a footstep. In the kitchen. An image shot through her mind. The cabinets, the drawers. The knives.

Her breath was coming in tight gasps. She shrank farther from the stairs, her thoughts flying frantically toward escape. Two upstairs bedrooms, plus a bathroom. And screens on all the windows. Could she make it through in time?

From below came more footsteps. The intruder had moved out of the kitchen. He was approaching the stairs.

Miranda fled into the master bedroom. Darkness obscured her path; she collided with a nightstand. A lamp wobbled, fell over. The clatter as it crashed to the floor was all the intruder needed to direct him toward this bedroom.

In panic she dashed to the window. Through the darkness she saw a portion of gently sloping roof. From there it would be a twenty-foot drop to the ground. The sash was already up. Only the screen stood between her and freedom. She shoved at it—and it refused to push free. Only then did she see that the screen had been nailed to the window frame.

Frantic now, she began to kick at the steel mesh, sobbing as each blow met resistance. Again and again she kicked, and each time the wire sagged outward, but held.

A footstep creaked on the stairway.

She aimed a last desperate kick at the mesh.

The window frame splintered, and the whole screen fell away and thudded to the ground. At once she scrambled over the sill and dropped down onto the ledge of roof. There she hesitated, torn between the solid comfort of shingles beneath her feet and the free-fall of escape. She couldn't see what lay directly below. The rosebushes? She grabbed hold of the roof and lowered her body over the edge. For a few seconds she clung there, steeling herself for the impact.

She let go.

The night air rushed up at her. The fall seemed endless, a hurtling downward through space and darkness.

Her feet slammed into the ground. Instantly her legs buckled, and she fell sprawling to the gravel. For a moment she lay there as the sky whirled overhead like a kaleidoscope of stars. A frantic burst of adrenaline had masked all the sensation of pain. Her legs could be shattered. She wouldn't have felt it. She knew only that she had to escape, had to run.

She staggered to her feet and began to stumble down the road. She rounded the bend of the driveway—

And was instantly blinded by a pair of headlights leaping at her from the darkness. Instinctively she raised her arms to shield her eyes against the onslaught. She heard the car's brakes lock, heard gravel fly under the skidding tires. The door swung open.

"Miranda?"

With a sob of joy she stumbled forward into Chase's arms. "It's you," she cried. "Thank God it's you."

"What is it?" he whispered, pulling her close against him. "Miranda, what's happened?"

She clung to the solid anchor of his chest. "He's there—in the cottage—"

"Who?"

Suddenly, through the darkness, they both heard it: the slam of the back door, the thrash of running footsteps through the brush.

"Get in the car!" ordered Chase. "Lock the doors!"

"What?"

He gave her a push. "Just do it!"

"Chase!" she yelled.

"I'll be back!"

Stunned, she watched him melt into the night, heard his footsteps thud away. Her instinct was to follow him, to stay close in case he needed her. But already she'd lost sight of him and could make out nothing but the towering shadows of trees against the starry sky, and beneath them, a darkness so thick it seemed impenetrable.

Do what he says!

She climbed into the car, locked the doors and felt instantly useless. While she sat here in safety Chase could be fighting for his life.

And what good will I do him?

She pushed open the door and scrambled out of the car, around to the rear.

In the trunk she found a tire iron. It felt heavy and solid in her grasp. It would even the odds against any opponent. Any unarmed opponent, she was forced to amend.

She turned, faced the forest. It loomed before her, a wall of shadow and formless threat.

Somewhere in that darkness Chase was in danger.

She gripped the tire iron more tightly and started off into the night.

THE CRASH OF FOOTSTEPS through the underbrush alerted Chase that his quarry had shifted direction. Chase veered right, in pursuit of the sound. Branches thrashed his face, bushes clawed at his trousers. The darkness was so dense under the trees that he felt like a blind man stumbling through a landscape of booby traps.

At least his quarry would be just as blind. *But maybe not as helpless,* he thought, ducking under a pine branch. *What if he's armed? What if I'm being led into a trap?*

It's a risk I have to take.

The footsteps moved to the left of him. By slivers of starlight filtering through the trees Chase caught a glimpse of movement. That was all he could make out, shadow moving through shadow. Heedless of the branches whipping his face he plunged ahead and found himself snagged in brambles. The shadow zigzagged, flitting in and out of the cover of trees. Chase pulled free of the thicket and resumed his pursuit. He was gaining. He could hear, through the pounding of his heart, the hard breathing of his quarry. The shadow was just ahead, just beyond the next curtain of branches.

Chase mustered a last burst of speed and broke through, into a clearing. There he came to a halt.

His quarry had vanished. There was no movement, no sound, only the whisper of wind through the treetops. A flutter of shadow off to his right made him whirl around. Nothing there. He halted in confusion as he heard the crackle of underbrush to his left. He turned, listening for footsteps, trying to locate his quarry. Was that breathing, somewhere close by? No, the wind....

Again, that crackle of twigs. He moved forward, one step, then another.

Too late he felt the rush of air, the hiss of the branch as it swung its arc toward his head.

The blow pitched him forward. He reached out to cushion the fall, felt the bite of pine needles, the slap of wet leaves as he scraped across the forest floor. He tried to cling to consciousness, to order his body to rise to its feet and face the enemy. It refused to obey. Already he saw the darkness thicken before his eyes. He wanted to curse, to rail in fury at his own helplessness. But all he could manage was a groan.

PAIN. THE POUNDING of a jackhammer in his head. Chase ordered it to stop, demanded it stop, but it kept beating away at his brain.

"He's coming around," said a voice.

Then another voice, softer, fearful. "Chase? Chase?"

He opened his eyes and saw Miranda gazing down at him. The lamplight shimmered in her tumbled hair, washed like liquid gold across her cheek. Just the sight of her seemed to quiet the aching in his head. He struggled to remember where he was, how he had gotten there. An image of darkness, the shadow of trees, still lingered.

Abruptly he tried to sit up, and caught a spinning view of other people, other faces in the room.

"No," said Miranda. "Don't move. Just lie still."

"Someone—someone out there—"

"He's gone. We've already searched the woods," said Lorne Tibbetts.

Chase settled back on the couch. He knew where he was now. Miss St. John's cottage. He recognized the chintz fabric, the jungle of plants. And the dog. The panting black mop sat near one end of the couch, watching him. Or was it? With all that hair, who could say if the beast even had eyes? Slowly Chase's gaze shifted to the others in the room. Lorne. Ellis. Miss St. John. And Dr. Steiner, wielding his trusty penlight.

"Pupils look fine. Equal and reactive," said Dr. Steiner.

"Take that blasted thing away," Chase groaned, batting at the penlight.

Dr. Steiner snorted. "Can't do much damage to a head as hard as his." He set a bottle of pills on the end table. "For the headache. May make you a little drowsy, but it'll cut the pain." He snapped his bag shut and headed for the door. "Call me in the morning. But not too early. And may I remind you—all of you—I do not, repeat, do *not* make house calls!" The door slammed shut behind him.

"What wonderful bedside manner," moaned Chase.

"You remember anything?" asked Lorne.

Chase managed to sit up. The effort sent a bolt of pain into his skull. At once he dropped his head into his hands. "Not a damn thing," he mumbled.

"Didn't see his face?"

"Just a shadow."

Lorne paused. "You sure there was someone there?"

"Hey, I didn't imagine the headache." Chase grabbed the pill bottle, fumbled the cap off and gulped two tablets down, dry. "Someone hit me."

"A man? Woman?" pressed Lorne.

"I never saw him. Her. Whatever."

Lorne turned to Miranda. "He was unconscious when you found him?"

"Coming around. I heard his groans."

"Pardon me for asking, Ms. Wood. But can I see that tire iron you were carrying?"

"What?"

"The tire iron. You had it earlier."

Miss St. John sighed. "Don't be ridiculous, Lorne."

"I'm just being thorough. I have to look at it."

Without a word Miranda fetched the tire iron from the porch and brought it back to Lorne. "No blood, no hair," she said tightly. "I wasn't the one who hit him."

"No, I guess not," said Lorne.

"Jill Vickery," Chase muttered.

Lorne glanced at him. "Who?"

The pain in Chase's head suddenly gave way to a clear memory of that afternoon. "It's not her real name. Check with the San Diego police, Lorne. It may or may not tie in. But you'll find she has an arrest record."

"For what?"

Chase raised her head. "She killed her lover."

They all stared at him.

"Jill?" said Miranda. "When did you find this out?"

"This afternoon. It happened ten, eleven years ago. She was acquitted. Justifiable homicide. She claimed he'd threatened her life."

"How does this fit in with anything else?" asked Lorne.

"I'm not sure. All I know is, half her job résumé was pure fiction. Maybe Richard found out. If he did—and confronted her..."

Lorne turned to Miss St. John. "I need to use your telephone."

"In the kitchen."

Lorne spent only a few minutes on the phone. He emerged from the kitchen shaking his head. "Jill Vickery's at home. Says she was home all evening."

"It's only a half-hour drive to town," said Miss St. John. "She could have made it, barely."

"Assuming her car was right nearby. Assuming she could slip right behind the wheel and take off." He looked at Ellis. "You checked up and down the road?"

Ellis nodded. "No strange cars. No one saw nothin'."

"Well," said Lorne, "whoever it was, I don't think he'll be back." He reached for his hat. "Take my advice, Chase. Don't drive anywhere tonight. You're in no shape to get behind a wheel."

Chase gave a tired laugh. "I wasn't planning to."

"I can take him up to the cottage," said Miranda. "I'll keep an eye on him."

Lorne paused and looked first at Miranda, then at Chase. If he had doubts about the arrangement, he didn't express them. He simply said, "You do that, Ms. Wood. You keep a *good* eye on him." Motioning to Ellis, he opened the door. "We'll be in touch."

Chapter Twelve

Light spilled from the hallway across the pine floor of the bedroom. Miranda pulled down the coverlet and said, "Come on, lie down. Doctor's orders."

"To hell with doctors. That doctor, anyway," growled Chase. He sat on the side of the bed and gave his head a shake, as though to clear it. "I'm okay. I feel fine."

She regarded his battered, unshaven face. "You look like a truck ran over you."

"The brutal truth!" He laughed. "Are you always so damn honest?"

There was a silence. "Yes," she said quietly. "As a matter of fact, I am."

He looked up at her. *What do you see in my eyes?* she wondered. *Sincerity? Or lies, bald, dangerous lies?*

It's still not there, is it? Trust. There'll always be that doubt between us.

She sat beside him on the bed. "Tell me everything you learned today. About Jill."

"Only what I read in the press file from San Diego." He reached down and began to pull off his shoes. "The trial got a fair amount of coverage. You know, sex, violence. Circulation boosters."

"What happened?"

"The defense claimed she was an emotionally battered woman. That she was young, naive, vulnerable. That her boyfriend was an abusive alcoholic who regularly beat her up. The jury believed it."

"What did the prosecution say?"

"That Jill had a lifelong hatred of men. That she used them, manipulated them. And when her lover tried to leave her, she flew into a rage. Both sides agreed on the facts of the killing. That while her lover was passed out drunk she picked up a gun, put it to his head and pulled the trigger." Exhausted, Chase lay back on the pillows. The pills were taking effect. His eyelids were already drifting shut. "That was ten years ago," he said. "An era Jill conveniently left behind when she came to Maine."

"Did Richard know all this?"

"If he bothered to check, he did. Only the last half of her résumé was true. Richard may have been so dazzled by the whole package he didn't bother to confirm much beyond the last job or two. Or he may have found out the truth only recently. Who knows?"

Miranda sat thinking, trying to picture Jill as she must have been ten years ago. Young, vulnerable. Afraid.

Like me.

Or was the prosecution's description a more accurate image? A man hater, a woman of twisted passions?

That's how they'll try to portray me. As a killer. And some people will believe it.

Chase had fallen asleep.

For a moment she sat beside him, listening to his slow and even breaths, wondering if he could ever learn to trust her. If she could ever be more to him than just a piece of the puzzle—the puzzle of his brother's death.

She rose and pulled the coverlet over his sleeping form. He didn't move. Gently she smoothed back his hair, stroked the beard-roughened cheek. Still he didn't move.

She left him and went downstairs. The boxes of papers confronted her, other bits and pieces of that puzzle. She separated them into files. Article files. Financial records. Personal notes from M, as well as from other, unidentified women. The miscellaneous debris of a man's life. How little she had known Richard! What a vast part of him he had kept private, even from his family. That's why he had so jealously guarded this north shore retreat.

In the fabric of his life, I was just a single, unimportant thread. Will I ever stop hurting from that?

She rose and checked the doors, the windows. Then she went back upstairs, to the master bedroom.

Chase was still asleep. She knew she should use the other room, the other bed, but tonight she didn't want to lie alone in the darkness. She wanted warmth and safety and the comfort of knowing Chase was nearby.

She had promised to look after him tonight. What better place to watch over him than in the same bed?

She lay down beside him, not close but near enough to imagine his warmth seeping toward her through the sheets.

Sometime during the night the dreams came.

A man, a lover, was holding her. Protecting her. Then she looked up at his face and saw he was a stranger. She pulled away, began to run. She found she was in a crowd of people. She began to search for a familiar face, a pair of arms she could reach out to, but they were all strangers, all strangers.

And then there he was, standing far beyond her reach. She cried out to him, held her hands out for him to grab. He moved toward her and her hands connected with warm and solid flesh. She heard him say, "I'm here, Miranda. Right here...."

And he was.

Through the semidarkness she saw the gleam of his face, the twin shadows of his eyes. His gaze was so still, so very quiet. Her breath caught as he took her face in his hands. Slowly he pressed his lips to hers. That one touch sent a shudder of pleasure through her body. They stared at each other and the night seemed filled with the sounds of their breathing.

Again, he kissed her.

Again, that wave of pleasure. It crested to a wanting for more, more. Her sleep-drugged body awoke, alive with hunger. She pressed hard against him, willing their bodies to meld, their warmth to mingle, but that frustrating barrier of clothes still lay between them.

He reached for her T-shirt. Slowly he pulled it up and over her head, let it drop from the bed. She was not so patient. Already she was undoing his buttons, sliding back his shirt, fumbling at his belt buckle. No words were spoken; none were needed. The soft whispers, the whimpers, the moans said more than any words could have.

So did his hands. His fingers slid across, between, inside all the warm and secret places of her body. They teased her, inflamed her, brought her to the very edge of release. Then, with knowing cruelty, they abandoned her, leaving her unsatisfied. She reached out to him, silently pleading for more.

He grasped her hips and willingly thrust into her again, but this time not with his fingers.

She cried out, a sound of joy, of delight.

At the first ripple of her climax he let his own needs take over. Needs that made him drive deep inside her, again and again. As her last wave of pleasure washed through her, he found his own cresting, breaking. He rode it to the very end and collapsed, sweating and triumphant, into her welcoming arms.

And so they fell asleep.

CHASE WAS THE FIRST to awaken. He found his arms looped around her, his face buried in the sweet-smelling strands of her hair. She was curled up on her side, facing away from him, the silky skin of her back pressed against his chest. The memory of their lovemaking was at once so vivid he felt his body respond with automatic desire. And why not, with this woman in his arms? She was life and lust and honeyed warmth. She was everything a woman should be.

And I'm treading on dangerous ground.

He pulled away and sat up. Morning light shone through the window, onto her pillow. So innocent she looked, so untouched by evil. It occurred to him that Jill Vickery once must have looked as pure.

Before she shot her lover.

Dangerous women. How could you tell them from the innocents?

He left the bed and went straight to the shower. Wash the magical spell away, he thought. Wash away the desire, the craving for Miranda Wood. She was like a sickness in his blood, making him do insane things.

Last night, for instance.

They had simply fallen into it, he told himself. A physical act, that was all, a chance collision of two warm bodies.

He watched her sleep as he dressed. With each layer of clothes he felt more protected, more invulnerable. But when she stirred and opened her eyes and smiled at him, he realized how thin his emotional armor really was.

"How are you feeling this morning?" she asked softly.

"Much better, thanks. I think I can drive myself back to town."

There was a silence. Her smile faded as she took in the fact he was already dressed. "You're leaving?"

"Yes. I just wanted to make sure you got out of here safely."

She sat up. Hugging the sheets to her chest, she watched him for a moment, as though trying to understand what had gone wrong between them. At last she said, "I'll be fine. You don't have to wait around."

"I'll stay. Until you get dressed."

A shrug was her response, as if it didn't matter to her one way or the other. *Good,* he thought. *No sticky emotions over last night. We're both too smart for that.*

He started to leave, then stopped. "Miranda?"

"Yes?"

He turned to look at her. She was still hugging her knees, still every bit as bewitching. To see her there could break any man's heart. He said, "It's not that I don't think you're a wonderful woman. It's just that . . ."

"Don't worry about it, Chase," she said flatly. "We both know it won't work."

He wanted to say, "I'm sorry," but somehow it seemed too lame, too easy. They were both adults. They had both made a mistake.

There was nothing more to be said.

'IT'S NOT AS IF ANY of this is incriminating," said Annie, flipping through the notes from M that were arrayed on her kitchen table. "Just your routine desperate-woman language. Darling. If you'd only see me. If only this, if only that. It's pathetic, but it's not murderous. It doesn't tell us that M—whoever she is—killed him."

"You're right." Miranda sighed, leaning back in the kitchen chair. "And it doesn't seem to tie in with Jill at all."

"Sorry. The only M around here is you. I'd say these letters could cause you more damage than good."

"Jill said there was a summer intern a year ago. A woman who got involved with Richard."

"Chloe? Ancient history. I can't imagine she'd sneak back to town just to kill an ex-lover. Besides, there's no *M* in her name."

"The *M* could stand for a nickname. A name only Richard used for her."

"Muffin? Marvelous?" Laughing, Annie rose to her feet. "I think we're beating a dead horse. And I'm going to be late." She went to the closet and pulled out a warm-up jacket. "Irving hates to be kept waiting."

Miranda glanced with amusement at Annie's attire: a torn T-shirt, scruffy running shoes and sweatpants. "Irving likes the casual look?"

"Irving *is* the casual look." Annie slung her purse ove
her shoulder. "We're sanding the deck this week. Loads o
fun."

"Will I ever get to meet this boat bum of yours?"

Annie grinned. "Soon as I can drag him to shore.
mean, the yachting season's gotta end one of these days."
She waved. "See ya."

After Annie had left, Miranda scrounged together a sala
and sat down at the kitchen table for a melancholy dinner
Irving and his boat didn't sound like much in the way o
companionship, but at least Annie had someone to keep he
company. Someone to keep away the loneliness.

Once, Miranda hadn't minded being alone. She'd eve
enjoyed the silence, the peace of a house all to herself. Nov
she craved the simple presence of another human being
Even a dog would be nice. She'd have to think about get
ting one, a large one. A dog wouldn't desert her the wa
most of her friends had. The way Chase had.

She set down her fork, her appetite instantly gone. Wher
was he now? Probably sitting in that house on Chestnu
Street, surrounded by all the other Tremains. He'd hav
Evelyn and the twins to keep him company. He wouldn't b
alone or lonely. He would be just fine without her.

In anger she rose to her feet and slid the remains of he
salad into the trash. Then she started for the door, deter
mined to get outside, to run around the block, anything t
escape the house.

At the front door she halted. A visitor stood on th
porch, hand poised to ring the bell.

"Jill," whispered Miranda.

This was not the cool, unflappable Jill she knew. This Ji
was white-faced and brittle.

"Annie's not here right now," said Miranda. "She . .
should be back any minute."

"You're the one I came to see." Without warning Jil
slipped right past into the living room and shut the doo
behind her.

"I—I was just on my way out." Miranda edged slowly for the door.

Jill took a sidestep, blocking her way. For a moment she stood there, regarding Miranda. "It's not as if I haven't been punished," she said softly. "I've done everything I could to put it behind me. Everything. I've worked like a madwoman these last five years. Built the *Herald* into a real newspaper. You think Richard knew what he was doing? Of course not! He relied on me. *Me.* Oh, he never admitted it, but he let me run the show. Five years. And now you've ruined it for me. You've already got the police shoveling up old dirt. You think the Tremains will keep me on? Now that they know? Now that everyone knows?"

"I wasn't the one. I didn't tell Lorne."

"*You're* the reason it's all come up! You and your pathetic denials! Why don't you just admit you killed him? And leave the rest of us out of it."

"But I didn't kill him."

Jill began to pace the room. "I've sinned, you've sinned. Everyone has. We're all equal. What sets us apart is how we live with our sins. I've done the best I could. And now I find it's not good enough. Not good enough to erase what happened...."

"Did Richard know? About San Diego?"

"No. I mean, yes, in the end. He found out. But it didn't matter to him—"

"It didn't matter that you killed a man?"

"He understood the circumstances. Richard was good that way." She let out a shaky laugh. "After all, he himself wasn't above a little sinning."

Miranda paused, gathered the courage for her next question. "You had an affair with him, didn't you?"

Jill's response was a careless shrug. "It didn't mean anything. It was years ago. You know, the new girl on the block. He got over it." She snapped her fingers. "Just like that. We stayed friends. We understood each other." She stopped pacing and turned to look at Miranda. "Now

Lorne wants to know where I was the night Richard was killed. He's asking *me* to come up with an alibi! You're casting the blame all around, aren't you? To hell with who gets hurt. You just want off the hook. Well, sometimes that's not possible." She moved closer, her gaze fixed on Miranda, like a cat's on a bird. Softly she said, "Sometimes we have to pay for our sins. Whether it's an indiscreet affair. Or murder. We pay for it. I did. Why can't you?"

They stared at each other, caught in a binding fascination for each other's transgressions, each other's pain. *Killer and victim,* thought Miranda. *That's what I see in her eyes. Is that what you see in mine?*

The telephone rang, shattering the silence.

The sound seemed to rattle Jill. At once she turned and reached for the door. There she stopped. "You think you're the exception, Miranda. You think you're untouchable. Just wait. In a few years, when you're my age, you'll know just how vulnerable you are. We all are."

She walked out, closing the door behind her.

At once Miranda slid the bolt home.

The phone had stopped ringing. Miranda stared at it, wondering if it had been Chase, praying that he would call again.

The phone remained silent.

She began to pace the living room, hoping Chase, Annie, *anyone* would call. Starved for the sound of a human voice, she turned on the TV. Mindless entertainment, that's what she needed. For a half hour she sat on the couch among Annie's discarded socks and sweatshirts, flicking nervously between channels. Opera. Basketball. Game show. Opera again. In frustration she flicked it back to basketball.

Something clattered in the next room.

Startled, she left the couch and went into the kitchen. There she found herself staring down at a plastic saucer rolling around and around on its side across the linoleum.

floor. It collapsed, shuddered and fell still. Had it tumbled off the drainboard? She looked up at the sink and noticed, for the first time, that the window was wide open.

That's not the way I left it.

Slowly she backed away. The gun—Annie's gun. She had to get it.

In panic she turned to make a dash for the living room—

And found her head brutally trapped, her mouth covered by a wad of cloth. She flailed blindly against her captor, against the fumes burning her nose, her throat, but found her arms wouldn't work right. Her legs seemed to slide away from her, dissolving into some bottomless hole. She felt herself falling, caught a glimpse of the light as it receded into an impossibly high place. She tried to reach out for it but found her arms had gone numb.

The light wavered, shrank.

And then it winked out, leaving only the darkness.

PHILLIP WAS BANGING AWAY at the piano. Rachmaninoff, Chase thought wearily. Couldn't the boy choose something a little more sedate? Mozart, for instance, or Haydn. Anything but this Russian thunder.

Chase headed out to the veranda, hoping to escape the racket, but the sound of the piano seemed to pound right through the walls. Resignedly he stood at the railing and stared toward the harbor. Already sunset. The sea had turned to red flame.

He wondered what Miranda was doing.

Wondered if he'd ever stop wondering.

This morning, when they'd driven off in their separate cars, their separate ways, he'd known their relationship had gone as far as it could. To go any further would require a level of trust he wasn't ready to give her. Their amateur detective work had come to a dead end; for now they had no reason to see each other. It was time to let the pros take over. The police, at least, would be objective. They wouldn't be swayed by emotions or hormones.

They still believed Miranda was guilty.

"Uncle Chase?" Cassie pushed through the screen door and came out to join him. "You can't stand the music, either, I see."

He smiled. "Don't tell your brother."

"It's not that he's a bad musician. He's just...loud." She leaned against one of the posts and looked up at the sky, at the first stars winking in the gathering darkness. "Think you could do me a favor?" she asked.

"What's that?"

"When Mom gets home, will you talk to her? About the *Herald*."

"What about it?"

"Well, with all that's come up—about Jill Vickery, I mean—it's beginning to look like we'll need a strong hand on the helm. We all know Dad groomed Phillip to be the designated heir. And he's a bright kid—I'm not putting him down or anything. But the fact is, Phillip's just not that interested."

"He hasn't said much about it, one way or the other."

"Oh, he won't say anything. He'll never admit the truth. That he's not crazy about the job." She paused, then said with steel in her voice, "But I am."

Chase frowned at his niece. Not yet twenty, and she had the look of a woman who knew exactly what she wanted in life. "You think you have what it takes?"

"It's in my blood! I've been involved from the time I could put pen to paper. Or fingers to keyboard. I know how that office works. I can write, edit, lay out ads, drive the damn delivery truck. I can *run* that paper. Phillip can't."

Chase remembered Cassie's term papers, the ones he'd glanced through at the cottage. They weren't just the chewing up and spitting out of textbook facts, but thoughtful, critical analyses.

"I think you'd do a terrific job," he said. "I'll talk to your mother."

"Thanks, Uncle Chase. I'll remember to mention your name when I get my Pulitzer." Grinning, she turned to go back into the house.

"Cassie?"

"Yes?"

"What do you think of Jill Vickery?"

Cassie frowned at the change of subject. "You mean as a managing editor? She was okay. Considering what she got paid, we were lucky to keep her."

"I mean, on a personal level."

"Well, that's hard to say. You never really get to know Jill. She's like a closed book. I never had any idea about that stuff in San Diego."

"Do you think she had an affair with your father?"

Cassie shrugged. "Didn't they all?"

"Do you think she was hurt by it?"

Cassie thought this over for a moment. "I think, if she was, she got over it. Jill's a tough cookie. That's the way I'd like to be." She turned and went into the house.

Phillip was still playing Rachmaninoff.

Chase stood and watched the last glow of sunset fade from the sea. He thought about Jill Vickery, about Miranda, about all the women Richard had hurt, including his own wife, Evelyn.

We're lousy, we Tremain men, he thought. *We use women, then we hurt them.*

Am I any different?

In frustration he slapped the porch railing. *Yes, I am. I would be. If only I could trust her.*

Phillip's pounding on the piano had become unbearable.

Chase left the porch, walked down the steps and headed for his car.

He would talk to her one last time. He would look her in the eye and ask her if she was guilty. Tonight he would get his answer. Tonight he would decide, once and for all, if Miranda Wood was telling the truth.

NO ONE ANSWERED Annie's front door.

The lights were on inside, and Chase could hear the TV He rang the bell, knocked, called out Miranda's name. Sti there was no answer. At last he tried the knob and foun the door was unlocked. He poked his head inside.

"Miranda? Annie?"

The living room was deserted. A basketball game, un watched, was playing out its last minute on the TV. A pai of Annie's socks lay draped over the back of the sofa. Ev erything seemed perfectly normal, yet not quite right. H stood there for a moment, as though expecting the forme occupants of the room to magically reappear and confron him.

The basketball game went into its fifteen-second count down. A last-ditch throw, across the court. Basket. Th crowd cheered.

Chase crossed the room, into the kitchen, and halted.

Here things were definitely not right. A chair lay top pled on its side. On the floor a saucer lay upside down Though the kitchen window was wide open, an odor hung in the room, something vaguely sharp, medicinal.

Quickly he searched the rest of the house. He found nei ther Miranda nor Annie.

With growing panic he hurried outside and glanced up and down the street. Except for the far-off barking of a dog, the evening was still.

No, not quite. Was that the sound of a car engine run ning? If seemed muffled or distant. He circled around the house and saw a small detached garage in back. The doo was shut. The sound of the car engine, though still muf fled, seemed closer.

He started toward the garage. Then, out of the corner o his eye, he sighted a flicker of movement. He turned just in time to spy a shadow slipping away, blending into the darkness.

This time, you bastard, Chase thought, *you don't ge away from me.*

Chase sprinted off in pursuit.

He heard his quarry dodge left, toward a thick hedge of bushes. Chase, too, veered left, scrambled over a low stone wall and broke into a sprint.

The fleeing shadow burst through the hedge and made a sharp right, into a neighboring yard littered with garden tools. Chase, intent on capture, didn't notice his quarry had swept up a rake. It came flying at him through the darkness.

Chase ducked. Tines first, it flew over his head, then clattered into a wheelbarrow behind him. Chase leaped back to his feet.

His quarry grabbed a pickax, flung it.

Again Chase dodged. He heard the whoosh of air as the lethal weapon looped past. By the time he'd recovered his balance the figure was off and running again, toward a stand of trees.

He'll be lost in the shadows! thought Chase. He mustered a final burst of speed, drew within reach. His quarry was tired. He could hear the other man's ragged breaths. Chase launched himself forward, grabbed a handful of shirt and held on.

His quarry, instead of trying to pull free, spun around and charged like a bull.

Chase was flung backward, into a tree. The shock lasted only an instant. Rage, not pain, was his first response. Shoving away from the tree, he flung himself at his attacker. Both men fell off balance, went skidding across the wet leaves. The attacker punched, and the blow caught Chase in the belly. With a new strength born of fury, Chase slammed his fist blindly at the squirming shadow. The man groaned, tried to lash out. Chase hit him again. And again.

The man went limp.

Chase rolled away from the body. For a moment he sat there, catching his breath, wincing at the pain in his knuckles. The other man was still alive—he could hear him breathing. Chase grabbed the inert figure by the legs and dragged him across the leaf-strewn lawn, toward a faint pool of light from a distant porch lamp. There he knelt to see who his prisoner was. In disbelief he stared at the face now revealed.

It was Noah DeBolt. Evelyn's father.

Chapter Thirteen

The steady growl of an engine slowly penetrated Chase's numbed awareness. The car in the garage...the closed door...

That's when the realization hit him. He lurched to his feet.

Miranda.

He sprinted across the yard to the garage. A cloud of fumes assailed him as he pushed through the door. Miranda's car was parked inside, its engine still running. In panic, he flung open the car door.

Miranda lay sprawled across the front seat.

He switched off the ignition. Coughing, choking, he dragged her roughly out of the car, out of the garage. It terrified him how lifeless she felt in his arms. He carried her to the lawn and laid her down on the grass.

"Miranda!" he yelled. He shook her hard, so hard her whole body shuddered. "Wake up," he pleaded. "Damn you, Miranda. Don't you give up on me. Wake up!"

Still she didn't move.

In panic he slapped her face. The brutality of that blow, the sting of her flesh against his, shocked him. He laid his ear to her breast. Her heart was beating. And there it was—a breath!

She groaned, moved her head.

"Yes!" he shouted. "Come on. Come on." She san
back into unconsciousness. He didn't want to do it, but h
had no choice. He slapped her again.

This time she moved her hand, a reflexive gesture to war
off the savage blows. "No," she moaned.

"Miranda, it's me! Wake up." He brushed back her hai
gently took her face in his hands and kissed her forehead
her temples. "Please, Miranda," he whispered. "Look a
me."

Slowly she opened her eyes. They were dazed and full o
confusion. At once she lashed out blindly, as though sti
fighting for her life.

"No, it's me!" he cried. He held her, hugged her tightl
against him. Her frantic thrashing grew weaker. He felt th
panic melt from her body until she lay quietly in his arms

"It's all over," he whispered. "All over."

She pulled away and stared up at him with a look of be
wilderment. "Who..."

"It was Noah."

"Evelyn's *father?*"

Chase nodded. "He's the one who's been trying to ki
you."

"You have no right to hold me, Lorne. You under
stand? *No right.*" Noah, his face bruised an ugly purple
stared at his accusers. Through the closed door came th
sounds of the police station: the clack of a typewriter, th
ringing phone, the voices of patrolmen headed out for nigh
duty. But here, in the back room, there was dead silence.

Quietly Lorne said, "You're not in any position to pu
rank, Noah. So talk to us."

"I don't have to say a thing," said Noah. "Not until Le
Hardee gets here."

Lorne sighed. "Legally speaking, yeah, you're right. Bu
it would sure make things easy if you'd just tell us why yo
tried to kill her."

"I didn't. I went to her house to talk to her. I heard the car running in the garage. I thought maybe she was trying to kill herself. I started to go in, to check on it. Then Chase showed up. I guess I panicked. That's why I ran."

"That's all you were doing there? Just paying Ms. Wood a visit?"

Noah gave him an icy nod.

"In a getup like that?" Lorne nodded at Noah's black shirt and trousers.

"What I wear happens to be my concern."

"Chase says differently. He says you dragged her in the garage, left her there and started the car."

Noah snorted. "Chase has a little trouble being objective. Especially where Miranda Wood is concerned. Besides, *he* attacked *me*. Who the hell's got the bruises, anyway? Look at my face. Look at it!"

"Seems to me you both got some pretty good bruises," said Lorne.

"Self-defense," claimed Noah. "I had to fight back."

"Chase thinks you're the one who's been going after her. That you set fire to her house. Drove at her with a stolen car. And what about tonight? Was that supposed to be a convenient little suicide?"

"She's got him all twisted around. Got him taking her side. The side of a murderer—"

"Who's the guilty party here, Noah?"

Noah, sensing he'd said too much already, said abruptly, "I'm not going to talk till Les gets here."

In frustration Lorne crumpled his paper coffee cup in his fist. "Okay," he said, dropping into a chair. "We can wait. As long as it takes, Noah. As long as it takes."

"IT'S NOT GOING TO STICK," said Miranda. "I know it won't."

They sat huddled together on a bench in the intake area. Ellis Snipe had brought them coffee and cookies. Perhaps it was his way of personally atoning for the ordeal the po-

lice had put them through. So many questions, so many
reports to be filed. And then, halfway through the interrogation, Dr. Steiner had shown up, called in by Lorne to
check on her condition. In the guise of a medical exam, he
had practically assaulted her with his stethoscope. *Breathe
deep, damn it! Gotta check your lungs. You think I like
making all these house calls? This keeps up, you two will
have to put me on retainer!*

The questions, the demands, had left her exhausted. It
was all she could manage, to sit propped up against Chase's
shoulder. Waiting—for what? For Noah to confess? For the
police to tell her the nightmare was over?

She knew better than that.

"He'll get out of it," she said. "He'll find a way."

"This time he won't," said Chase.

"But I never saw his face. I can barely remember what
happened. What can they charge him with? Trespassing?"
Miranda shook her head. "This is Noah DeBolt we're
talking about. In this town, a DeBolt can get away with
murder."

"Not Richard's murder."

She stared at him. "You think he killed Richard? His
own son-in-law?"

"It's starting to fall together, Miranda. Remember what
that lawyer FitzHugh told us? The real reason Richard gave
Rose Hill to you? It was to keep the land out of Evelyn's
control."

"I don't see what you're getting at."

"Who's the one person in the world Evelyn listens to?
Trusts? Her *father*. Noah could have talked her into selling
the land."

"You think this is all for control of Rose Hill? That's not
much of a motive for murder."

"But the threat of bankruptcy is. If his investment collapsed, Noah would be left holding acres of land he could
never develop. Worthless land."

"The north shore? Then you think Noah was the money behind Stone Coast Trust."

"Which makes Tony Graffam nothing but a front man. A patsy, really. My guess is, Richard found out. He had those financial records from Stone Coast, remember? The account numbers, the tax returns. I think he matched one of those accounts to Noah."

"Richard could have ruined him right then and there," she pointed out. "All he had to do was run the story in the *Herald*. But he canceled it."

"It's the way their relationship worked, Richard and Noah. They were always out to cut each other down. But not in public, *never* in public. It was a private rivalry, just between them. That's why Richard didn't print the article. It would've exposed his own father-in-law. And brought the family's dirty linen out into the public eye."

Miranda shook her head. "We'll never prove it. Not after Noah's lawyer gets through with the smoke and mirrors. You've been away from this island too long, Chase. You've forgotten how it is. The DeBolts, they're the equivalent of gods in this town."

"Not any longer."

"Then there's the matter of evidence. How do you prove he killed Richard?" She sighed, an admission of defeat. "No, *I'm* the convenient suspect. The one they'll convict." She sat back wearily. "The one they'll put away."

"That won't happen, Miranda. I won't let it happen."

Their gazes met. For the first time she saw what she'd been longing to see in his eyes. Trust. "Then you think I'm telling the truth."

"I know you're telling the truth." He touched her face. As his hand stroked down the curve of her cheek she closed her eyes and felt herself melting, flowing like warm liquid against him. "I think I've known it all along. But I was afraid to admit it. Afraid to consider the other possibilities...."

"It wasn't me, Chase. It wasn't." She slid into his arms, and there she found warmth and courage, all the courage she'd somehow lost in these past soul-battering days. *Believe me,* she thought. *Never stop believing me.*

They were still locked in that embrace when Evelyn Tremain walked in the station door.

Miranda felt Chase stiffen against her, heard his sharp intake of breath. Slowly she raised her head and turned to see Evelyn and the DeBolt family attorney, Les Hardee, standing a few feet away.

"So it's come to this, has it?" Evelyn said quietly.

Chase said nothing.

"Where is my father?" said Evelyn.

"In the room down the hall," said Chase. "He's talking to Lorne."

"Without me?" cut in the attorney. He headed swiftly down the hall, muttering, "A clear violation of rights...."

Evelyn hadn't moved. She was still staring at them. "What sort of lies are you spreading about my father, Chase?"

Slowly Chase stood to face her. "Only the truth, Evelyn. It may be hard to take, but you'll have to accept it."

"The *truth?*" Evelyn let out a disbelieving laugh. "An officer calls me, tells me my father's been arrested for assault. Assault? *Noah DeBolt?* Who's lying, Chase? My father? You?" She looked at Miranda. "Or someone else?"

"Lorne will explain the charges. You'd better talk to him."

"Because you won't? Is that it? Oh, Chase." She shook her head. "You've turned your back on your own family. We love you. And look how you hurt us." She turned, faced the corridor. Softly she said, "I just hope Lorne has the good sense to know the truth when he hears it." Taking a deep breath, she started down the hall.

"Wait here," Chase said to Miranda.

"What are you going to do?"

He didn't answer. He just kept walking away, in pursuit of Evelyn.

Stunned, Miranda watched him vanish around the corner. She heard a door open, then close behind him, shutting her out. She wondered what was going on in that room, what words were being exchanged, what deals forged. She had no doubt there *would* be deals, declarations of Noah's innocence. His attorney would do his best to twist the story around, make it seem like some crazy misunderstanding. Somehow they'd manage to make Miranda look like the guilty party.

Please, Chase, she thought. *Don't let them sway you. Don't start doubting me again.*

She stared down the hall and waited.

And she feared the worst.

"THE CHARGES ARE preposterous," said Evelyn. "My father's never broken a law in his life. Why, if he gets too much change back from a clerk, he'll go across town to return it. How can you accuse him of assault, much less attempted murder?"

"Mr. Tremain here has the bruises to prove it," said Lorne.

"So does my client!" cut in Les Hardee. "All that proves is, they traded blows in the dark. A case of mistaken identity. Two men blindly duking it out. At the very worst, you can accuse my client of idiotic behavior."

"Thanks a lot, Les," grunted Noah.

"The point is," said Hardee, "you can't hold him. The damage—" he glanced at Chase's bruised face, then at Noah's face, even more bruised "—appears to be mutual. And as for that nonsense about trying to kill Miranda Wood, well, where's your evidence? She was facing a jail term. Of course she was depressed. Of course she'd consider suicide."

"What about the fire?" pointed out Chase. "The car that almost ran her down? I was there, I saw it. *Someone's* trying to kill her."

"Not Mr. DeBolt."

"Does he have alibis?"

"Do *you* have evidence?" Hardee shot back. He turned to Lorne. "Look, let's call a halt to this farce. I'll take the responsibility. Release Mr. DeBolt."

Lorne sighed. "I can't."

Evelyn and Hardee stared at the diminutive chief of police.

"I'm afraid there *is* evidence," said Lorne, almost apologetically. "Ellis found a bottle of chloroform behind the garage. That kind of argues against suicide, doesn't it?"

"Nothing to do with me," said Noah.

"Then here's some more evidence," cut in Chase. It was time to gamble, time to shoot the wad. He was going to make a guess here; he only hoped it was the right one. "You know that money from the Bank of Boston? That hundred thousand dollars used to bail out Miranda Wood? Well, I had a banker friend of mine slip into the computer. Match that money transfer to an account."

"What?" Lorne turned to Chase in surprise. "You know who paid the bail?"

"Yes." *Here goes*, thought Chase. "Noah DeBolt."

It was Evelyn who reacted first, with a rage that transformed her face into an ugly mask. The look was directed at her father. "You did *what?*"

Noah said nothing. His silence was all Chase needed to back up his hunch. Right on target.

"It can be officially confirmed," said Chase. "Yes, it was your father who paid the bail."

Evelyn was still staring at Noah. "You let her out?"

Noah's head drooped. In an instant he'd been transformed into a very old, very tired-looking man. "I did it for you," he whispered.

"For me? For *me?*" Evelyn laughed. "What other favors have you done for me, Daddy?"

"It was for you. Everything was for you—"

"You crazy old man," muttered Evelyn. "You must be going senile."

"No." Noah's head shot up. "I would've done anything, don't you see? I was protecting you! My little girl—"

"Protecting me from what?"

"From yourself. From what you did...."

Evelyn turned away in disgust. "I don't know what the hell he's raving about."

"Don't turn your back on me, young lady!"

"You can see he needs a doctor, Lorne. Try a psychiatrist."

"This is the thanks I get!" Noah roared. "For keeping you out of *prison?*"

Instant silence. Evelyn, white-faced, turned to confront her father. "Prison? For what?"

"Richard." Noah, his rage suddenly spent, sank slowly back against the chair. Softly he said, "For Richard."

"You thought... that I—" Evelyn shook her head. "Why? You knew it was that—that bitch!"

Noah merely looked away. With that one gesture he gave his answer. An answer that lifted a weight so heavy from Chase's soul he felt he was floating. It was a burden he could only now acknowledge had been there all along, the burden of proof. With that one gesture, the last blot of suspicion was washed away.

"You know Miranda's innocent," said Chase.

Noah dropped his head in his hands. "Yes," he whispered.

"How?" cut in Lorne.

"Because I had her followed. Oh, I knew about the affair. I knew what he was up to. I'd had enough of it! I wasn't going to see him hurt Evelyn again. So I hired a man, told him to watch her. To follow her, take photos.

Catch 'em in the act. I wanted Evelyn to know, once and for all, what a bastard she'd married.''

"And the night he was killed, you had Miranda under surveillance?" asked Lorne.

Noah nodded.

"What did your man see?"

"Of the murder? Nothing. He was busy following the woman. She left the house, walked to the beach. Sat there for an hour or so. Then she went home. By then my son-in-law was already dead."

Exactly what she said, thought Chase. *It was all the truth, right down to the last detail.*

"Then your man never saw the killer?" said Lorne.

"No."

"But you assumed your daughter..."

Noah shrugged. "It seemed . . . a logical guess. He had it coming. All these years of hurting her. You think he didn' deserve it? You think she wasn't justified?"

"But I didn't do it," said Evelyn.

Her words went ignored.

"Why did you bail out Miranda Wood?" asked Lorne.

"I thought if she went to trial, if her story held together there was a chance they'd start to look at other suspects."

"You mean Evelyn."

"Better to have it over and done with!" blurted out Noah. "If there was an accident, that would end it. No more questions. No more suspects."

"So you wanted her out of jail," said Chase. "Out on the street, where you could reach her."

"That's enough, Noah!" cut in Hardee. "You don't have to answer these questions."

"Damn you, Les!" snapped Evelyn. "You should have told him that earlier!" She looked at her father, her expression a mixture of pity and disgust. "Let me set your mind at rest, Daddy. I didn't kill Richard. The fact you thought I did only shows how little you know me. Or I you."

"I'm sorry about this, Evelyn," said Lorne quietly. "But now I'm going to have to ask you a few questions."

Evelyn turned to him. Her chin came up, a gesture of stubborn pride, newfound strength. For the first time in all the years he'd known her Chase felt a spark of admiration for his sister-in-law.

"Ask away, Lorne," she said. "You're the cop. And I guess I'm now your prime suspect."

Chase didn't stay to hear the rest. He left the room and headed down the hall to find Miranda. *Now it can be proved. It was true, every word you said.* They could start from the beginning, he thought. He suddenly strode ahead with new hope, new anticipation. The shadow of murder was gone, and they had a chance to do it over, to do it right.

He rounded the corner eagerly, expecting to see her sitting on the bench.

The bench was empty.

He went over to the clerk, who was typing out Noah's arrest report. "Did you see where she went?"

The clerk glanced up. "You mean Ms. Wood?"

"Yes."

"She left the station. About, oh, twenty minutes ago."

"Did she say where she was going?"

"Nope. Just got up and walked out."

In frustration Chase turned to the door. *You never make it easy for me, do you?* he thought. Then he pushed through the door and headed out into the night.

ALL DAY OZZIE HAD BEEN restless. Last night, all that frantic running around and police activity had driven the beast nearly mad with excitement. A day later and the agitation still hadn't worn off. He was all nerved up, clawing at the door, whining and tip-tapping back and forth across the wood floor.

Maybe it's my fault, Miss St. John thought, gazing in disgust at her hysterical dog. *Maybe my mood has simply rubbed off on him.*

Ozzie crouched at the front door like a discarded fur coat, staring pitifully at his mistress.

"You," said Miss St. John, "are a tyrant."

Ozzie merely whimpered.

"Oh, all right," said Miss St. John. "Out, out!" She opened the door. The dog bounded out into the twilight.

Miss St. John followed the beast down the gravel driveway. Ozzie was dancing along, his fur bouncing like black corkscrews. Truly an ugly animal, thought Miss St. John, the same thought that occurred to her on every walk. That he was worth several thousand dollars for his pedigree alone only went to show you the worthlessness of pedigrees, be they for dogs or people. But what Ozzie lacked in beauty he made up in energy. Already he was trotting far ahead and veering up the path, toward Rose Hill.

Miss St. John, feeling more like dog than mistress, followed him.

The cottage was dark. Chase and Miranda had left that morning and now the place stood deserted and forlorn. A pity. Such charming cottages should not go empty, especially not in the summertime.

She climbed the steps and peered through the window. Shadows of furniture huddled within. The books were back in the shelves. She could see the gleam of their spines lined up against the wall. Though they'd combed those books and papers thoroughly, she still wondered whether they had missed something. Some small, easily overlooked item that held the answers to Richard Tremain's death.

The door was locked, but she knew where the key was kept. What harm would there be in another little visit? She'd always felt just a bit proprietary when it came to Rose Hill. After all, she'd played near here almost every day as a child. And as an adult she'd made a point of keeping an eye on the cottage, as a favor to the Tremains.

Ozzie seemed happy enough, padding about in the yard.

Miss St. John retrieved the key from the planter, unlocked the door and went inside.

It seemed very still, very sad in that living room. She turned on all the lamps and wandered about, her gaze combing the nooks and crannies of the furniture. They'd already made a search of those places. There was no point repeating it.

She went through the kitchen, through the upstairs bedrooms, came back down again. No hunches, no revelations.

She was turning to leave when her gaze swept past the area rug, set right in front of the door. That's when a memory struck her, of a scene from *Tess of the D'Urbervilles*. A confessional note, slipped under the closed door, only to be pushed accidentally under the adjacent rug. A note that was never found because it lay hidden from view.

So vivid was that image that when she bent and pulled up the edge of the rug she was not at all startled to see a sealed envelope lying there.

The note was from M. The intended recipient had never found it, never read it.

...This pain is alive, like a creature gnawing at my organs. It won't die. It refuses to die. You put it there, you planted it, you gave the embryo all those years of nourishment.

And then you walked away.

You say you are doing me a kindness. You say it is better to break off now, because, if it goes on longer, it will only hurt more. You don't know what it is to hurt. Once you claimed to be love's walking wounded. Once, I thought to save you.

You were the serpent I hugged to my breast.

Now you say you've found a new savior. You think she'll make you happy. But she won't. It will be the same with her as it was with the others. You'll decide she isn't perfect. No one who's ever loved you, really loved you, has ever been good enough for you.

But you're getting old, flabby, and still you think that somewhere there's a young and perfect woman just longing to make love to your wrinkled old carcass.

She doesn't know you the way I do. I've had years to learn all your dirty little secrets. Your conceits and lies and cruelty. You'll use her, the way you've used all the others. And then she'll be tossed on the heap with the rest of us, another woman terribly hurt.

You should suffer where you've sinned. A good clean slice—

Miss St. John, still clutching the letter, abruptly left Rose Hill and hurried home.

With shaking hands she made two phone calls. The first was to Lorne Tibbetts.

The second was to Miranda Wood.

Chapter Fourteen

Miranda was near the point of exhaustion by the time she climbed up Annie's porch steps. It had been only a ten-minute walk from the police station, but the distance she had traveled had been emotional, not physical. Sitting alone on that bench, shut out from the fancy deal-making between attorneys and cops, she'd come to the sad realization that Noah DeBolt would never be charged with any crime worse than trespassing. That she, Miranda, was too convenient a suspect to be let off the hook. And that Chase, by walking down the corridor, by joining Evelyn and Noah behind that closed door, had made his choice.

Didn't they say that crisis brought families together? Well, the arrest of patriarch Noah DeBolt was one hell of a crisis. The family would rally.

Miranda was not, could never be, part of that family.

She stepped in the front door. Annie was still not home. Silence hung like a shroud over the house. When the phone suddenly rang, the sound was almost shocking to her ears.

She picked up the receiver.

"Miranda?" came a breathless voice.

"Miss St. John? Is something wrong?"

"Are you home alone?" was Miss St. John's bizarre reply.

"Well, yes, at the moment—"

"I want you to lock the door. Do it now."

"No, everything's all right. They've arrested Noah DeBolt—"

"Listen to me! I found another letter, at Rose Hill. That's what she was after, don't you see? The reason she kept going to the cottage! To get back all her letters!"

"Whose letters?"

"M."

"But Noah DeBolt—"

"This has nothing to do with Noah! It was a crime of passion, Miranda. The classic motive. Let me read you the letter...."

Miranda listened.

By the time Miss St. John had finished, Miranda's hands were numb from clutching the receiver.

"I've already called the police," said Miss St. John. "They've sent a man to pick up Jill Vickery. Until then, keep your doors locked. It's a sick letter, Miranda, written by a sick woman. If she comes to the house, *don't let her in.*"

Miranda hung up.

At once she missed the sound of a human voice, any voice, even one transmitted through telephone wires. *Annie, come home. Please.*

She stared at the phone, wondering if she should call someone. But who? It was only as she stood there, thinking, that she noticed several days' mail mounded haphazardly by the telephone, some of it threatening to spill over onto the floor. A half-dozen household bills mingled with ad circulars and magazines. Annie's bookkeeping must be as sloppy as her housekeeping, she thought, straightening the pile. Only then did she notice the newsletter from the alumni association of Tufts University—Annie's old alma mater. It lay at the edge of the table, four photocopied pages stapled together, personal notes from the class of '68, with a mass-mailing label on front. Of no particular interest to Miranda—except for one detail.

It was addressed to Margaret Ann Berenger.

You're the only M I know, Annie had said.

And all the time, she'd known another.

It doesn't mean she's the one.

Miranda stood staring at that label. Margaret Ann Berenger. Where was the proof, where was the link between Annie and all those letters from M?

It suddenly occurred to her. *A typewriter.*

A manual model, Jill had said, with an *e* hammer in need of cleaning. It would be a large item, difficult to hide. A quick check of all the closets, all the cabinets, confirmed that there was no manual typewriter in the house. Could it be in the garage?

No, she'd been in the garage. It was barely large enough to hold a car, much less store household items.

She checked, anyway. No typewriter.

She went back into the house, her mind racing. By now Jill might already be under arrest. Annie would hear of it in no time, would know the search for the real M was on. Her first move would be to get rid of the incriminating typewriter, if she hadn't already done so. It was the one piece of evidence that could link Annie to Richard's murder.

It could prove my innocence. I have to find it, before she destroys it. I have to get it to the police.

There was one more place she had to look.

She ran from the house and got into her car.

Moments later she pulled up in front of the *Herald* building. It was dark inside. The latest issue had just been put to bed. No one would be working late tonight, so she'd have the building to herself.

She let herself in the front door with her key—the key she'd never gotten around to turning in. With a twinge of irony she remembered that it was Richard who'd told her to keep it. He was certain he could talk her into returning to the job.

Well, here she was, back again.

She moved up the aisle of desks and went straight to Annie's. She flicked on the lamp. The top drawer was unlocked. Among the jumble of pens and paper clips she found some loose keys. Which one would open Annie's locker? She gathered them all up and headed down the stairwell and into the women's room.

She turned on the light. A flowered couch, mauve wall-paper, Victorian prints sprang into view. Jill's decorative touch couldn't disguise the fact it was a closed-in dungeon of a room, without a single window. Miranda moved to the bank of lockers. There were six of them, extra wide to accommodate employees' heavy coats and boots during the winter months. She knew which one belonged to Annie. It had the sticker that said I've Got PMS. What's Your Excuse?

She inserted the first key into the lock. It didn't turn.

She tried the second key, then the third. The lock popped open.

She swung open the door and frowned at the contents. On the top shelf were mittens, a pair of old running shoes, a wool scarf.

On the bottom shelf a sweater lay draped over a towel-wrapped bundle. Miranda took out the bundle. The object inside was heavy. She unwrapped the towel, revealed the contents.

It was an old blue-green Olivetti with pica type.

She slid in a scrap of paper and with shaking hands typed the name Margaret Ann Berenger. The *e* loop was smudged.

An overwhelming sense of relief, almost euphoria, at once washed over her. Quickly she shut the locker and re-wrapped the typewriter. As she gathered it up in her arms, a puff of air blew past her cheek. That was all the warning she had, that soft whisper of wind through the door as it opened and shut behind her.

Miranda turned.

The intruder stood in the doorway, her hair a mass of windblown waves, her face utterly devoid of emotion.

Miranda said softly, "Annie."

In silence Annie's gaze settled on the typewriter in Miranda's arms.

"I thought you were with Irving," said Miranda.

Annie's gaze slowly rose once again to meet Miranda's. Sadness now filled those eyes, a look of pain that seemed to spill from her very soul. *Why did I never see it before?* thought Miranda.

"There is no Irving," said Annie.

Miranda shook her head in confusion.

"There never was an Irving. I made him up. All the dates, all those evenings out. You see, I'd drive to the harbor. Park there and just sit. Hours, sometimes." Annie took a deep breath and, shuddering, let it out. "I couldn't take the pity, Miranda. All that sympathy for an old maid."

"I never thought that—"

"Of course you did. You all did. Then there was Richard. I wouldn't give him the satisfaction of knowing that—" Her voice broke. She wiped her hand across her eyes.

Slowly Miranda set the typewriter down on the bench. "Knowing what, Annie?" she asked softly. "How badly he hurt you? How alone you really were?"

A shudder racked Annie's body.

"He hurt us both," said Miranda. "Every woman he ever touched. Every woman who ever loved him. He hurt us all."

"Not the way he hurt me!" Annie cried. The echo of her pain seemed to reverberate endlessly against those stark walls. "Five years of my life, Miranda. That's what I gave him. Five years of secrets. I was forty-two when we met. I still had time for a baby. A few short years left. I kept hoping, waiting for him to make up his mind. To leave Evelyn." She wiped her eyes again, smearing a streak of mascara and tears across her cheek. "Now it's too late for me. It was my last chance and he took it from me. He *stole* it from me. And then he ended it." She shook her head, laughing through her tears. "He said he was only trying to be kind. That he didn't want me to waste any more years on him. Then he said the thing that hurt me most of all. He said, 'It was just your fantasy, Annie. I never really loved you the way you thought I did.'" The look she gave Miranda was the gaze of a tortured animal's. "Five years, and he tells me that. What he didn't tell me was the truth. He'd found someone younger. You." There was no hostility, no anger in her voice, only quiet resignation. "I never blamed you, Miranda. You didn't know. You were just another victim. He would have left you, the way he left us all."

"You're right, Annie. We were all his victims."

"I'm sorry. I'm so sorry, Miranda." Annie slid her hand into her jacket pocket. "But someone has to suffer for it." Slowly she withdrew the gun.

Miranda stared at the barrel, now pointed at her chest. She wanted to argue, to plead, anything to make Annie lower the gun. But her voice had frozen in her throat. She could only stare at the black circle of the barrel and wonder if she would feel the bullet.

"Come, Miranda. Let's go."

Miranda shook her head. "Where—where are we going?"

Annie opened the door and gestured for Miranda to move first. "Up the stairs. To the roof."

No ONE WAS HOME.

Chase circled around Annie's house to the garage and found that the car was gone. Miranda must have returned, then left again. He was standing in the driveway, wondering where to look next, when he heard the phone ringing inside the house. He ran up the porch steps and into the living room to answer the call.

It was Lorne Tibbetts. "Is Miranda there?" he asked.

"No, I'm looking for her."

"What about Annie Berenger?"

"Not here, either."

"Okay," said Lorne. "I want you to leave the house, Chase. Do it right now."

Chase was stunned by the unexpected command. He said, "I'm waiting for Miranda to show up."

He heard Lorne turn and say something to Ellis. Then, "Look, we got evidence snowballing down here. If Annie Berenger shows up first, you keep things nice and casual, okay? Don't rattle her. Just calmly leave the house. Ellis is on his way over."

"What the hell's going on?"

"We think we know who M is. And it's not Jill Vickery. Now get out of there." Lorne hung up.

If it isn't Jill Vickery . . .

Chase went to the end table and opened the drawer. Annie's gun was missing.

He slammed the drawer shut.

Where are you, Miranda?

The next thought sent him running outside to his car. There might still be time to find them. He'd missed Miranda by only five, maybe ten minutes. They couldn't have gone far, not yet. If he circled around town, kept his eyes open, he might be able to find her car.

If they were still in the area.

I can't lose you. Now that we can prove your innocence. Now that we have a chance together.

He swung the car around. With tires screeching, he raced back toward town.

"Go on. Up the last flight."

Miranda paused, her foot on the next step. "Please, Annie . . ."

"Keep moving."

Miranda turned to face her. They were already on the third-floor landing. One more flight and then the door to the roof. Once she'd marveled at the beauty of this stairwell, at the carved mahogany banister, the gleaming wood finish. Now it had become a spiral death trap. She gripped the railing, drawing strength from the unyielding support of solid wood.

"Why are you doing this?" she asked.

"Go on. Go!"

"We were friends once—"

"Until Richard."

"But I didn't know! I had no idea you were in love with him! If only you'd told me."

"I never told anyone. I couldn't. It was his idea, you see. Keep it quiet, keep it our little secret. He said he wanted to protect me."

Then I'm the only one left who knows, thought Miranda. *The only one still alive.*

"Move," said Annie. "Up the stairs."

Miranda didn't budge. She looked Annie in the eye. Quietly she said, "Why don't you just shoot me now? Right here. If that's what you're going to do anyway."

"It's your choice." Calmly Annie raised the gun. "I'm not afraid of killing. They say that it's hardest the first time you do it. And you know what? It wasn't really hard at all. All I had to do was think about how much he hurt me. The knife seemed to move all by itself. I was just a witness."

"I'm not Richard. I never meant to hurt you."

"But you will, Miranda. You know the truth."

"So do the police. They found that letter, Annie. The last one you wrote."

Annie shook her head. "They arrested Jill tonight. But you're still the one they'll blame. Because they'll find the typewriter in your car. What a clever girl you'll seem, making up all those letters, planting them in the cottage. Throwing suspicion on poor innocent Jill. But then the guilt caught up with you. You got depressed. You knew jail was inevitable. So you chose the easy way out. You climbed to the roof of the newspaper building. And you jumped."

"I won't do it."

Annie gripped the gun with both hands and pointed it at Miranda's chest. "Then you'll die here. I had to kill you, you see. I found you planting the typewriter in Jill's office. You had a gun. You ordered me into the stairwell. I tried to grab the gun and it went off. A tidy end for everyone involved." Slowly she cocked back the pistol hammer. "Or would you rather it be the roof?"

I have to buy time, thought Miranda. *Have to wait for a chance, any chance, to escape.*

She turned and gazed up at the last flight of stairs.

"Go on," said Annie.

Miranda began to climb.

Fourteen steps, each one a fleeting eternity. Fourteen lifetimes, passing, gone. Frantically she tried to visualize the roof, the layout, the avenues of escape. She'd been up there only once, when the news staff had gathered for a group photo. She recalled a flat stretch of asphalt, punctuated by three chimneys, a heating duct, a transformer shed. Four stories down—that would be the drop. Would it kill her? Or was it just high enough to leave her crippled on the sidewalk, a helpless mound of broken bones, to be dispatched with a few blows by Annie?

The door to the roof loomed just above. If she could just get through that door and barricade it, she might be able to buy time, to scream for help.

Only a few steps more.

She stumbled and fell forward, catching herself on the stairs.

"Get up," said Annie.

"My ankle—"

"I said, get up!"

Miranda sat on the step and reached down to massage her foot. "I think I sprained it."

Annie took a step closer. "Then crawl if you have to! But get up those stairs!"

Miranda, her back braced firmly against the step, her legs wound up tight, calmly kept rubbing her ankle. And all the time she thought, *Closer, Annie. Come closer....*

Annie moved up another step. She was standing just below Miranda now, the gun frighteningly close. "I can't wait. Your time's run out." She raised the gun to Miranda's face.

That's when Miranda raised her foot—in a vicious, straight-out kick that thudded right into Annie's stomach. It sent Annie toppling backward down the stairs, to sprawl on the third-floor landing. But even as she fell she never released the gun. There was no opportunity to wrestle away the weapon. Annie was already rising to her knees, gun in hand. Her aim swept up toward her prey.

Miranda yanked open the rooftop door and dashed through just as Annie fired. She heard the bullet splinter the door, felt wood chips fly, sting her face. There was no latch, no way to bolt the door shut. So little time, so little time! Fourteen steps and Annie would be on the roof.

Miranda glanced wildly about her, could make out in the darkness the silhouette of chimneys, crates, other unidentifiable shapes.

Footsteps thudded up the stairs.

In panic Miranda took off into the shadows and slipped behind a transformer shed. She heard the door fly open, heard it bang shut again.

Then she heard Annie's voice, calling through the darkness. "There's nowhere to run, Miranda. Nowhere to go but straight down. Wherever you are, I'll find you...."

CHASE SPOTTED IT from a block away: Miranda's old Dodge, parked in front of the *Herald* building. He pulled up behind it and climbed out. A glance through the window told him the car was unoccupied. Miranda—or whoever had driven it here—must be in the building.

He rattled the front door to the *Herald*. It was locked. Through the glass he saw a lamp burning on one of the desks. Someone had to be inside. He banged on the door and called, "Miranda?" There was no answer.

He rattled the door again, then started around to the back of the building. There had to be another way in, an unlocked window or a loading door. He had circled the corner and was moving down one of the alleys when he heard it. Gunfire.

It came from somewhere inside the building.

"Miranda?" he yelled.

He wasted no more time searching for unlocked entrances. He grabbed a trash can from the alley, carried it around to the front of the building and hurled it through the window. Glass shattered, flying like hail across the desks inside. He kicked in the last jagged fragments, scrambled over the sill and dropped onto a carpet littered with razorlike shards. At once he was running past the desks, moving straight for the back of the building. With every step he took he grew more terrified of what he might find. Images of Miranda raced through his head. He shoved through the first door and confronted the deserted print shop. Newspapers—the next issue—were bundled and stacked against the walls. No Miranda.

He turned, moved down the hall to the women's lounge. Again, that surge of terror as he pushed through the door.

Again, no Miranda.

He turned and headed straight into the women's rest room, pushing open stall doors. No one there.

Ditto for the men's room.

Where the hell had that gunshot come from?

He ran back into the hall and started up the stairwell. Two more floors to search. Offices on the second floor, storage and news file rooms on the third. Somewhere up there he'd find her.

Just let me find you alive.

MIRANDA HUGGED THE SIDE of the transformer shed and listened for the sound of footsteps. Except for the hammering of her own heart she heard nothing, not even the softest crunch of shoes on asphalt. *Where is she? Which way is she moving?*

Quickly Miranda glanced to either side of her. Her eyes had began to adjust to the darkness. She could make out, to the left, a jumble of crates. Right beside them were the handrails of a fire escape. A way off the roof! If she could just make it to that edge, without being seen.

Where was Annie?

She had to risk a look. She crouched down and slowly inched toward the corner. What she saw made her pull back at once in panic.

Annie was moving straight toward the transformer shed.

Miranda's instinct told her to run, to attempt a final dash for freedom. Logic told her she'd never make it. Annie was already too close.

In desperation she scrabbled for a few bits of gravel near her feet. She flung it high overhead, aiming blindly for the opposite end of the roof. She heard it clatter somewhere off in the darkness.

For a few terrifying seconds she listened for sounds—any sounds. Nothing.

Again she edged around the corner of the transformer. Annie was following the sound, toward the opposite edge of the roof, stalking slowly toward one of the chimneys. A few steps farther. One more...

Now was her chance—her only one! Miranda ran.

Her footsteps sounded like drumbeats across the asphalt roof. Even before she reached the fire escape she heard the first gunshot, heard the whine of the bullet as it hurtled past. No time to think, only move! She scrambled for the fire escape, swung her leg over onto the first metal rung.

Another gunshot exploded.

The bullet's impact was like a punch in the shoulder. Its force sent her toppling sideways, over the roof's edge. She caught a dizzying view of the night sky, then felt herself falling, falling. Instinctively she reach up, clawed blindly for a handhold. As she tumbled over the edge of the fire escape landing, her left hand closed around cold steel—the railing. Even as her legs slipped away, dangling beneath her like dead weights, her grip held. She tried to reach up with the other arm but it wouldn't seem to obey her commands. She could only raise it to shoulder height, and then her hand closed only weakly around the outside edge of the landing. For a second she clung there, her feet hanging uselessly. Then she managed to brace one foot against the brick face of the building. *Still alive, still here!* she thought. *If I can just pull myself over the rail—get back onto the landing...*

The flicker of a shadow moving just above made her freeze. Slowly she lifted her gaze and stared into the gun barrel. Annie was standing at the roof's edge, aiming directly at Miranda's head.

"Now," said Annie softly. "Let go of the fire escape."

"No. No—"

"Just open your fingers. Lean back. A fast and easy way to die."

"It won't work. They'll find out! They'll know you did it!"

"Jump, Miranda. *Jump.*"

Miranda stared down at the ground. It was so far away, so very far.

Annie swung one leg over the roof's edge, aimed her heel at Miranda's hand gripping the rail and stamped down.

Miranda screamed. Still she held on.

Annie raised her heel, stamped again, then again, each blow crushing Miranda's left hand.

The pain was unbearable. Miranda's grip loosened. She lost her foothold, was left dangling free. Her left hand, throbbing in agony, could stand the abuse no longer. Her right hand, already weak and growing numb from the bullet wound, didn't have the strength to hold her weight. She gazed up in despair as Annie raised her heel and prepared to stamp down one last time.

The blow never fell.

Instead, Annie's body was jerked up and backward, like a puppet whose strings have been yanked all at once. She let out an unearthly screech of rage, of disbelief. And then there was a thud as her body, hurled aside, slammed onto the rooftop.

An instant later Chase appeared at the roof's edge. He leaned over and grabbed her left wrist. "Take my other hand! Take it!" he yelled.

Bracing her feet against the brick wall, Miranda managed to raise her right arm. "I can't...can't reach you...."

"Come on, Miranda!" He leaned farther, his body stretching over the edge. "You have to do it! I need both your hands! Just reach up, that's all! I'll grab it, darling. Please!''

Darling. That single word, one she'd never heard before on his lips, seemed to spark some new source of strength deep inside her. She took a breath and strained toward the heavens. *That's as far as I can go*, she thought in despair. *No farther.*

That's when his hand closed around her wrist. At once she was held in a grip so tight she never feared, even for an instant, that she would fall. He dragged her up and up, over the roof's edge.

Only then did her strength give out. She had no need of it now, not when Chase was here to lend her his. She tumbled into his arms.

No tree had ever felt so solid, so unbendable. Nothing, no one could hurt her in the fortress of those arms. He said, "My God, Miranda, I thought—"

Instantly he fell silent.

A pistol hammer clicked back.

They both spun around to see Annie standing a few feet away. She wobbled on unsteady legs. With both hands she clutched the gun.

"It's too late, Annie," said Chase. "The police know. They have your final letter. They know you killed Richard. Even now they're looking for you. It's over."

Annie slowly lowered the gun. "I know," she whispered. She took a deep breath and looked up at the sky. "I loved you," she said to the heavens. "Damn you, Richard. *I loved you!*" she screamed.

Then she raised the gun, put the barrel in her mouth and calmly pulled the trigger.

Chapter Fifteen

This time the ministrations of cranky Dr. Steiner were insufficient. Only a hospital—and a surgeon—would do. An emergency ferry run was ordered and Miranda was loaded aboard the *Jenny B* with Dr. Steiner in attendance. The hospital in Bass Harbor was alerted to an incoming patient: gunshot wound to the right shoulder, patient conscious and oriented, blood pressure stable, bleeding under control. The *Jenny B* pulled away from the dock with two passengers, a crew of three and a corpse.

Chase wasn't aboard.

He was at that moment fidgeting in a chair in Lorne Tibbetts's back office, answering a thousand and one questions. A command performance. A woman, after all, was dead; an investigation was called for; and as Lorne so succinctly put it, the choice was between talk or jail. All the time Chase sat there, he was wondering about the *Jenny B*. Had it reached Bass Harbor yet? Was Miranda stable?

Would Lorne ever finish with the damn questions?

It was two in the morning when Chase finally walked out of the police station. The night was warm, warm for Maine, anyway, but he felt chilled as he walked to his car. No more ferries to Bass Harbor tonight. He was stranded on the island until morning. At least he knew that Miranda was out of danger. A phone call to the hospital had told him she was resting comfortably, and was expected to recover.

Now he wondered where to go, where to sleep.

Not Chestnut Street. He could never sleep under Evelyn's roof again, not after the damage he'd done to the DeBolt family. No, tonight he felt rootless, cut off from the DeBolts, from the Tremains, from the legacy of his rich and haughty past. He felt born anew. Cleansed.

He got in the car and drove to Rose Hill.

The cottage felt cold, devoid of life or spirit, as if any joy that had ever existed within had long since fled. Only the bedroom held any warmth. This was where he and Miranda had made love. Here the memory of that night, that one night, still lingered.

He lay on the bed and tried to conjure up the memory of her scent, her softness, but it was like trying to catch your own reflection in water. Every time you reach out to hold it, it slips from your grasp.

The way Miranda had slipped from his grasp.

She's not one of us, Evelyn had once said. *She's not our kind of people.*

Chase thought of Noah, of Richard, of Evelyn. Of his own father. And he thought, *Evelyn's right. Miranda's not our kind of people.*

She's far better.

"HAPPY ENDINGS," said Miss St. John, "are not automatic. Sometimes one has to work for them."

Chase took the advice, and the cup of coffee she handed him, in silence. The advice was something he already knew. Hadn't experience taught him that happy endings were what you found in fairy tales, not real life? Hadn't his own marriage proved the point?

But this time it will be different. I'll make it different. If only I could be certain I'm the one she wants.

He sipped his cup of coffee and absentmindedly scratched Ozzie's wild black mop of hair. He didn't know why he was petting the beast, except that Ozzie seemed so damn appreciative. A glance at his watch told Chase he had plenty of time to catch the twelve-o'clock ferry to Bass Harbor. To Miranda.

All night he'd lain sleepless in bed, wondering about their hances, their future. The specter of his brother couldn't be o easily dispelled. Just a few short weeks ago Richard had een the man she loved, or thought she loved. Richard had aken her innocence, used her, nearly destroyed her. *And ow here I am, another Tremain. After what Richard did o her, why should she trust me?*

Events, emotions had moved at lightning speed these past ew days. A week ago he had called her a murderess. Only ours ago he had come to accept her innocence as gospel ruth. She had every right to resent him, to never forgive im for the things he'd once said to her. So many cruel and errible words had passed between them. Could love, real ove, grow from such poisoned beginnings?

He wanted to believe it could. He had to believe it could. But those doubts kept tormenting him.

When Miss St. John had come knocking at the cottage loor at ten o'clock with an offer of coffee and a morning hat, he'd almost welcomed the intrusion, though he sus- ected her invitation was inspired by more than neighborly indness. Word of the night's goings-on must already be uzzing about town. Miss St. John, with her mile-long an- ennae, had no doubt picked up the signals and was prob- bly curious as hell.

Now that she'd been brought up to date, she was going o offer an opinion, whether he wanted to hear it or not.

"Miranda's a lovely woman, Chase," she said. "A very ind woman."

"I know" was all he could answer.

"But you have doubts."

He sighed, a breath that seemed weighted with pain and ncertainty. "After all that's happened . . ."

"People are entitled to make mistakes, Chase. Miranda nade one with your brother. It wasn't a terrible sort of nistake. It had nothing to do with cruelty or bad inten- ions. It had only to do with love. With misjudgment. The nistake was real. But the emotions were the right ones."

"But you don't understand," he said, looking up at her. "My doubts have nothing to do with her. It's *me,* whether she can forgive me. For being a Tremain. For being the symbol of everything, everyone who's ever hurt her."

"I think Miranda's the one who's searching for forgiveness."

He shook his head. "What should I forgive *her* for?"

"You have to answer that."

He sat in silence for a moment, rubbing the ugly head of that ugly dog. *What do I forgive you for? For showing me the real meaning of innocence. For making me question every stuffy notion I was brought up to believe in. For making me realize I've been an idiot.*

For making me fall in love with you.

With sudden determination he put down his coffee cup and rose to his feet. "I'd better get going," he said. "I've got a ferry to catch."

"And then what happens?" asked Miss St. John, walking him to the door.

Smiling, he took her hand—the hand of a very wise woman. "Miss St. John," he said, "when I find out, you'll be the first to know."

She waved as he headed out to his car. "I'll count on it!" she yelled.

Chase drove like a crazy man to the ferry landing. He arrived an hour early, only to find a long line of cars already waiting to board. Rather than risk missing the sail, he decided to leave his car and board as a foot passenger.

Two hours later he walked off onto the dock in Bass Harbor. No taxis here; he had to hitch a ride to the hospital. By the time he strode up to the patient information desk, it was already two-thirty.

"Miranda Wood," said the volunteer, setting down the phone receiver, "was discharged an hour ago."

"What?"

"That's what the floor nurse said. The patient left with Dr. Steiner."

Chase felt ready to punch the desk in frustration. "Where did they go?" he snapped.

"I wouldn't know, sir. You could ask upstairs, at the nurses' station, second floor."

Chase was about to head for the stairwell when he suddenly glanced up at the wall clock. "Miss—what time does the ferry return to Shepherd's Island?" he asked.

"I think the last one leaves at three o'clock."

Twenty minutes.

He hurried outside and glanced up and down the street for a taxi, a bus, anything on wheels that might take him to the landing. They *had* to be at the landing. Where else would she and Dr. Steiner go, except back to the island?

It was the last ferry of the day and he'd never catch it in time.

Happy endings are not automatic. Sometimes one has to work for them.

Okay, damn it, he thought. *I'm ready to work. I'm ready to do anything it takes to make this turn out right.*

He took off at a sprint down the street. It was two miles to the ferry landing.

He ran every step of the way.

THE DECKHAND YELLED, "All aboard!" and the engines of the *Jenny B* growled to life.

Standing at the rail, Miranda stared out over the gray-green expanse of Penobscot Bay. So many islands in the distance, so many places in the world to run to. Soon she'd be on her way, leaving memories, good and bad, behind her. There was just this one last journey to Shepherd's Island, to tie up all those loose ends, and then she could turn her back on this place forever. It was a departure she'd planned weeks ago, before Richard's murder, before the horrors of her arrest.

Before Chase.

"I still say it was an idiotic idea, young lady," said Dr. Steiner, hunched irritably on a bench beside her. "Checking out just like that. What if you start to bleed again?

What if you get an infection? I can't handle those comp‑
cations! I tell you, I'm getting too old for this business. T
old!''

"I'll be just fine, Doc," she said, her gaze focused on ‑
bay. "Really," she said softly, "I'll be just fine...."

Dr. Steiner began to mutter to himself, a grumpy mor‑
logue about disobedient patients and how hard it was to ‑
a doctor these days. Miranda scarcely listened. She had ‑
many other things on her mind.

A quiet exit, some time alone—yes, all in all, it was b‑
ter this way. Seeing Chase again would be too confusi‑
What she needed was escape, a chance to analyze what s‑
really felt for him. Love? She thought so. Yes, she was s‑
of it. But she'd been wrong before, terribly wrong. *I do‑*
want to make the same mistake, suffer the same cons‑
quences.

And yet ...

She gripped the railing and gazed off moodily at the ‑
lands. The wind had come up and it whistled across t‑
water, blew its cold salt breath against her face.

I do love him, she thought. *I know I do.*

But it's not enough to make a future. Too much stood ‑
the way. The ghost of Richard. The shadow of mistru‑
And always, always, those metaphorical train tracks ‑
whose wrong side she'd grown up. It shouldn't make a d‑
ference, but then, she was merely Miranda Wood. Pe‑
haps, to a Tremain, it made *all* the difference.

"Bow line's free!" called the deckhand.

The engines of the *Jenny B* throttled up. Slowly she pi‑
oted to starboard, to face the far-off green hillock that w‑
Shepherd's Island. The deckhand strode the length of t‑
boat and released the stern line. Just as it slipped free the‑
came a shout from the dock.

"Wait! Hold the boat!"

"We're full up!" yelled the deckhand. "Catch the ne‑
one."

"I said *hold up!*"

"Too late!" barked the deckhand. Already the *Jenny B* was pulling away from the dock.

It was the deckhand's sharp and sudden oath that made Miranda turn to look. She saw, far astern, a figure racing toward the end of the pier. He took a flying leap across the growing gap of water and landed with only inches to spare on the deck of the *Jenny B.*

"Son of a gun," marveled the deckhand. "Are you nuts?"

Chase scrambled to his feet. "Have to talk to someone—one of your passengers—"

"Man, you must want to talk *real* bad."

Chase took a calming breath and glanced around the deck. His gaze stopped at Miranda. "Yeah," he said softly. "Real bad."

Miranda, caught standing against the rail, could only stare in astonishment as Chase walked toward her. The other passengers were all watching, waiting to see what would happen next.

"Young man," snapped Dr. Steiner. "If you sprained your ankle, don't expect me to fix it. You two and all your damn fool stunts."

"My ankle's fine," said Chase, his gaze never leaving Miranda. "I just want to talk to your patient. If it's all right with her."

Miranda gave a laugh of disbelief. "After a leap like that, how could I refuse?"

"Let's go up front." Chase reached for her hand. "For this, I don't need an audience."

They walked to the bow and stood by the rail. Here the salt wind flew at them unremittingly, whipping at their clothes, their hair. Above, gulls swooped and circled, airborne companions of the plodding *Jenny B.*

Chase said, "They told me you checked out early. You should have stayed in the hospital."

Miranda hugged herself against the wind and stared down at the water. "I couldn't lie in that bed another day. Not with so many things hanging over me."

"But it's over, Miranda."

"Not yet. There's still that business with the police. And I have to settle with my lawyer."

"That can wait."

"But I can't." She raised her head and faced the wind. "I want to leave this place. As soon as I can. Any way I can."

"Where are you going?"

"I don't know. I've thought about heading west. Jill Vickery walked away from her past. Maybe I can, too."

There was a long silence. "Then you're not staying on the island," he said.

"No. There's nothing here for me now. I'll be getting the insurance money from the house. It will be enough to get me out of here. To go some place where they don't know me, or Richard, or anything that happened."

The water broke before the bow of the *Jenny B* and the spray flew up, misting their faces.

"It's not an easy thing," she said, "living in a town where they'll always wonder about you. I understand now why Jill Vickery left San Diego. She wanted to wash away the guilt. She wanted to get back her innocence. That's what I want back, Chase. My innocence."

"You never lost it."

"Yes, I did. That's what you thought. What you'll always think of me."

"I know better now. I have no more questions, Miranda. No more doubts."

She shook her head. Sadly she turned away. "It's not as easy as that, to bury the past."

"Okay, so it's not." He pulled her around to face him. "It's never easy, Miranda. Love. Life. You know, just this morning, Miss St. John said a very wise thing to me. She said happy endings aren't automatic. You have to work for them." He reached up and framed her face in his hands. "Don't you think this happy ending is worth working for?"

"But I don't know if I believe in them anymore. Happy endings."

"Neither did I. But I'm beginning to change my mind."

"You'll always be wondering about me, Chase. About whether you can trust me—"

"No, Miranda. That's the one thing I'll *never* wonder about."

He kissed her then, a sweet and gentle joining that spoke not of passion but of hope. That one touch of his lips seemed to rinse away the terrible grime of guilt, of remorse, that had stained her soul.

The renewal of innocence. That's what he offered; that's what she found in his arms.

It seemed only a short time later when the gulls suddenly burst forth into a wild keening, a raucous announcement that land was close at hand. The couple standing at the bow did not stir from each other's arms. Even when the boat's whistle blew, even when the *Jenny B* glided into the harbor, they would still be standing there.

Together.

Take 4 bestselling love stories FREE

Plus get a FREE surprise gift!

Special Limited-time Offer

Mail to Harlequin Reader Service®

3010 Walden Avenue
P.O. Box 1867
Buffalo, N.Y. 14269-1867

YES! Please send me 4 free Harlequin Intrigue® novels and my free surprise gift. Then send me 4 brand-new novels every month. Bill me at the low price of $2.24 each plus 25¢ delivery and applicable sales tax, if any.* That's the complete price and—compared to the cover prices of $2.99 each—quite a bargain! I understand that accepting the books and gift places me under no obligation ever to buy any books. I can always return a shipment and cancel at any time. Even if I never buy another book from Harlequin, the 4 free books and the surprise gift are mine to keep forever.

181 BPA AJJE

Name	(PLEASE PRINT)	
Address	Apt. No.	
City	State	Zip

This offer is limited to one order per household and not valid to present Harlequin Intrigue® subscribers.
*Terms and prices are subject to change without notice. Sales tax applicable in N.Y.

UINT-93R

©1990 Harlequin Enterprises Limited

Calloway Corners

In September, Harlequin is proud to bring readers four involving, romantic stories about the Calloway sisters, set in Calloway Corners, Louisiana. Written by four of Harlequin's most popular and award-winning authors, you'll be enchanted by these sisters and the men they love!

MARIAH by Sandra Canfield
JO by Tracy Hughes
TESS by Katherine Burton
EDEN by Penny Richards

CAL93

Harlequin is proud to present our
best authors and their best books.
Always the best for your
reading pleasure!

Throughout 1993, Harlequin will bring you
exciting books by some of the top names in
contemporary romance!

In August,
look for
Heat Wave by

BARBARA
DELINSKY

A heat wave hangs over the city....

Caroline Cooper is hot. And after dealing with crises all
day, she is frustrated. But throwing open her windows to
catch the night breeze does little to solve her problems.
Directly across the courtyard she catches sight of a man
who inspires steamy and unsettling thoughts....

Driven onto his fire
escape by the sweltering heat, lawyer Brendan Carr
is weaving fantasies, too—around gorgeous Caroline.
Fantasies that build as the days and nights go by.

Will Caroline and Brendan dare cross the dangerous
line between fantasy and reality?

Find out in HEAT WAVE by Barbara Delinsky...
wherever Harlequin books are sold.